Robin Blake

ORIGINAL SINS

Magoo Editions

Published by Magoo Editions

Copyright © 2024 Robin Blake.

Printed in Great Britain by Book Printing UK
www.bookprintinguk.com
Remus House, Coltsfoot Drive, Peterborough, PE2 9BF

Catalogue details of this book are available from the British
Library and other copyright libraries.

ISBN 978-1-9196323-4-6

For my granddaughters
Esme and Ivy

Contents

All the human boy knows of the human girl will be found in my stories of him; it is not very much.

Eden Philpotts
in *The Human Boy*

Cots

1952

I knew the word cot.

'Let's get you into the cot,' Clara said.

Sometimes I wriggled and protested but she put me in all the same and I immediately settled down. My cot was painted pale blue. It was my world. It had wooden bars and soft bedding. The bedding smelt more familiar than anywhere else that I knew.

If I grasped the bars I could pull myself up and look on tiptoes over the rail and see more of the room. There were two high windows. The windows were draped but through the shining gaps came shafts of yellow sunshine in which motes of dust danced.

I was waiting for David to come back. Daddy had taken David away in the car in the morning. Clara had held me in the crook of her arm to wave him goodbye. David had a red cap on and a brown bag on a strap. Clara told me he would come back later.

It was peaceful without him but I was waiting for him to come back. We would go running around in circles with our arms outstretched pretending to be planes. David would be laughing and making me laugh. He would shout rhymes Daddy taught him like 'One Man Went to Mow'.

I had long ago learned to cry when I wanted Mummy or Clara. I cried now and Mummy came. She picked me out of the cot and planted me on the ground to change the nappy.

'Soon you won't need these, Christopher,' she whispered. 'You'll have a little brother or sister who will want them instead of you.'

Then she lifted me up and held me in her arms and told me I was good. I felt her lips on my face. I felt the pressure and little suck of her kiss and then her nose nuzzling my cheek.

I knew that word good and I also knew bad. They were not anything I could eat, or keep, or chuck away.

1

They were inside me, and what I was made of. If I lay still while my nappy was changed I was good. If I did something that I must not do I was naughty, which meant I was bad.

Maria was born then. I was told I must not go into where the baby lay. But when no one was looking I did. I went into the dark bedroom and saw the cot. It was much smaller than my cot. I saw the baby sleeping in it. I knew not to tell anyone so I kept it forever as a secret.

Soon afterwards they stopped putting me into the blue cot. Clara said I was no longer the baby now that there was a new one, so I had to sleep in another bed, one without bars, and become a boy.

I didn't know how to become a boy.

I had three friends who were called Diggle, Daggle and Susan. No one could see them. They lived in a house in the garden, inside a rhododendron bush, where they invited me to tea. I never saw them but I believed in them without question. When the leaves shifted in the wind I understood it was Diggle, Daggle and Susan walking in the garden.

I confessed to them that I had gone into the dark room, and seen the baby, and so must turn into a boy. Diggle, Daggle and Susan told me that they knew how you turn into a boy and said they would help me.

Six years passed and I no longer remembered that I'd once believed in Diggle, Daggle and Susan. That was because now, without quite knowing how, I had become a boy after all.

The Ropes

1958

When I saw the Castle for the first time, the other boys of my Year had been there for longer than a whole term. Even so, the friendships across the Year had not been settled. Boys tried out experimental pairings based on shared interests (cars, chess, stamps, Biggles stories), or because they came from the same part of the country, or for some other mutual attraction. But these were provisional attachments, subject to sudden rifts, as well as to lazier driftings apart. The Castle was a fluid marketplace in friendship in which we switched and swapped pals like Horniman's tea cards.

Arrival

So I came late onto the scene. Everyone else had started in September, but I didn't arrive until one Sunday three weeks after New Year. We had driven in the Rover more than a hundred miles across the high part of the Pennines, travelling most of the day so that when we arrived at the Castle it was dark. I made out the silhouette in the moonlight of a severe-looking eighteenth century mansion with two square wings jutting out to enclose the gravel forecourt on three sides. I held tight to my mother's hand as my father led us up grand steps, little used and mossy, whose double flights curled inward towards each other like a crab's claws. I stood between my parents in my new, scratchy, grey uniform, as my father touched the bell beside the double front door. It trilled somewhere inside. The upper halves of the doors were of window glass but I wasn't tall enough to see anything inside except the ceiling. Low powered bulbs glowing in a brass chandelier. Patterned plaster, an elaborate arrangement of ribs and bosses alternating with pendants that hung down and looked like asparagus.

A shadow flicked across the glass and the door was scraped open by a thin, stooping man with a pinched face. He wore complicated black robes and a hood that folded flat across the back of his shoulders. He held a smouldering cigarette between his fingers.

'So!' he said when he had greeted and shaken hands with my parents. 'Our latest addition: Conroy C.'

His face wore a twisty smirk that was his default expression when speaking to, or about, a boy.

'This is Father Sigbert,' my father said with strained jauntiness. 'The headmaster.'

With a jerk of his body, Father Sigbert bent and looked into my face and I smelled the bitter burnt tar on his breath.

'I trust he wasn't *car-sick* on the way,' he said.

I had not been car-sick, though I may have looked as if I had. The monk's remark was no doubt intended to convey his care, but in my mind it insinuated that to have been sick was a transgression. Fear contracted my stomach. I knew nothing of the codes, rules and conventions of the world I was about to be pitched into.

Stepping back, Father Sigbert gestured my parents through the door and towards a great baronial fireplace, around which were arranged an oak settle, a pair of armchairs and a standard lamp. Tea arrived, trolleyed in by a fat woman who immediately withdrew into the shadowy area at the back of the hall and banged a door. I looked after her but could see only the foot of a dark polished stair and the high doorway through which she had vanished.

The grown-ups sat and chatted about our journey while sipping tea. I peered around. The hall, I later learned, was used only for the reception of parents, governors and important clerics such as the Bishop, or the Abbot from across the valley. On such occasions, and only then, a fire of birch and spruce logs was lit.

Parting

It became time for my parents to leave. Calling upon two passing boys for their help, Father Sigbert went briskly outside with my father to haul my trunk from the boot of the Rover and have it dragged into the building. My mother kept me by her side at the fire, holding my hand and stroking my head. I later wished I had attended better to these last few minutes with her. Instead, I was listening to the distant clatter and shouting of other boys in some distant room. Then, beneath this, I made out another sound from deep in the belly of this unmapped, unimaginable, labyrinthine building: a ceaseless rumbling and growling. It was the heating furnace, but I thought of the hungry Minotaur.

Within a few minutes Father Sigbert returned to my mother and told her Joe was waiting in the car. He called my father 'Joe' because once they had been boys together at the school – the College, that ranged, with the monastery beside it, three miles away on the opposite side of the valley. This was where I was destined one day to complete my own education.

My mother hugged me, kissed the top of my head, hugged me again and retreated to the door. I followed her only as far as the top of the steps and watched as, putting on a show of levity, she skipped down to the gravelled ground, leaving the faintest trace of her perfume in the cold air. She turned and looked back, gave a wan smile and waved, then slipped into the passenger seat of the car. Father Sigbert shut her door with a clump, and I raised my arm high over my head and swung it from side to side. The Rover's lights came on, the starter whined, whinnied and coughed the engine into life. With a brief burp of rubber on gravel the car half-circled and, after a second louder wheel-burp and a puff of exhaust smoke, my parents had gone. As the headlights disappeared the darkness surrounding the Castle became even darker.

Father Sigbert bounded up the steps and brought me back inside. A boy with protruding ears and round National Health glasses came trotting into the hall.

'Come here, Collinshaw!'

The boy froze then turned and came over to us.

'This is Conroy, a tardy arrival,' said Father Sigbert. 'Show him the Ropes, will you?'

The Ropes

'What are the Ropes?' I asked.

Collinshaw ignored the question. He seemed in a hurry. He walked ahead of me so briskly that I was nearly running to keep up. He opened the high door at the back of the hall. Through it I saw a huge room with floor-to-ceiling Elizabethan windows and paneling inlaid with a geometrical pattern. The windows were decorated with knights' shields in stained glass. The room was full of long tables and benches and smelled of cooked cabbage.

'This is the old bit of the Castle,' said Collinshaw. 'It used to be called the Great Chamber. Now it's just the refectory.'

He swung round and marched off. I followed until we reached a long room with boys all dressed like us in grey shorts and shirts. They were sticking stamps into albums, playing Owzat!, reading the *Eagle* — anything like that. The room had a ping-pong table and was lined with small square cupboards.

'The gallery,' said Collinshaw. 'Those are our lockers. You can find yours for yourself. It's got your name on it.'

He was off again, leading me two at a time up some stone stairs and opening one of a pair of brass handled double doors. A smell wafted out that I knew from Sundays at home – stale incense smoke laced with floor polish.

'The chapel,' said Collinshaw.

Before I had seen anything of the interior, he let the door swing back and was off again. Next he showed me a room crammed with green-blanketed beds.

'A typical dormitory,' he whispered. 'You don't talk in here — ever.'

We toured the long washroom, with two rows of basins down the middle and an open area with eight showerheads. We finished the tour in the teaching block. Collinshaw took me into one of the classrooms.

'You're in this one with Mr Dunn. He's got a deformed arm and his nose drips. Sit down.'

I sat down behind the nearest desk. Collinshaw paced up and down in front of the blackboard.

'Now, I've got to tell you the school rules. Pay attention. First, Stick offences.'

'What are they?'

Collinshaw closed his eyes for a moment, willing himself to be patient.

'I'm just going to tell you. I'll only say everything once so listen carefully. Stick offences are the following.'

He counted them off on his fingers.

'Fooling around in class, running in the building, excessive shouting in the building, being improperly dressed, being late for Mass without an excuse, being late for meals ditto, lessons ditto, Benediction ditto, games ditto.'

'What's ditto?'

He gave me a pitying look.

'It means the same, obviously. Where was I? Badly made bed, untidy bed area, wasting food, wasting lav paper, writing in ink in school books. That's all the things you get the Stick for. Got them?'

'You haven't told me what the Stick actually is?'

'You'll find out. The slipper's worse. You get that for cheeking a master, being out of bounds, talking after lights-out, talking during Mass, blaspheming against Our Lord, ditto Our Lady, using swear words, lying, stealing more than sixpence and fighting. That's the slipper. If you do silly things that are not actually bad sins you get lines. You have to write out a sentence like "I must not pick my nose even if it's got hard snot in it" a hundred times. Also for not finishing your prep or not paying attention in class or not having an Osmiroid or a protractor. For all that kind of thing you get detention. Right. I'll give you three questions then I have to go. Keep it snappy.'

'What's an Osmi–thing? What you said.'

'A pen that you can write in italic script with. They're compulsory. Next.'

'What's detention?'

'When you have to miss something nice that's happening, for example the film on Wednesday, or cubbing.'

'What's cubbing?'

'That's when we go to the woods on half-day. It's wizzo fun.'

'And what's blaspheming?'

He clicked his tongue.

'I said only three questions. Now I've got to go. Me and Mulligan are trying to work out our next move in a game of postal chess that we've got to send off tomorrow.'

Benediction

A boy appeared at one end of the gallery laboriously ringing a handbell with both hands. Everyone started to return their games, books and copies of *Eagle* to their lockers, and then to file out onto the stairwell that led up to the chapel. I followed. The chapel had rows of rush-seated chairs with kneelers and flat elbow-rests on top for the use of the boy behind. There were also narrow troughs below to keep missals in. Everyone was filing into their places and taking out their missals.

'I don't know where to sit,' I said to the monk who was standing at the back. He looked annoyed.

'Sir,' he said.

I looked at him. What did he mean?

'I don't know where to sit, *Sir*,' he said.

He cupped his hand behind his ear.

'Let me hear you.'

I repeated the words,

'You must be our late arrival. The one who had the mysterious infection?'

'It was a virus.'

'It was a virus, *Sir*,' he said.

'It was a virus, Sir.'

'Well, anyway, yours is the vacant chair in the second row. What's your name?'

'Christopher, Sir.'

'No, no, your surname.'

'Conroy, Sir.'

'Right. That's what you're called around here. We don't use first names. You call me Sir, and I call you Conroy. On the other hand, in the *third* person, I'm Father Kentigern, though you are still Conroy. Do you understand?'

I did, more or less, though not who this Third Person was. I went forward and took my place in the second row from the front. There was a label slotted into a thin brass frame on the back of the chair with "Conroy C.J." written on it in careful italic handwriting. The place on my right was occupied by a boy smaller than me named Deuchar, and the one on my left belonged to a much plumper boy named Corcoran. Both had their missals open on the page for Benediction.

Here for the first time was something familiar. The altar was clothed in green and had a red sanctuary candle-lamp hanging next to it. On the altar was what I knew to be the monstrance, though it was still covered by a silk veil. Then Father Sigbert came down the aisle wearing a gold-embroidered cope and we opened our hymnals at the number shown on the hymn-board. We stood up to sing.

Soul of my Saviour, sanctify my breast…

At the end of the hymn we knelt. Next to me Corcoran was behaving oddly. He was rocking back and forth with his head bowed over the missal and sniffing. Glancing down, I noticed that he had a deckle-edged snapshot marking the page. It showed two grown-up people, a man and a woman, laughing happily with their arms draped around each other. With his head hovering over the words of Benediction, and this snapshot next to them, Corcoran was crying. He was trying not to show it but I saw his teardrops spotting the faces of his parents and the words of *O Salutaris Hostia*.

Tarka

There were nine beds in the dormitory. We had all put on our pyjamas and got into bed, supervised by our dormitory captain from the third Year. Father Kentigern marched in with two large brown jars, one in each hand.

'Dynamite or concrete!' he intoned shaking the jars, which made a rattling sound.

No one responded and he strode into to the next dormitory, where he called out again.

'Concrete or dynamite!'

I heard Father Kentigern's voice calling out twice more as it receded through the two dormitories beyond. Then he returned, without the two jars, and stood in the connecting doorway between ours and the next room. He opened a book called *Tarka the Otter* and began to read aloud from chapter six. In this episode the young otter and his mother come across an old grizzled dog-otter, twice the size of Tarka, who wants to play in the water with Tarka's mother, while butting Tarka to drive him away. Tarka tries every trick he knows, whistling to his mother and repeatedly crying *Ic-yang*, 'but she was heedless of her cub's cries, as she dived with the dog in play'.

Tarka dances this way and that along the edge of the water but try as he might he can't get his mother's attention. Finally the old dog-otter loses patience, comes out of the water and hurls himself at Tarka with violence in his teeth and eyes. Tarka runs for his life.

'Already,' read Father Kentigern, 'his mother had forgotten, and perhaps would never again remember, that she had loved a cub called Tarka.'

He snapped the book shut.

'Good night boys,' he called and switched off the light.

I lay curled up in the dark and thought about Tarka, and soon my pillow was soaked through with tears.

Letter Home

The blackboard extended almost right across the classroom wall, the one that the rows of desks faced. When Mr Dunn wrote on it he started at the extreme left, near the top and proceeded in jerks, his chalk whacking and screeching as he lurched sideways on his way to the other end of the board. His writing could not help slowly sinking downward as he went, giving a lop-sided look to his labours.

He had written LETTER HOME followed by the day and date written in full and then the words BULLET POINTS. He finished with a large solid dot at the beginning of the next line then, jamming the stub of chalk into the hole made by the frozen curled fingers of his left hand, swung around to face us.

'All right chaps,' he said. 'This week's letter to your besotted parents. You all know the drill. Bullet points please. Yes, Carani.'

'Match against the Priory, Sir.'

'Result, boy?'

'They won 12-9, Sir.'

11

'Bad show.'

He wrenches the chalk from its notch, writes this information next to the dot, makes another dot on a new line and turns again.

'Next point. Romero.'

'The film, Sir.'

'Well, what was it?'

'Norman Wisdom, Sir.'

'Does this film perchance have a title?'

'*The Square Peg*, Sir.'

Mr Dunn wrote this up followed by "a comedy. We laughed a lot."

And so it continued; weather (rainy), Feast of St Aidan (half-holiday), visit by the Bishop for—.

He swiveled around.

'A boiled sweet for the boy who can spell "Confirmation".'

Several arms sprouted into the air.

'Sir! Sir!'

'Nelson,' said Mr Dunn.

Nelson had not raised his hand. He stood up slowly and in a mumbling voice began to spell.

'C-O-N-F-E-R—.'

'Wrong. Sit down. Deuchar knows, don't you boy?'

Deuchar stood and carefully gave the correct spelling. Mr Dunn took a cellophane wrapped sweet from a jar on his desk, bowled it overarm across the room towards Deuchar who had to scrabble around on the floor to find it. Mr Dunn finished the bullet point: *the Bishop for Confirmation of senior boys*.

With the bullet points established the class twisted the caps off our Osmiroids and bent to the task over our pads of Basildon Bond notepaper. My letter completed itself quickly, taking up all of the front of the sheet and half of the back. To fill up the empty space I added a P.S.

'Mr Dunn looks exactly like Mr Punch. His arm is parylised. It is like a salarmi. The fingers are no good exept for keeping the chalk in. He has watery snot dripping out of his nose when it is cold. He is our form master.'

I folded the paper, slid it into the envelope and wrote *Mr and Mrs Conroy* and our address. Then I licked the gum and pressed the flap down. When Mr Dunn came round collecting our letters he frowned when he saw what I'd done.

'Conroy! Have you sealed your envelope?'

'Yes, Sir.'

He clicked his tongue.

'Next time leave it open. I won't tell you again.'

Skates

My earliest friend was Deuchar. He held himself in a hunched, asymmetrical way, with his arms close to his body, as if trapping something under his school blazer. He made me think of Chuchundra, the musk-rat in Kipling's story, ever fearful of threats and never venturing into the centre of the room. But from his position in the sidelines Deuchar was an astute observer of his classmates.

'Everybody wants to be friends with Carani and Nelson,' he said. 'Carani knows an awful lot of different things and funny songs and jokes. He's Italian but he's got the gift of the gab. Nelson's Irish but he hasn't. My father says that's an irony. Anyway it doesn't matter to Nelson because of the things he can do.'

'Like what?'

'For one thing he's a super skater. And wait till you see him swimming.'

Even before I saw him swimming I watched Nelson and realised that I too wanted to be his friend. Some hope. He was undeniably handsome. He was the only one in the Year who actually looked older than his eight or nine years, even in his short grey trousers and Clark's sandals. But Deuchar was right: Nelson showed up best in his swimming trunks. He had the easiest, laziest, most stylish crawl you could imagine. Looking back, I think Nelson came as near to being James Dean as any child could. Physical grace came as naturally to him as breathing.

Swimming we had once a week, but there was roller skating at break almost every day.

'Don't you have any skates?' said Deuchar.

'No. I wish I had. What about you?'

It was the beginning of morning break and we were in the boot room changing our indoor shoes. We each had a large pigeon-hole for outdoor shoes and rugger boots, but skates could be kept there too. Deuchar showed me his skates. They had metal wheels and clamps that you pinched to the soles of your shoes by tightening a key and when you skated the wheels made a harsh discordant noise on the tarmac. Even I could tell these skates were years out of date. Luckier boys like Nelson, and also Romero who was American and never lacked for anything, had modern Jacko-skates, which were attached to your feet by lace-up cuffs made of red leather. They also had silent wheels in hardened rubber, shaped like an aircraft's undercarriage. Deuchar's skates were more like a steam engine by comparison.

'I can show where to get some but it's a deathly secret. Have you got any money?'

'A pound. I had to give it to Father Kentigern to keep in the Bank. Plus I've still got a shilling that my grandmother gave me. How much are the skates?'

'You'll need three-and-six for Jacko-skates or one-and-six for old ones like mine.'

We were able to apply to Father Kentigern for money from the Bank on Wednesday and Saturday morning. Anything more than a shilling, he would ask what it was for. My heart thudding, I replied as Deuchar had instructed me.

'Can I have two shillings for a bottle of ink, Sir.'

'You don't have to pay for ink from your own money, you know. You can charge it.'

'I don't think I should, Sir.'

'Why is that?'

I hadn't considered this question. I thought desperately, and an answer came to me.

'I was clumsy, Sir. I broke the one I had.'

'I see. That is commendable. Very well but two shillings is more than you'll need. I'll allow you one and six.'

He shelled the money out and entered it in the debit column of his Bank Book.

Greeks and Romans

The Castle was divided horizontally into three Year Groups, and vertically into four houses. The houses were Trojans, Athenians, Spartans and Romans. Carani while learning to tie flies for trout fishing with Father Finbar had asked Sir why the houses were called that.

'He says that there's a main thing that every house stands for,' Carani told us next day. 'Athenians stand for fairness and being reasonable at all times.'

Carani was an Athenian.

'What did he say about the other houses?' we wanted to know.

'Like the Spartans,' said Nelson. Nelson was a Spartan.

'Spartans are hard and fit but a bit vain. Eee-gee, Sir says, in history they were always combing their hair.'

'And what about the Romans?'

'They do what they're told and are incredibly organised. The Romans built Hadrian's Wall and the Great North Road and things like that.'

'You haven't said what the Trojans are like.' I said. I was a Trojan.

'Oh well, Trojans lose battles and never ever cry about it. Ha-ha!'

'Is that true?' cried a chorus of Trojans.

'Yes, but don't worry, they're still pretty good at war. All the houses are good at war – that's the whole point. You've got to read the Iliad and Aristotle and Livy to understand, Sir says.'

'Ha-ha! Harry Stottle – who's that?' shouted Biggins.

'Shut up Biggins, you loon,' said Carani.

'What's the Iliad?' I said.

'It's a poem written about a million trillion years ago about the Trojan war.'

I had never heard of the Trojan War. I found the Iliad in the dusty bookshelves that lined the classroom corridor and once I started reading it I couldn't stop. I found that Hector, the strongest and bravest of the Trojans, was killed by Achilles, because he'd killed Achilles's best friend Patroclus. It obviously wasn't a fair fight – I mean between Achilles and Hector. The gods made it unfair because they sacrificed heroes whenever they felt like it. It was like in chess: the gods were Kings and Queens and the humans — even the heroes — were just pawns.

Hector was strong and good-looking, and by far the best warrior in the Trojan army. He should have been able to defeat proud and bad-tempered Achilles, but the gods weren't on his side so he was killed. Hector had no best friend able to get revenge on Achilles for his death, but only some feeble brothers like Paris, who was handsome but lazy, lying around eating grapes and spooning with Helen. I saw why being a Trojan meant you had to be a good loser. But I felt like crying for Hector, especially at the bit where his body gets dragged through the dirt behind Achilles's chariot.

Old Tyler

At Break I ran by double steps down to the boot-room to meet Deuchar.

'I've got the money from Father Kentigern. I had to tell a lie to get it. Now I've got two and six. Where do we get the skates from?'

'From Old Tyler.'

'Who's that?'

'The caretaker. His lair's next to the boiler-room. Every year boys leave pairs of skates behind and Old Tyler takes them over. He lends them to other boys for money that haven't got skates.'

'What's he like?'

'He was in the First World War, in the navy.'

'In a battleship?'

'No. Destroyers. But he's a communist now. He'd get the sack if Father Sigbert found out so it's a deathly secret.'

We left the boot-room and penetrated deeper into the cellar, where the boiler room was. Next to this we found a dusty space in the middle of which a bare bulb illuminated an old kneehole desk and a sagging armchair, where a lined and grimy old man lounged smoking a pipe. An extraordinary assortment of stuff was piled up around him: old bookcases, dented filing cabinets, stoved-in cupboards, classroom desks, seatless chairs, a ruined piano, two eviscerated radios, a bird-cage, a stack of car batteries, three or four blackened oil-lamps, a washboard, an old bicycle and several tea-chests. The walls were lined with shelving on rusty brackets, stacked with cardboard boxes,

'What d'you want?' growled the old man.

'Conroy wants some skates,' said Deuchar.

The caretaker hauled himself out of his chair and bent to scrutinize my face. He wore brown overalls smutched with oil. It was impossible to tell how old he was. His nose was bulbous and deeply pitted all over.

'You Conroy are you, nipper?'

'Yes, Sir.'

'Don't call me Sir. Mr Tyler's my name.'

He shuffled across to one of the loaded shelves and took down a box that had once been filled with Haig's whisky. He brought it under the light and I saw it contained a heap of rusty metal-wheeled skates.

'They're all I've got in stock at the minute. But believe you me, a drop of oil and they'll roll just like new, yurr. Help yourself, just give me two and six and you can take them away.'

I drew Deuchar to one side.

'You said they were one and six,' I whispered.

'That's what they are, usually.'

I spoke to Old Tyler.

'Deuchar says they should be one and six.'

'That's what they are, nipper. Plus a tanner deposit returnable at the end of term with the skates in the same condition as what they were given out in.'

'That's still only two shillings,' I protested.

Old Tyler delved into one of the many pockets in his overalls and brought out something small and metal, which he held up, giving me a gappy, tobacco-stained leer.

'But it's another tanner for the key, ain't it? Yurr. Without that you'll never be able to fix them to your shoes.'

Sins

Every third Friday after tea we had to go to Confession. Old Father Giles, who lived in the Castle but, being so ancient, didn't teach or do much of anything, was the most popular confessor. This was because he didn't know any of our names and was deaf and assumed to be verging on senility. On my first time I lined up outside his room with about eight other boys.

My turn came and I went in. The desiccated figure of the old monk was sitting in a chair next to a pri-dieu. He wore a habit, with the hood over his head, that was as worn and ragged as he was. Around his neck he had draped a long, green, silk stole ending in tassels that lay on the floor. He gestured for me to kneel.

This felt very strange. At home I had made my First Confession to Father Hosker in a proper closed confessional, where the priest sat on the other side of a window fitted with grille and a curtain. Even then I

18

was tongue-tied. I recited the preliminary words that had been drilled into me all right, but I became overwhelmed by shyness when it came to telling him my sins. Father Hosker prompted me in a patient, kind voice. He suggested a few things I might have done – to which I would reply "yes Father" or "no, Father"– after which he moved on to say the Latin words of absolution and told me to say three Hail Marys as a penance. So I had fallen into the habit of letting Father Hosker lead me through my sins. At the end it was always three Hail Marys.

'Bless me Father for I have sinned,' I now said to Father Giles, 'and it is four weeks since my last confession.'

I stopped as usual, waiting for the priest to come up with some putative misdemeanours for me to confirm, or deny. Father Giles would have none of it.

'Well?' he said testily after a pause of ten seconds, putting his hand behind his ear.

'I don't know, Sir.'

'You don't *know*? Why d'you think you're here? Haven't you examined your conscience?'

'Well, yes, Sir, but I couldn't think of anything.'

'You couldn't *think* of anything? Don't waste my time, boy. Go outside and stand at the back of the queue and when you come in again I want to hear your sins. Is that quite clear? Next!'

It was while I was standing in the queue again that I thought of the lie I'd told to Father Kentigern. The lie about the bottle of ink. It was as if my soul shrank within me but I knew I would have to admit the falsehood to Father Giles.

'I told a lie, Sir,' I said ten minutes later, when I was again kneeling on the pri-dieu.

'What lie?'

'I said I'd broken a bottle of ink when I hadn't.'

'Why?'

'Because I wanted to get Father Kentigern to give me extra money from the Bank, for a pair of skates.'

19

'A funny kind of a lie, boy. Did you get the skates?'

'Yes, Sir.'

He sighed and began to mutter rapidly in Latin, ending with the words I recognized – *Ego te absolvo a peccatis tuis in nomine Patris, et Filii et Spiritus Sancti. Amen* – while tracing the sign of the cross with two fingers in front of my nose.

'A decade of the rosary for your penance. Go and sin no more.'

I left the room and went into the Chapel, where I went to my place, knelt and raced through the penance. I left with an overpowering sense of uplift and relief, tearing down the stairs to the classroom block and taking the last three stairs in one joyful leap. While still in the air I collided with Father Finbar who had appeared at the bottom carrying a neat stack of exercise books.

'Look out!' he cried, much too late.

I bounced off him and floundered down until I lay on the ground. At the same time the exercise books had exploded from his arms and were scattered across the floor. I picked myself up and began scrabbling around to collect them.

'What on earth do you think you were doing Conroy?'

'I don't know, Sir. Sorry, Sir.'

I presented him with the exercise books, now in a disorderly heap.

'You may be sorry, but you will be even sorrier,' he said, trying to square up the pile. 'You perfectly well know the rule.'

He raised his head and looked me in the eyes.

'You will go for the Stick tomorrow.'

The Stick

Tomorrow came after what felt like three days. My stomach was leaden and without appetite, and my mind was choked with yellow slimy dread, like a clogged gutter.

You had to present yourself outside the Book Room just before lunch. The Book Room was at the very end of the range of classrooms. When I got there I found another boy already waiting. Every one else had gone up to wash their hands for lunch. The Book Room door lay open: evidently Father Sigbert, who administered the Stick, had not yet arrived.

'What are you here for?' murmured the other boy, an older member of my own house, the Trojans.

'Running.'

'Oh.'

He didn't sound impressed.

'I cracked a dirty joke in Maths,' he told me after a moment. 'You had this before?'

'No.'

'Well you look like a scared rabbit. Or, to put it another way, you look like a bowl of cold custard.'

'Does it hurt? The Stick I mean?'

'Of course it hurts. It's meant to hurt. But when you've had it thousands of times, like I have, you just get used to it.'

'I've seen boys after it in the Wash Room putting their hands in water.'

'Yes. It's a good idea.'

'But do you use hot water or—,'

'Shh! He's coming.'

Father Sigbert swept into sight at the end of the empty corridor, carrying a sheet of paper. When he reached us he consulted it.

'Ah, yes,' he said, businesslike. 'Littlemore and Conroy. Where's Garfield?'

'Here, Sir.'

Garfield, who was notably plump, had speed-walked down the corridor behind Father Sigbert and was out of breath.

'You're late, Garfield. You must be here before me, as well you know.'

21

Garfield took his place behind me. Father Sigbert folded the paper and pushed it into the pocket of his habit. He went into the Book Room and held the door.

'First!'

Littlemore adopted a sauntering gait as he went inside and closed the door. Garfield and I looked at each other.

'What are you here for?' he whispered.

'Running. Or rather, jumping down the stairs.'

'Father Michael found I hadn't made my bed properly, worse luck.'

We could hear a murmuring of voices, mostly Father Sigbert's, from the far side of the door, followed by a sharp sudden crack like a piece of wood splintering. Then another. And another. We heard a brief murmur from Father Sigbert, followed by three more evenly spaced sharp cracks. Then the door burst open and Littlemore emerged. All his cockiness had deserted him. His face was contorted and his arms were crossed across his chest so that he could squeeze his hands into his armpits. He stumbled, almost running, past us and up the corridor.

'Next!'

I froze. A few seconds passed.

'I said next! That's you, Conroy.'

I crept into the Book Room.

'Shut the door.'

I did as I was told and stood opposite Father Sigbert, looking anywhere but directly at him. The Book Room was a narrow space between two long walls entirely covered in bookshelves. I saw that most were loaded with stacks of *Kennedy's Latin Primer*, *Pendlebury's Arithmetic*, *Fabulae Faciles*, and the like, but some had new exercise books, boxes of pencils and sticks of chalk. There was a small window so dirty as to let in little light and the air smelled of dust, must and ink.

'Father Finbar says you nearly caused him a serious accident.'

He was speaking quietly, without emphasis. His lips had that — not exactly a smile, but a kind of ironic curl about them.

'Yes, Sir. But I didn't actually see him coming because he was—.'

'Precisely, Conroy. You didn't *actually* see him coming. You are not to run on the stairs, or in the corridor, or anywhere inside the Castle. Someone might get hurt. So you must take your punishment. Hold out your hand with the palm upwards.'

He brought a black object from under his scapula: my first look at the Stick. In reality it was a ferrule — a piece of galvanized rubber half an inch thick and shaped just like a rubber dog-bone that had been steamrolled flat. Gingerly I offered my right hand. My fingers were slightly curled and Father Sigbert reached out with one hand and straightened them with appalling patience. Then with the other he raised the Stick and smacked it down, twice, on my palm before asking me to extend my other hand. It took about ten seconds for the pain to start.

Cubbing

On the horizon to the south of the Castle, lay the Wolery, a thick wood to which the whole Year went every Wednesday afternoon. This was called cubbing. For ninety minutes boys could do anything they wanted to do, except light a fire. They did a lot of running around and tree climbing. They built huts. They formed armies and engaged in complicated games of hide and seek.

Carani's and Nelson's army was the biggest. They didn't let everybody join so the rest formed a rejects' unit, usually consisting of Corcoran, Deuchar and me. From time to time Nelson and Carani would expel one of their army and he would come and join us. That's how Skinner came in, and at one point Romero too.

'Carani is ant-eye-American,' Romero said, when he arrived one Wednesday. 'So I'll join up with you if you're not ant-eye-American.'

I assured him we weren't, even though sometimes I was. Anyway I always lived in hope that Romero would lend me his Green Lantern comics. But after two weeks of exile, he wheedled his way back into Nelson's and Carani's army by handing round sweets called M&Ms, which Deuchar said were just American Smarties. I never got a peep at Green Lantern.

Nelson and Carani had a fort. One of its ramparts was the trunk of a fallen beech tree. They built two further ramparts out of boughs and branches to make a triangular enclosure, with a hut in the middle. The fort was in a raised position so they could spot attackers coming from any direction. These attackers were all imaginary, as our army did not try to attack or besiege their fort. We were too few.

Nor did we have a fort of our own, only a hut. Every now and then Nelson's and Carani's army would launch an offensive and pull our hut down, so that we had to re-build it.

'I'm fed up with always having to re-build the hut,' said Deuchar. 'Let's make a secret base underground, which they can't pull down even if they find it.'

In another part of the Wolery we found a hole in a bank facing a clearing, that had once been a badger's sett. For two successive Wednesday afternoons we scraped away with sticks and eventually it was big enough for one of us to crawl all the way inside. We called it the Den.

The Use of the Penis

One morning, instead of Mr Dunn, Father Sigbert came into our classroom. His face, never cheerful, looked ready to pronounce a death sentence.

'I have something to tell you of the greatest importance,' he said. 'Some of you might find it embarrassing, or even amusing. If so, keep your embarrassment or amusement to yourself. What I am about to tell you appertains to the private parts of your body. Is everyone paying attention?'

He raked the class with his small grape-green eyes. We all looked down, no one daring to meet that gaze.

'Very well. Now, you have between your legs a tube. It is called your penis. Its function as far as may concern you today is as a hose to empty your bladder periodically of urine. You need to do this because urine is full of poisons collected from your blood by your kidneys and it has to be expelled. Now, you have two Christian duties when it comes to your penis. Listen carefully. Are you listening, Biggins?'

'Yes, Sir,' said Biggins miserably. He flushed to a rich shade of crimson.

Father Sigbert held up one finger.

'First, you must keep it clean. *Clean*, Biggins, with soap and with water, either in the shower or in the bath. Is that clear, Biggins?'

'Yes, Sir,' croaked Biggins.

'And second,'

He held up a second finger.

'You must not otherwise play with it, or let anyone else play with it — ever. Is that understood? Not *ever*. Skinner, you have an unpleasantly vacant expression on your face — is that understood?'

'Yes, Sir,' said Skinner who likewise blushed to something like the colour of a raspberry.

'And the rest of you – is that understood?'

'Yes, Sir,' we all mumbled.

'Good,' said Father Sigbert. 'Because the sin of impurity, whenever it is committed, grievously insults the Blessed Virgin. That is all I have to say to you this morning. Mr Dunn will be here in a moment to get on with your scheduled lesson. '

Facts of Life

'I know another use for your penis,' said Romero. 'My father told me.'

We were putting on our outside shoes at the beginning of break.

'Go on. What is it?'

But Romero wasn't about to sell his information cheap. He bent over his shoelaces, tying them with exaggerated care.

'Someone might hear. I'll tell you outside.'

Romero was the only boy in the school whose parents were divorced. That, combined with his being technically American, set him apart from the rest of us. It was not that he was a pariah, or that he was bullied like Carani's hanger-on Skinner. Romero's exoticism and his different outlook were trump cards in the game of life at the Castle: they impressed us but also affronted us, as if in playing those cards Romero were cheating and getting away with it. His father served at a U.S. Air Force base somewhere in Lincolnshire, and Romero could sometimes deploy secret stores of forbidden chewing gum and Hershey bars direct from a special American shop called the PX, as well as comics of Batman, Superman and The Green Lantern. These comics gave him huge trading power beyond the capacity of the rest of us, who knew only *Beano*, *Dandy*, *Topper* and *The Eagle*. Romero could also speak with authority about cocktail parties, cars with automatic gear-boxes and what it was like to fly in an airliner. On the other hand he was much given to boasting about the superiority of the United States in every aspect of life, which made him frequently tiresome.

Tiresome or not, everyone in earshot wanted to hear what Romero had to say about the other use of the penis. A group of us trailed outside after him.

A light crust of frosted snow lay on the ground. Romero led us up to the skating rink, which was out of use because of the ice, and ducked under the parapet fence. He stood in the angle of one corner while the rest of us, staying outside the rink, gathered around him.

'Go on, then,' said Carani. 'Tell us what your father said.'

'You have to promise not to sneak to anyone that I told you.'

'We promise,' said Carani. 'Now spout, you cretin.'

'Cross your hearts then,' Romero said

'And hope to die,' we chanted.

And so it was that Romero broke the news — and it was news to most of us — of the mechanics of reproduction and how babies are made. He reinforced it with a visual aid, a gesture of a circle made out of the thumb and finger of one hand through which he poked the index finger of his other. There was a moment of awed silence then Nelson, who had listened intently to Romero's explanation, sniggered explosively, putting his hand to his nose with the sound sputtering out between his fingers. Then he and Carani wandered away, punching each other on the arm as they went, and I heard Nelson say the word, the short ugly word that Romero had taught us, the word that meant what he had been describing: the word that was symbolized by the gesture Romero had made with his fingers.

Cross-eyes

We sat round one end of the long table in the refectory. It was tea. The fat woman from the kitchen, and another thinner one, came round with giant brown enamel teapots, pouring the hot tea. They were called Sally and Freda. We had apples, margarine, lumps of cheese, strawberry jam and thick slices of white bread.

Carani was carefully using his knife to remove the core of an apple while keeping the rest of the fruit whole.

27

'My bro says never eat the pips or you get appendicitis. He's a medic at Barts.'

'What's a medic?' said Skinner.

'He's studying to be a doctor so he can cure your cross-eyes.'

'I haven't got cross-eyes.'

'You will if you don't stop thinking about Sally's titties,' said Romero.

Nelson gave his trademark explosive guffaw and the rest of us laughed with him, pointing at Skinner.

'What's Bart's where your bro is anyway?' said Biggins.

'A hospital in London,' said Carani. 'There's Bart's, Guy's and Tommy's. Bart's is best.'

Pushing the core out of the apple with his thumb and leaving the rest of the fruit whole, he began to describe his brother's student life. He was always playing ball games like rugby and golf, and going to pubs to play drinking games like 'Cardinal Puff' and 'Up Jenkins'. And of course he took nurses to dances and the theatre.

'Does he spoon with them? Does he kiss them? Yeurgh!' said Biggins, pretending to throw up.

'Of course not, stupid. He's not going to marry anyone till he's passed his exams. He just takes them out. He took one to *The Mousetrap*. It's a play about a murder by Agatha Christie. He told me the plot and I guessed who done it.'

'Who?'

Carani had cut a piece of cheese the right size to fit exactly into the cored apple. He now began coating this in jam.

'I'm not telling,' he said. 'You're sworn to secrecy on penalty of a thousand pounds fine, or being tortured if you can't pay up. There's probably a sound-proofed dungeon under the theatre where they put people on the rack who get caught telling people who done it and can't pay a thousand pounds.'

He carefully slid the plug of jammy cheese into the apple.

'Hey, Carani,' said Biggins, watching him.

Carani looked up.

'What?'

Biggins was pointing at Carani's apple.

'Look what you've just done.'

Carani looked. For a moment he was nonplussed, but the rest of us burst into uncontrollable cackles and pumped our elbows into each others' sides. But Carani's mood had changed. He frowned and put the apple down on his plate. He was grimacing. He made no attempt to eat the apple.

The Dispensary

Nurse Horgan always wore a royal blue tunic-dress and a starched white cap that wasn't a cap at all but more like a misplaced starched collar pinned to her steel-grey hair. She had a look in her eye that would pull a cork.

If you got an injury or felt ill you went to Nurse in the Dispensary, a narrow room that smelled of TCP. If you had a graze she'd briskly clean it out and paint it with gentian violet. In case of illness she'd listen to your symptoms and, with a look on her face of profound skepticism, would reach for a glass thermometer, which she would shake vigorously to force the column of mercury down and then ram it into your mouth below the tongue.

'No talking, now,' she warned, pinching your wrist and consulting her watch again.

Often Nurse would be out of the Dispensary and you would have to wait outside until she came along. One day, not long after we'd heard Romero's news about the uses of the penis, I was waiting there when Carani came up.

'What're you doing here?' he said.

I showed him my bloody knee, with its shredded skin and embedded grit.

'Looks bad. Is it sore?'

'Yes.'

'It'll be a lot sorer when she's finished with you.'

He took up position next to me. I didn't ask why he was lining up to see Nurse and he didn't tell me. But after a while he said, in a lowered voice,

'Do you think it's all true?'

'What?'

'That thing Romero said. That thing about … you know.'

He looked around to check we were not observed, then made the Gesture.

'Oh that!' I said. 'I don't know. It might be.'

'I don't think it's true. I think it's a bit horrible.'

This was so unlike Carani. He was someone who always saw the bright side of anything. Or the funny side. I guessed he was thinking about his parents doing it. I'd had the same thought, of course, with the same mental recoil. But the best way to face up to it was the way most of us did: treat it as a joke, a farce.

'It's funny. I think it's funny. I think it's as funny as Norman Wisdom,' I said.

'Well I don't. I think it's nasty.'

Blasphemy

Apart from that time outside the Dispensary, I never saw Carani make the Gesture, though it became a craze for many of us: a sure way of getting a laugh, or of breaking an awkward silence. One morning Father Sigbert was saying Mass and Lyon, wearing a black cassock and white surplice, was server. He had just taken the water and wine up to be poured into the chalice and was returning to his place at the bottom of the altar steps. He looked slyly along the row where we were sitting. His hands were at his chest in the prayer position, with fingers pointing straight up and palms pressed together. He separated his hands to pull up the cassock as he came down the steps and then, just before he turned to kneel, he brought his hands together again, but this time making a ring of

30

finger and thumb and pushing the index finger of his other hand through it: in – out, in – out. The Gesture.

We could not control ourselves. We spluttered and snorted into our hands and nudged our neighbours. Then we realised Father Sigbert had heard us. He was leaning forward over the altar muttering the Offertory prayer, but he stopped praying and twisted his head around until he could see us. We froze.

After a moment Father Sigbert resumed the prayer. I craned around and looked at the back of the chapel. Father Kentigern was standing by the door. He had his hands folded beneath his scapula. His face looked implacably stern. I couldn't tell from his face what he had seen, if anything. But I feared the worst.

Complicity

'Be in no doubt about this,' said Father Sigbert. 'Father Kentigern told me the vile smutty blasphemous thing Lyon did in the middle of Holy Mass. And I myself heard and saw all of you laughing.'

Those of us who had been sitting in the front row in the chapel were standing now in a shallow curved line before Father Sigbert.

'I am not angry, but I am shocked, and I am hurt. Father Kentigern is also shocked and hurt. It was an act of the grossest disrespect for Our Lord, as if Lyon had spat in His face; as if he'd jeered and sneered at the purity of Our Blessed Lady. As a result...'

He paused and examined our faces, assessing the degree of our complicity in Lyon's crime.

'Lyon's whole future at this school has been in question. I have had to speak to the Abbot. I have had to speak to his parents. Finally it has been decided to give him a second chance. However I expect you – all of you – to reflect on your own shameful part in this episode. You sniggered. You laughed. And I hope you are thoroughly ashamed of yourselves because, if not, you yourself will have no future in this school.'

The Slipper

We were put in detention for two successive films, and had to write out the words of the *Salve Regina* twenty times. Lyon, however, was to get the Slipper. The Slipper differed from the Stick in that you got it in the evening, between bed-time and lights-out. You were called to Father Sigbert's own room in your dressing gown and pyjamas, and had to listen to a jaw. Then you had to take off your dressing gown and bend over Father Sigbert's bed. Father Sigbert had a slipper with a leather sole. It was a huge slipper, probably about size fourteen, and he smacked your bottom with it as hard as ever he could and he went on smacking until you were blubbing and begging him to stop.

And he sometimes went on after that.

Father Sigbert's room had two doors: one from the corridor that was used to go in and out of the room, and a connecting door with one of the dormitories, which was permanently locked. But when someone got the Slipper, the boys in that dormitory could hear every stroke, and every victim's cry.

During the preceding day Lyon's face was white and he hardly said a word. Everyone tried to be nice to him, patting him on the back and saying good-luck. He didn't reply.

It was private reading in bed that night, as Father Kentigern was out somewhere. A Captain came in looking self-important.

'Lyon,' he said. 'You're for it now. Father Sigbert wants you in his room. Hurry up.'

Lyon, who had not been reading, but lying mummy-like under his bedclothes, got out of bed and reached for his dressing gown. The rest of us all had books open, but we were watching him. After he had fished his slippers out from under the bedside table and fumbled them on, he headed out of the dormitory. No one said a word. We were listening to the fading shuffle of his step as he went down the stairs.

The dormitory captain didn't interfere as we closed our books, left our beds and trailed down into the dorm that was next to Father Sigbert's room. We stood together in silence between the two rows of beds, our eyes fixed on the locked connecting door. We could hear Father Sigbert's voice droning on behind it, but not what he was saying. We then heard Lyon's voice more clearly, trying to interject.

'Oh, but Sir—.'

And Father Sigbert angrily cutting him off.

'Be quiet, and do as I say!'

At this point Lyon's courage dissolved entirely. His voice rose to a high pitch of panic and fear.

'I won't do it again, Sir. I promise. I won't do it again.'

'Get down there! Get down and keep still!'

'Oh, please, Sir! Let me off, Sir. I promise, Sir. I promise I'll be good.'

He was sobbing now, his cries trembling in terror.

'I'll do anything, Sir. Don't, Sir! Oh please, Sir!'

Father Sigbert was implacable.

'I SAID GET DOWN! STOP WRIGGLING! BE STILL!'

Lyon's sobs were muffled now, as his face was pressed into Father Sigbert's bed cover. There was a pause and then a fearful whack, sounding like a gunshot and followed, after a two second pause, by a hideous noise from Lyon, a screeching, open-mouthed, extended, snot-filled howl of pain. This was cut off by a second whack, and then a third, and a fourth, each one sounding louder and harder than the one before, and each bringing more howls from Lyon, as well as different kinds of cry ranging from sobs and squeals to one or two ululating screams.

There was a pause and Lyon's sobs subsided, but not for long. We heard more murmuring from Father Sigbert, and then came another ferocious whack. Now each of us was counting in our heads, with increasing amazement. Five … six … seven … eight … nine … ten ….

Then it stopped; it stopped at last. And we clearly heard Father Sigbert again.

'Now go off to bed, and reflect on why I have unfortunately been obliged to do this. Go on! Out of my sight.'

For the first time since assembling there, we looked at each other. No one spoke. It was understood as by a silent pact that Lyon never would, never could, be reminded of this.

And we never used the Gesture again.

The Fight

1959

At the Castle it was all right to talk about your father. You could quote him and even boast about him, which some boys did incessantly. But you didn't risk to make any mention of your mother. Not ever.

Nor did you say anything about someone else's mother, unless you wanted to get into a fight. Perhaps that is what Nelson did want, all along. Yet the last word you would have used when describing Nelson was pugnacious. Carani, certainly: he specialised in talking, fighting talk included. But not Nelson. He was one of those quiet boys. He was the brooding, cool type.

The one relationship amongst us all that stood as permanent as stone was the one between these two: Carani and Nelson. Everyone knew it. Carani and Nelson were the surest and most solid of best friends.

That is until Nelson said that thing about Carani's mother.

Sledging

When a heavy snowfall came, the Castle slipped into a mood quite different from the usual simple rigidities. For a week life was lighter, minds were freer. Organized games stopped and in the afternoons we went out onto the sloping field between the Wolery and the Castle to toboggan, make snowmen, and have running chaotic snowball fights that would last all the afternoon.

The school had a stock of ancient Davos sledges but some boys had sledges of their own. The most prized of these was the Flexible Flyer, a sleek and enviable design, low on the snow and with slender iron runners that could be shifted by handle grips to

35

make you go left or right. Snowmen were built up and down the hill and you had to sledge down slaloming between them. I saw the normally solemn and reserved Corcoran cackling with laughter as he plunged down the slope on a school sledge, quite unable to steer. He went smack into a life-size snowman that wore a school cap and Collinshaw's national health glasses. Corcoran rolled off the sledge and onto his back, waving his arms and legs in the air like a puppy, still laughing, as Mulligan and Collinshaw jumped out from behind the snowman and pelted him with snowballs.

Boxing

The frost and snow lasted into a second week and now Sergeant-Major Hanrahan set up a boxing ring in the gymnasium, with a canvas stretched on the floor, four posts connected by thick ropes and two stools in opposite corners. We were to have a tournament.

Our training included standing in a circle around him as he launched a medicine ball randomly and fast towards any of us, aiming at the stomach, which he told us was called, for boxing purposes, the Solar Plexus. If lack of concentration caused us not to catch the ball it would wind us, but Sarge would just laugh. When it happened to me, and I gasped in pain, he said,

'Ever heard the expression "The Readiness Is All", Conroy? Well, it's the secret of successful boxing. Anticipation. Remember it or you'll always be a loser.'

One day he brought in a canvas bag full of leather boxing gloves and hung up two punchbags, one at each end of the gym. The drill was to lace on gloves and run circuits of the gym at intervals. Whenever you came to a punchbag you gave it as many pummels as possible before giving way to the next boy that arrived behind you.

The Sergeant-Major was a stocky man with large head topped by a grizzled crew-cut. After the circuit training we would all be gathered around the ring while he demonstrated ringcraft, shadow boxing and dancing from rope to rope, corner to corner, until he was puffed out. Having regained his breath he would invite boys in turn to climb inside the ropes and air-box with him. He brought all his punches fractionally up short, while moving, weaving, shuffling, changing feet, pressing forward and skipping back.

Then he would taunt us.

'Come on, boy, hit me! You can do better than that! Lead! Lead! Not like that. Like this. To the body. To the chin. No, no, no! Not like that. Like THIS!'

And he would throw a left hook to within half an inch of your stomach, and an upper cut to just short of your chin, then feint, bend his body to the left, to the right, snapping his head back or ducking it forward as you flailed your fists at him, never actually landing a blow.

'Defence needs to be instinctive,' Sarge would say, 'But attack is a question of awareness. You have to take your opportunities, take advantage of your opponent's lapses. Defence can stop your opponent winning, but defence won't win you the fight. Seeing your opponent's guard drop, his attention wander, and acting instantly on it: that's decisive. That's what winners do.'

I only twice saw a boy lay a glove on Sergeant-Major Hanrahan. One was Carani, who by sheer manic persistence managed to get one of his swinging gloves to bury itself in the Sarge's stomach. The gym master was taken by surprise and we heard his "Oof!" as he bent forward momentarily, before straightening up and jogging backwards on the balls of his feet into the centre of the ring.

'Good! Very good, Carani. Not very stylish, but good all the same.'

The other boy, naturally, was Nelson, the most stylish of us all, not excluding the teacher. He would move and feint, crouch in the cover-up with his elbows forward, gloves presented in front of his head, then duck and weave and jab straight leads in exactly the way Sarge had expounded. He was also faster than Sarge and, after leaning out of reach of one of Sarge's jabs, he moved in again lightning quick and landing a left-and-right combination on the top of his opponent's lowered head.

After Gym

After gym you stripped off by the lockers and, with a towel around you and clutching a bar of Coal Tar Soap you went for a shower. We did this day after day, but my memory holds one time in particular. I was on my way, dripping, back to the locker room when I noticed Nelson. He was framed in the doorway as I approached, standing beside his locker and shedding his gym clothes. A dusty beam of rich winter's afternoon sun lit him from the unseen window behind. When he was naked he twisted and leaned to pick up his towel and just for a moment, before he wrapped it around his waist, I felt a strange pulse inside me. I saw what the living human body was. Not like the Greek Warrior in the Castle hallway. That by comparison was hard, cold, muscle-bound and dead. This was a body alive, so perfectly clothed with skin and layered with muscle, so proportional and easy and beautiful in itself, that it created desire just by being looked at, just by moving in the light.

I flicked a glance around. Carani was coming up behind me and I saw that he, too, was looking at Nelson wrapping the towel around his hips.

The Tournament

In the tournament we would box over two rounds of two minutes each. I was matched against Rowling. He was small, wiry and energetic. He had poppy eyes, a bobbly nose and straight hair that flopped down across his forehead. His father was a Brigadier.

'Watch out Conroy,' he said when the draw for the matches was posted. 'I'm going to give you a bloody nose.'

I didn't like the idea. I didn't want to fight — not Rowling, anyway, because I rather liked him. But truth was I was afraid —of being hurt but, worse, of being shown up. I admitted this in my own mind but of course I couldn't have said it openly. Listening to Sarge talk about cowardice — 'having a yellow streak down your back' as he was fond of putting it — was enough to teach you that. So I would have to fight Rowling willy-nilly in front of everybody else and not show my dread.

To begin with Rowling adopted a wide-legged stance, like someone about to use a scythe. He put on a theatrical half-snarl and waved his fists, waiting for me to advance on him. I inched forward, holding my own fists up in what I hoped was the approved way. Ranged around the ring the rest of the Year was shouting. I heard Rowling's name called out. I heard my name. It seemed incredible.

At home I had seen Henry Cooper fight Brian London on television, watching with my father. I tried to crouch as I had seen Cooper do, crouch and push forward, jab towards the body or head, then stand up and jog backwards, before moving in again, leaning forward, menacing, for the kill. In Cooper's case the kill would come when he unleashed his trademark left hook, known as 'Enry's 'Ammer'. I felt the acute lack of this decisive weapon.

Rowling, on his part, was not much like Brian London. London was mountainous. He would lumber around the ring, flail with his fists, fall back on the ropes absorbing punches, flail again and then wrap his arms around Cooper's body like an exhausted dancing partner. Occasionally he would let go and land whacking shots around Cooper's ears.

This was the kind of fight the boys wanted. It was the kind of fight Sarge wanted.

'Go on Conroy,' he rasped. He was in the ring with us as our referee. 'Get into him. *Into* him I said. Don't hang back! Move, Rowling, move boy! Move, for pity's sake! Go on Conroy. Nail him. He's there for the taking. Rowling get on your toes or he'll have you. '

I advanced another few inches, weaving my fists around in front of my face as if in two minds about going for the head or the body. In spite of Sarge's urging, I felt an invisible wall stopping me getting within range of Rowling. As he remained rooted, this meant neither of us was able to hit the other. The audience started hooting and booing. They wanted punches. They wanted blood.

Then, all at once, Rowling was upon me. He had made a little leap in the air and landed on his toes, which sprung him forward and within reach — or rather putting me within his reach. I felt a thudding blow on my cheek and lowered my head instinctively. I felt another blow on my temple, knocking me sideways onto the ropes.

I ricocheted back towards Rowling in a way that he wasn't expecting and though I wasn't in balance I swung a fist at him. It hit his side. I swung another that went into his stomach. He grunted. I revolved and for a moment my back was towards him. He pummeled me with a few blows on my back. I swung around and faced him. We circled each other for a few moments, breathing fast. The audience was yelling, finally getting what it wanted. Come on Conroy! Hit him, Rowling!

Ding!

Skinner had sounded the bell for the end of the round. On my corner stool, as Deuchar my second fanned my face vigorously with a towel, I felt hot and elated. Rowling and I were putting on a show and I seemed to be giving as good as I got.

In the second round, we had hardly squared up than Rowling had at me again with a glancing left hook and I felt a stinging pain around my mouth. He was grinning, or so I thought. My elation turned into a surge of anger. What was so funny? I lashed at his face and it snapped back.

'Ow!' he shouted.

I had hit him, as it happened, flat on the nose. Now it was Rowling's turn to be angry. With a furious snarl he surged towards me and I put out a straight arm so that he bounced off my fist. For a moment I thought he might go down as blood poured down his mouth and chin: rich, red, glistening blood, gushing out of both of his nostrils. I was almost electrified by the sight and now went forward in attack for the first time, jabbing and jabbing and receiving no reply. As Rowling reeled backwards Skinner rang the bell for the end of the contest.

Sarge gave Rowling some paper towelling to staunch the nosebleed and then stood centre ring holding each of us by the wrist. A moment later he had yanked my arm into the air.

'Well done, Conroy,' said Carani afterwards. 'I've never seen so much blood. Rowling's nose looked like a running tap. Jolly well done.'

Arrows

While the snow was still lying a man came to show us archery. We were told he had once represented the country in it.

First of all, helped by Father Michael, he put up a big circular target stuffed with straw on the grass in front of the Castle. It was covered by a paper with a red circle in the middle, a middle ring of yellow and a blue outer ring. First of all the instructor gathered us around him to show how a bow was strung and how they made arrows. His breath had a sweet caramelly perfume to it. He had brown blotches on his bald head and a pot belly.

'Archery is one of the oldest sports in human history, gentlemen, as it was a favourite pastime of the Egyptian Pharoah Ramases II and of course the Trojan prince Alexandrus, known as Paris — for some reason that I don't know as he wasn't French, ha-ha! Now, let me show you how it's done.'

He put on a pair of special leather wrist-guards and then fingerless gloves. Picking up the bow he took an arrow from a container he called a quiver that stood inside a wire stand under his right hand. He fitted the arrow in place — 'we call it "notching" the arrow' — and stood facing the target, with his forward foot just behind a string line that he had pinned into the grass.

'This is a concentration sport,' he said, 'a precision sport, whether practised on a moving or a fixed target. You see my position? Legs apart, with my weight on the back one so that it's braced. Always remember that you are bending the bow with both arms simultaneously, not just with the arm that draws the string. So as you raise the bow you pull the string back to your cheek as near to the ear as you can, while pushing the bow arm forward until it is straight and braced. Then you sight the target, check that everything is steady and let fly — like this.'

There was a satisfying twang but his arrow shot high to the left missing by a good three feet.

'That, boys, is what we call a "sighter". Just to get a feel for the wind and so on.'

He took another arrow and shot again. This one missed by a similar margin on the right hand side.

'Oops!' he said. 'Over-compensated. Third time lucky, eh, boys! Ha-ha!'

He notched a third arrow and drew the bow. I could tell that he was really trying now, as he sniffed very hard, held his breath and narrowed his eyes to slits. But his straightened bow arm was trembling from the effort and, as he released the bowstring, his body seemed to twitch. The arrow sailed harmless and high over the target.

'Bugger!' he said, not quite under his breath, and then, more loudly, 'Did you see that pigeon that flew across my line of sight? Totally queered the pitch. But never mind me. Let's see how Father can do, shall we?'

Father Michael tied the ends of his scapula together to keep them out of the way, then took the bow and an arrow and adopted the position. His arrow stuck into the target just outside the outer ring.

'Well done, Sir!' we shouted. 'Good shot!'

We lined up to try for ourselves. The bow was surprisingly stiff and most of us struggled to pull the arrow two thirds of the way back, so that it inevitably landed short. The worst shot was by Skinner. The bow was only half bent when it took control of him and he teetered back, let go at random, and sent the arrow high into the air. Then Nelson stepped forward and easily bent the bow. He looked as if he'd been doing it all his life. He sighted carefully and let the arrow go. It went straight to the yellow ring, an inch or two short of a bull's eye.

'Crikey!' said the instructor. 'You've done this before, young man. Who's next?'

Next was Carani. His shot missed by a couple of inches. He lowered the bow and scowled at the target as if to intimidate it. Without asking permission he picked another arrow from the quiver, notching it quickly in the bowstring a second time. He pulled and pushed almost savagely until the bow was fully bent and, sighting for a moment, he let fly. His arrow buried itself in the blue outer circle.

'One more,' he said.

He picked up an arrow, notched it and bent the bow so fast that no one could stop him. He braced himself until he was steady and shot. The arrow went into the target just inside centre spot. He grinned.

'Bull's eye,' he said, handing the bow back to the instructor.

'Give me another shot,' demanded Nelson.

The instructor seemed bemused. He handed over the bow and watched as Nelson, toeing the line, notched an arrow while it was still lowered towards the ground. In a smooth movement he raised the bow and arrow together, drawing the string as he did so in a single easy movement. He sighted for a couple of seconds and let go.

The arrow thudded into the straw just beside Carani's.

Wearing the Green

I had to collect a parcel from the Post Room. It proved to be a small green box sent by my grandmother for St Patrick's Day, which contained a bunch of shamrock still rooted in a little bed of Irish soil. You got it a few days ahead of time, giving you the chance to revive it with water and light before cutting it and pinning it to the lapel of your blazer on the day. All the Irish boys would get them. I was wearing mine when I went up to Carani's desk between History and Maths.

Granny Mooney had also enclosed in the package a cellophane envelope containing an assortment of stamps.

'Carani, have you got any stamp swaps?' I said. 'I just got sent a packet of assorted and there are some super triangular Hungarian Olympic ones.'

Carani ignored the question.

'What's that?' he said, pointing to my lapel with a sneer.

Carani knew perfectly well what it was.

'It's from my grandparents in Cork.'

'What're they sending you duckweed for?'

'It's not,' I said. 'It's shamrock.'

'No, it's duckweed! Duckweed! Duckweed!'

Carani thought this tremendously funny.

'Shut up Carani,' I said.

'Ha-ha! You're a bogtrotter,' he said. 'What are you? Say it. Say "I'm a bogtrotter".'

'No, I won't.'

'You will.'

'I won't.'

'You will.'

'CARANI!'

We never noticed that silence had fallen around us. Mr Finnegan had entered the classroom. He advanced on Carani and whacked him on the back of the head with the flat of his hand. Mr Finnegan, too, was wearing shamrock.

'I will not have Anti-Irish abuse at any time in my class, Carani, let alone on this sacred feast day. Understand? Do you know the lines "Now and in time to be, Wherever green is worn, All changed, changed utterly: A terrible beauty is born"'?

'No, Sir.'

'Shame on you. Write them out fifty times by tomorrow. Now, everyone, open your Pendlebury at page 41, if you please.'

After this Carani and I were on non-speaks.

A Pike in the Deep

Why did boys go from speaks to non-speaks and back again as if the previous states had not existed? Two days later Carani was acting as if our St Patrick's Day exchange had never happened.

'Father Finbar says there's a monster pike in the Small Lake,' he said. 'In the deeps of it.'

'Then we must try not to fall in,' said Deuchar.

We were down below the Castle, Nelson, Carani, Deuchar and me, each of us in wellies and carrying a net and a jam jar. We were collecting tadpoles from the lake for Father Finbar's fish tank that he'd set up in the classroom corridor. The Small Lake, nearer to the Castle than the substantial Big Lake, was still a sizeable body of water, seventy-five yards long and with two wooden stages or fishing platforms jutting out, one at each end. Leaving the other two to occupy the nearer of these platforms, Deuchar and I walked around to take up our station at the far end. We filled our jam jars with cloudy water threaded with weed and were kneeling and trawling the lake for specimens when I looked up. Nelson and Carani were doing the same at the other end of the water.

'What's this?' said Deuchar.

He had raised his net and found a small and almost translucent fish writhing in it. It had two sharp spines like needles sticking up from its back.

'Probably one of the giant pike's grandchildren.'

'I'm going to keep it. If I let it go it'll only be eaten by its grandfather. Maybe Father Finbar will let it live in the tank.'

He was just easing the little fish into his jam jar when we heard loud voices from Nelson's and Carani's platform. We looked up and saw that they were jostling each other in some argument. The next moment Carani was in the water with a splash but, instead of trying to get back to Nelson and the stage, he was paddling further into the middle of the lake, laughing and spitting water. He seemed to be enjoying himself but within a short time it became clear that, because of his wellies, swimming was not easy. Then he went under.

Nelson stood staring at the place where he had last seen Carani. Right next to him, hanging from a post, was a lifebelt, except it wasn't a belt. It was a big white and orange ring, like a giant polo mint. But as far as Nelson was concerned the lifebelt might not have been there. He just stared at the rippling surface of the water as if fascinated.

A voice roared out of the trees behind him.

'Nelson! Throw the lifebelt! NELSON!'

Then there was a thunder of rubberbooted steps on the landing stage and Father Kentigern, wearing a blue overall and woolly hat, launched himself like a human torpedo past Nelson and into the water. Three powerful swimming strokes got him to the place where Carani had disappeared. He took a huge breath and performed a duck-dive. The last we saw of him was his rubber boots kicking the air.

We waited in suspense, our eyes on the exact spot where the boots had gone under. The surface of the Lake was already getting smoother and there was still no sign of either Carani or Father Kentigern. I had a peculiar feeling. I could hear no birdsong or wind in the trees. Time had paused.

'The giant pike must have got Carani,' whispered Deuchar. 'Father Kentigern will be fighting the monster down on the depths.'

'He'll run out of air soon,' I said.

Now at last Nelson unhooked the lifebelt and sent it spinning towards the middle of the Lake. Simultaneously there was an explosion of water and two heads broke the surface. Next thing, ignoring the lifebelt, Father Kentigern was swimming one-arm side-stroke towards the bank, with Carani clasped under his spare arm. Deuchar and I abandoned our position and ran to the spot where they'd be coming ashore. We got there just as Father Kentigern, puffing and gasping, found his depth and began to wade towards the bank, half carrying and half towing Carani. We pulled at his sodden overall to help him out. He had lost his woollen hat.

Father Kentigern laid Carani down on his front, head to one side, and pressed his back two-handed. There was no sign of life. He pressed again, leaning into the press with all his weight, then relaxed and did the same a third time. Now at last Carani twitched and convulsed and a quantity of muddy, slimy water gushed from his mouth. His legs kicked and pretty soon he was retching and coughing, and sitting up, with a bewildered look on his face. Father Kentigern lifted him in his arms and marched away with him along the shore of the Lake up towards the Castle.

'We'd better get our nets and the jar,' said Deuchar.

As we left the Lake to return to the Castle, the orange lifebelt was slowly spinning on the surface of the water, alongside Father Kentigern's woolly hat. There was no sign at all of Nelson.

The Fishtank

'He's a Stickleback, Father Finbar says,' said Deuchar. 'I'm going to call him Sticky.'

With our noses close to the glass of the fish tank, Deuchar, Corcoran and I were watching the spiny little individual that Deuchar had taken from the lake. A squadron of tadpoles wriggled in the water around him as he hovered with his face towards the stream of bubbles from the aerator, holding the position with flicks of its tail and fins

'What's he doing that for?' said Corcoran

'He's dreaming of his old life in the lake,' I said.

'He should be glad he was saved from being eaten by the pike.'

'This is worse, actually, because it's not his home,' said Deuchar, with a sigh that condensed for a moment on the glass of the fishtank. 'This water's too clean and bright. It should be green and gloomy. If you ask me he doesn't like us looking at him all the time. He's got nowhere to hide.'

'And he's scared of being eaten by Poseidon,' said Corcoran.

Poseidon was the crayfish that had been introduced into the tank even before Sticky. Father Finbar had christened him. He spent most of its time lurking behind a rock that lay half sunk in the fine white sand of the tank floor. Poseidon's armoured body was black and his arms ended in pincers with serrations like saws, or the teeth of a small crocodile. Antennae sprouted from his brow and he had evil little eyes that missed nothing.

'Do you think Carani was grabbed by a giant crayfish at the bottom of the lake?' said Corcoran.

'Sir says it was just that his wellies filled up and he got tangled up in weeds or something.'

'It could even have been the pike that caught him,' I said. 'The monster pike.'

'He would have had a wound,' Deuchar pointed out. 'Slashed by its teeth. And a hole in his welly, with one or two of his toes taken off. A crayfish pincer might not've broken through the rubber of his wellies, but still held him under.'

The Lie

Not long after that we were cubbing and I was holed up inside the Den with the smell of earth in my nose. I'd hidden the mouth of the Den with a leafy branch that looked as it if was a young tree growing in the bank. I was imagining I was in an R.L. Stevenson novel, hiding from pursuing Hanoverian soldiers. But lying in a narrow hole with nothing happening outside soon becomes boring and I was just about to crawl out and run off to join Deuchar and Corcoran, who were yet again re-building the hut, when I heard voices. I looked out through the leaves and saw Carani and Nelson, just the two of them, coming towards me. They sat down on the trunk of a dead tree that lay along one side of the clearing, exactly in my line of sight.

'Do you mean you really can't remember anything?' said Nelson.

'I remember us going down to the lake and walking onto the landing stage. That's all. The rest is just a blank. Nurse says it's the shock.'

'Don't you even remember falling in?'

'No. Nothing until I woke up in the Sick Room. Tell me what happened, Nelson.'

'You fell in. You were fooling around and you stepped off into the air – and landed sideways in the water. You paddled around for a bit laughing and then you just went under. Father Kentigern says your wellies filled up with water and you sank.'

'So what did you do?'

'I threw in the life belt and then I got off my wellies and dived straight in after you, to save you. I was just swimming towards the middle of the lake when Father Kentigern dived in past me and pulled you out of the deep.'

'What a swiz. Thanks a million trillion anyway, Nelson. Even if you didn't actually save me it's the thought that counts. I was nearly a goner.'

'Well, if Father K. hadn't saved you, I would have instead, wouldn't I?'

I heard the lie and I let it go by for the moment. After all, what Nelson said was the expected truth. Not only was he Carani's best friend, he was by miles the best swimmer in the Year. So of course he would've got his wellies off, dived straight in and swum to where he'd seen Carani go under. Of *course* he would've.

Except that he never did.

Low Grade Vitality

'Heh-heh,' said Old Tyler. 'So you came back from the dead. How was the Underworld?'

It was still Easter Term but next term would be cricket and Carani and I were in the Boot Room, oiling our cricket bats in readiness. Sergeant-Major Hanrahan was going to hold some indoor nets to sort out the hares from the rabbits, so he said.

I had grown closer to Carani in these days. We were both keen on cricket, though my team was Lancashire and his was Worcestershire. We possessed similar, quite old bats. Mine was printed across the splice with the facsimile signature of Cyril Washbrook, now barely visible. Carani's was an equally battered Denis Compton autograph bat.

Old Tyler, shuffling out from the cellar gloom of his Lair, had stopped and spoken this interesting question.

'I don't know,' said Carani. 'I don't think I was quite dead, actually.'

'Not what I heard. Came back from the dead is what I heard, yurr. Which reminds me of somebody else I could name.'

'Who's that, Mr Tyler?'

'Oh, er, yurr. Better not say.'

'I thought you were an Atheist, ' I said. 'Atheists don't believe in the Underworld, or Heaven, or anything like that.'

He scratched the bulb of his nose and then pulled the palm of his hand down across his mouth.

'I was ribbing you. There's always a scientific explanation for any queer thing. I'll give you a similar for-instance. There was this bloke I was in the War with, on convoy duty in the North Atlantic. In winter it was so bloody freezing even the icicles were complaining. One morning they came across this rating frozen rigid after a night on deck watch. So they threw him in the sick bay to thaw out but when he did, they reckoned he was dead as a kipper. Yurr. They sewed him up in a bag ready to tip him into the drink and send off the telegram to his folks saying he'd copped it, but next thing – no word of a lie – this midshipman came along and bumped into the body somehow and, bugger me, that body moved under the canvas and all at once he was alive and breathing again. I had a talk with him later. I asked him the same question as I just asked you. How was the Underworld?'

'What did he say?'

'Couldn't say, same as you couldn't say. Of course, it didn't stop the blokes on his Watch talking about a miracle. But me, I know why he couldn't say. Because there's no such thing as a miracle, see? What happened, the scientists have got a word for it: Low Grade Vitality. It's what occurred in your case, boy, until Father frightened you back to life. Reversible shut-down of vital signs. So, my shipmate didn't go nowhere. He was just out like a light bulb, which then happened to get turned on again. Mark my words, there's a scientific explanation for everything.'

'But Father Kentigern didn't frighten me, Mr Tyler,' said Carani.

'Whatever it was, he knew what to do, so be thankful.'

51

Old Tyler went on his way and Carani poured some more linseed oil into his bunch of rag, before starting to caress it into the wood of the bat.

'I wish I'd been rescued by Nelson, that's all,' he said. 'Sir got to me first, but it was a deadly close race and I wish Nelson had got to me first.'

I picked up the bottle of linseed oil and poured some more onto the blade of my bat. I began rubbing. I had the thought that I ought to tell him what I knew. I didn't but it was sorely troubling.

Looking for Medicine Balls

Nelson and Carani were still, officially as you might say, best friends. But since that day at the lake their relationship had subtly changed. They no longer spent time exclusively in each other's company, but each held court to a certain extent over a different circle of boys. Carani's group included me, Biggins, Deuchar and Corcoran. Nelson seemed to be spending a lot more time than he used to with Romero. He liked to hear tales of the Marines stationed at the Base – how they trained and had fun; how they talked.

Around the middle of term came St Benedict's Day, a Whole Holiday, when an excursion was organized for our Year by Father Kentigern. It meant getting into a bus and going to a Dale, so a lot of boys took model boats to float on the river, and some took swimming trunks. Others came equipped for rounders and French cricket. But first we all had to play a game which Father K called a Wide Game.

'There are two teams chosen by lot,' he said, after he'd blown his whistle and gathered us all under a great oak tree, which stood in the big meadow alongside the riverbank. 'Your names appear on the team sheets that I've pinned to the tree here. The blue team's Command Post is the wooden hut over there. The red team is based in the tin hut on the other side. So here is the object of the game. I've brought a dozen medicine balls from the gym and hidden them in various places within a perimeter of five hundred yards. They are mostly in or around the fringes of the surrounding woods, or in the river bank. The team that brings the most medicine balls back to their Command Post wins. You're allowed to intercept members of the other team and pinch medicine balls before they get them back, but once a ball is back at the Command Post it's untouchable. Rugger rules apply. Tackles are allowed but no hitting, kicking, biting, gouging or grabbing people's soft bits. One whistle to start, three loud blasts to stop and return to base for lunch. All right?'

As it turned out Carani and Nelson were in opposite teams. Carani was in the Reds with me. When we went to our base we found red armbands, which we put on. There was a lot of excitement and chatter. Boys were all for tearing off at once to look for medicine balls. Then Carani raised his voice.

'Shut up and listen. We've got to have a plan. It's much better than cubbing, more like a real war. We should get into groups so when we find the medicine balls we can protect them as we get them back. And three of us should stay here in base.'

'To guard against attacks?' said Biggins.

'Exactly. To watch over our medicine balls.'

I expected that Carani would stay at the Command Post. But he didn't want to miss the action so the job went to Biggins, who recruited Skinner and Deuchar, as they would not be very good in a fight. The rest of us formed into threesomes, and I was in a unit with Carani and a boy called Shelley. The sky was cloudy and threatening rain as the units sallied forth in various directions.

We had got one Medicine Ball safely back to Biggins and now Shelley was climbing a tree because he swore he could see another high in the branches. With half an eye on him, Carani and I were poking around in some bracken nearby while also keeping an eye out for marauding Blues.

'I suppose Nelson and Romero will be filling the Blue team with ideas from the U.S. Marines,' Carani said. 'Give me the Royal Marines any day. Which do you prefer?'

I didn't really know the difference, but I could tell he wanted me to say the Royal Marines, so I did.

'Nelson's gone potty about everything American,' Carani said. 'He gave me some gum to chew yesterday. I said I'd rather drink petrol and he said the Yanks call that gas short for gasoline. I said that's a stupid name, and he said I should have said what a *dumb* name, only it wasn't one. And when I tried to tell him what dumb really means he wouldn't listen.'

It was not often you heard negative remarks from Carani about Nelson. I sensed that this was a good moment to shed my burden of guilty knowledge.

'Carani,' I said. 'You know Nelson's supposed to have dived into the water to save you from drowning in the lake, except Father K got there first?'

'Yes. That's what he told me, anyway.'

'That you missed your step and fell in, and he threw in the lifebelt, then got out of his wellies and dived in? And then Father K dived past him?'

Carani frowned and gave me a mistrustful look.

'It's what he told me, because I've got amnesia about it. But how do you know that's what he said to me?'

I needed a lie because, for some reason, I was shy of telling him I had eavesdropped on his tête-à-tête with Nelson.

'It's what he told other people,' I said.

This might even have been true. If it wasn't, it was a small lie, a white one. Not like the stinking great lie I'd heard Nelson tell.

'So? Why shouldn't he? It's what happened, isn't it?'

I looked directly into his brown, guileless eyes.

'Actually, no,' I said. 'Actually I saw the whole thing from the other landing stage. Deuchar and I saw exactly what happened.'

'What did you see?'

'You didn't just fall in. You were having a row and I think he barged you in. And he didn't throw in the lifebelt when he said he did. He only threw it when it was too late. And he didn't get his wellies off or dive in after you. He just stood and stared like a complete clot at the place you went under. He never even got his feet wet.'

Carani had stopped combing the bracken. He was staring at me, with his mouth open.

'He pushed me in?' he said.

I realised I had gone too far. I didn't know that Nelson had actually pushed Carani into the water. But I told myself he easily might have, which meant that, again, I hadn't quite told a lie. So I said,

'Ask Deuchar. He was there too.'

'And according to you Nelson didn't dive in to save me?'

That at least was true. I was on safer ground.

'No. We were watching. He didn't.'

Before we could say any more a Medicine Ball landed on the ground between us with a thump.

'See?' called out Shelley from above. 'I told you there was one up here.'

The worst words

During break soon after St Benedict's I was skating with Deuchar on our rumbling wheels when Carani came up alongside. Like us, he laboured along on ancient metal-wheel skates clipped to his shoes. All around a frantic game of skate-hockey, played with improvised sticks and a tennis ball, was going on among the more fluent skaters.

Nelson was in the heart of the game, gliding about on his Jacko-skates, gracefully swerving around non-players like a skier performing Christie turns, then sprinting to pounce on the ball and whacking it as hard as he could before looping back in a perfect arc to his previous position. It was half way along one of these arcs that he collided head on with Carani.

Both of them went down. Carani was initially pushed into reverse. He leaned forward to regain control but his skates came together and then went wide apart before he cannoned into the surrounding fence and went to the floor in a heap. Nelson couldn't maintain his balance. He was rolling on one skate and tilting sideways, with his other leg cocked up like a pissing dog, his arms wagging back and forth. He managed to bring the wayward leg down, but in trying the straighten his body he leant back too far, his skates went from under him and he upended onto his bum.

'Look out you clumsy bloody clot!' Nelson shouted from the floor. 'Are you blind? Why don't you look where you're going?'

It was rare, almost unknown, for Nelson to get waxy like this, and Carani was taken by surprise. He had got to his knees and began to examine the heels of his hands, which he had grazed breaking his fall. He was smiling ruefully.

'Oh, *really*, Nelson,' he said. 'That was actually your fault.'

All activity in the immediate vicinity of the accident had stopped and boys stood around watching its aftermath.

'I was only skating slowly and you were zooming around utterly regardless,' went on Carani, pointing at Nelson. 'So *you're* the clot, not me. '

Nelson was getting up now. Slowly he straightened and, skating to the rail, leaned on it with his elbows. He affected nonchalance.

Carani had not finished.

'You're also the clot who didn't dive in to save me from the bottom of the lake, even though you told me you did.'

Nelson formed his lips into a tight contemptuous smile. Before replying he flicked a glance towards

Romero who was standing nearby. Then he looked back towards Carani and said slowly, almost lazily,

'Want to know what I think? I think you're a mother-fucker, Carani. So why don't you fuck off and fuck your prostitute mother?'

Nelson had picked the worst words he knew — *fuck, prostitute* — and planted them in Carani's mind, together with the Castle's greatest unmentionable subject, *your mother*. Carani stared, unable at first to take the words in, or what Nelson meant by saying them. But a match had been struck and put to the fire and now, all at once, it ignited. With a cry like an animal, he lunged towards Nelson, pulled him away from the rail and started punching him on the body, the head – anywhere. He was grunting and had gone tomato red in the face, with his eyes in slits and an unfunny grin, as he pummeled and pummeled. Meanwhile Nelson tried to ward off the blows with his hands. It is impossible to fist-fight on wheels and both of them immediately began spinning helplessly around until they could do nothing but go down. When this happened Carani was at first on top and punching Nelson in the body as rapidly as he could.

But then Nelson seemed to recollect himself – that he was taller than Carani and stronger. That he was an athlete. With a violent jerk, he rolled out from under and got above Carani, then fell onto him so that it was now Carani's turn to get a pummeling. Not for long, though. Father Finbar came up at a run, vaulted over the railing and sprinted across the tarmac to separate them.

'Who would have thought it?' said Deuchar when the excitement was over and we were jogging back to the Castle for the next lesson. 'Nelson was meant to be Carani's official best friend. But now he hates his guts. Do you suppose he hated him all the time, in fact?'

It was the nearest thing that I heard to an explanation of what Nelson did. But there was something else in my mind. I remembered how Nelson had looked across at Romero and I wondered if he had rehearsed those words. Was what Nelson said to Carani a *calculated* insult?

The Challenge

The disgusting, vile words Nelson had used at the rink were not voiced again. And they were never referred to by another boy in Carani's presence. But that didn't mean they were forgotten.

He and Nelson didn't talk directly to each other but passed messages through go-betweens. Carani was tending the fire of his anger. He was always reading books about heroes and villains in olden times, so he was fond of the lore of knighthood and chivalry, challenge and combat. Now, because of his anger, and the insult that caused it, he was inspired to issue a challenge to Nelson. There would have to be another fight, he said, and this time a final, decisive one.

He wrote the challenge out. I was with him when he did it. I guess he wanted a witness of some sort. Also he wanted a second, who would actually deliver the challenge.

I, R. Carani, he wrote, *hereby issue a challenge to T. Nelson to fight because he insulted me and my family with poisonous words. This message is hereby carried by my second C. Conroy. Nelson has to tell him the name of his second and he will make the arrangements with Conroy. (signed) R. Carani*

I folded the challenge and put it in my pocket. I had a proud feeling, knowing he had chosen me as his second. I would give the challenge to Nelson, I said, when I saw him next.

It so happened that I next saw him sitting in what we were supposed to refer to as the Places, but which were always called the Bogs. His shorts were around his ankles in one of the stalls — the stalls whose doors had long since been taken away.

Nelson read the challenge, then looked up at me.
'So?'

58

'You have to do what he says. Tell me the name of your second.'

'Why do I have to? What law says I have to?'

'The law of honour,' I said, which I considered a terrific reply. I was thinking of the *Iliad* and the fight between Paris and Menelaus, which was supposed to settle the Trojan War without more bloodshed. That was a matter of honour, which even weak-willed Paris couldn't get out of.

Nelson said nothing. He just sighed as if tired of the whole thing.

'So, who *is* your second, then?' I said, pointing to the letter in his hand. 'We have to make the arrangements.'

'Oh well, Romero I suppose,' said Nelson with a shrug.

Seconds

I got the chance to talk to Romero when he joined me outside the Post Room at break to collect parcels. We were only allowed in there one at a time. Nearby was Matron's headquarters, where sheets were laundered and pressed, so our noses were full of the scents of starch, damp cotton and Omo. Matron was also in charge of the Post Room.

'I'm Carani's second in his challenge on Nelson,' I said.

'I know,' he said.

'And you're Nelson's second.'

'Right,' he said.

'We've got to decide on a place for it.'

'And a time.'

'I know. And the rules.'

Before we got any further Matron called him in.

Later the same day we were able to whisper together while crossing the hall on our way into lunch.

'Nelson says OK, he'll fight, but he bags the choice of weapon.'

'What weapon does he bag?'

'He says boxing gloves.'

We were just alongside the naked Greek warrior. I looked up and noticed the disdainful curl of his lip.

Next day I found Romero playing ping-pong in the gallery.

'Carani agrees to boxing gloves at dawn,' I said.

Romero had possession of the Champ's bat, which was coloured red. One boy after another picked up the blue Challenger's bat and tried to dethrone him, but he was dismissing them one by one with delicate spinning drop-shots, or hurtling drives that flew off the edge of the table. Even Nelson was not better at ping-pong than Romero, which is why Nelson never played him.

'At dawn?' said Romero, working his opponent from side to side, forehand to backhand.

'Not actually at dawn, obviously. But boxing gloves, anyway.'

'And boxing rules.'

I considered for a moment.

'But Sarge keeps the boxing gloves locked up. Where are we going to get some from?'

Romero aimed an ambitious looping backspin shot intended to land on the extreme edge of the table. It was too long by a quarter of an inch.

'Now look what you've made me do, Conroy, you blighter.'

He handed the red bat across to the opponent and walked discontented away from the table.

'Well, where *are* we going to get boxing gloves from?' I said.

He shrugged.

'From Old Tyler, I guess.'

Later Carani took me aside.

'About the challenge. What's the latest?'

'Romero and me are going to try and get boxing gloves off Old Tyler. We'll have to tell him what they're for.'

'Better if I talk to him. He'll do what I ask. He likes me.'

Weapons of Choice

'So what d'you want boxing gloves for?' said Old Tyler, shooting another shovel-full of coal into the furnace.

Old Tyler had unbuttoned the top of his overalls and slipped his arms out, leaving his torso covered only by a dirty white vest. His bare arms showed off his tattoos. On one forearm was an anchor above a scroll on which was written "H.M.S. Vulcan". The other displayed a heart pierced by an arrow with the name "Mae-Lou" inside. On his biceps there were respectively a mermaid with oversized breasts and a picture of a man with a mass of hair and tangled beard, under which was written the name "Karl Marx".

'I'm fighting Nelson,' said Carani. 'It's a matter of honour. He insulted my— . Someone in my family.'

Old Tyler's face, glistening with sweat, had an unearthly glow in the orange furnace-light. He hastily shoveled a last lot of coal then banged the furnace door shut.

'Why don't you tell Sergeant-Major Hanrahan?' he said. 'He'll give you gloves.'

'We can't. We're not supposed to fight. We get the Slipper if we are caught fighting.'

'Ha! Unless Hanrahan arranges it himself, of course. Queensbury Rules — yurr. Hypocrites, all of them. Don't say I said that. Come into the Office.'

He propped the shovel against the wall and led us back into the room where I had first met him. Collapsing into the ruined armchair he picked up a pipe and lit it, sending up thick signals of smoke. He was quite still for a moment, looking up in thought at the ceiling which was hung with a network of grimy cobwebs. We waited in suspense.

'Yurr, I dare say I can oblige,' Old Tyler said at last. 'Probably do you both good: clear the air, yurr. Got three or four pairs of gloves somewhere about.

61

They'll be old and a bit torn and chewed-up, but you can patch 'em. Haven't seen them recently, mind. '

He placed the pipe in the ashtray on his desk and, uttering a groan, levered himself up. He crossed bow-legged to his shelves, took down some boxes and looked inside them, inserting his hand and stirring the contents. None evidently contained boxing gloves. He took down more boxes and searched them in a similar way.

'Chess pieces,' he said. 'Carpet bowls ... shuttlecocks ... croquet hoops ... mallet heads. They do love their games in this place. Hold hard. What's this?'

He pulled out a ferrule, the rubber advanced in decay and threaded with cracks.

'Gosh, it's an old Stick,' said Carani. 'How did you get that, Mr Tyler?'

'I get all sorts, when nobody's got further use for them. This one had plenty of use on its time, mind. Yurr. Even the Navy don't do that no more.'

He dropped it back into the box. His face had an odd look, as if he had just smelled excrement.

'Here's one glove, leastways.'

He'd lifted a single boxing glove out. He held it up by its drawstring and it revolved in the air. Dusty, dull, the leather hardened and creased.

'There might be another half to the pair. Let's see.'

He opened another box and gave a cry of triumph.

'See here, boys. I got a plethora of them. Know what a plethora is?'

'A lot,' I said.

'Yurr. A lot. A cornucopia. Six or seven pair to choose from at least. Take your pick.'

Carani examined the contents of the box. He tried some of the gloves on and finally settled on two pairs. They were in no better condition than the first one we'd seen, but they fitted.

'They're exactly the same as each other,' he said. 'That's all right. He's got hands the same size as mine.'

'What about the torn parts?'

'I can mend them with some Elastoplast I've got in my wash-bag,' said Carani.

'You should save that for your own cuts,' said Old Tyler. ' Here, I got some insulating tape.'

He yanked open his desk drawer and brought out a ring of black tape, which he handed over.

'That'll be a bob on account,' said Old Tyler, holding out his palm. 'I'll give you a tanner back when you return them gloves, with the tape you don't use.'

'Do we have to pay?' said Carani.

'Yurr. Nothing's for nothing down here.'

We each found a sixpence in our pocket, and handed it over.

'Swizz about the shilling,' I said as we left. 'But at least we got some gloves.'

'Yurr,' said Carani.

The Ring of Bracken

Everyone agreed the fight would have to be during cubbing. It was the only chance of getting away from a master for any length of time. The previous week we had chosen a clearing within the densest part of the Wolery, where the ground was more or less flat, and covered with a carpet of dead wet leaves. We arranged a barrier of fallen branches around the edge to create a make-shift boxing ring.

'It'll do,' said Carani when we showed it to him. 'But I think you should take away the branches and use dead bracken. There's piles of it around. It's safer for when I knock him out of the ring because there won't be anything to break his legs on. And, by the way, why's it called a ring when it's square?'

Nelson also inspected the ring, now edged by lines of heaped bracken. He nodded his head and merely said,

'Who's going to be referee?'

We looked at each other. Nobody had thought of that. Then Collinshaw shot up his arm.

'I'll do it,' he said. 'I know the rules. No hitting below the belt, etcetera.'

It was Collinshaw who insisted on the timing of the contest.

'It's got to be three rounds of two minutes each,' he said. 'That's normal. We haven't got a bell so the timekeeper will have to shout when time's up. Who's got a second hand on their watch?'

Skinner had, and he had been timekeeper before, when Sarge was in charge.

Single Combat

A week later I stood with Carani at cubbing, easing the gloves onto his hands. The whole Year was there, tense with suppressed excitement, almost all of them betting hypothetically on Nelson.

'Don't forget what Sarge told us,' I said, tying up the drawstrings of Carani's gloves. 'You've got to defend and avoid his punches, then you can bide your time and hit him when you get the best chance.'

Someone had found a large log and put it in Nelson's corner inside the ring for him to sit on between rounds. Now Deuchar came up carrying another for Carani, who sat down on it without a word. In the week leading up to this he had been his usual self, cracking jokes and taking the Mickey out of people. But there had been no jokes today, and no teasing. He had never been so quiet, and now seemed to be thinking hard — thinking, I had no doubt, of the vicious words Nelson had used about his mother. I looked across at the opposite corner. Nelson also had his gloves on now and Romero was whispering into his ear and laughing. Nelson looked at ease. He stood up, bounced on the balls of his feet and knocked his gloved fists together. Carani stood up also.

Romero and I stepped out across the boundary bracken, taking the log-stools with us. Everybody gathered round the edge of the ring. Both boxers stood ready in their corners while Collinshaw took up position in the middle. He was looking at Skinner, who had his eyes trained on his watch. They were waiting for his second hand to reach the vertical.

'Six ... five ... four ....' called Skinner.

'THREE ... TWO ... ONE,' we all called out together.

'BOX!' shouted Skinner.

The two boxers raised their fists and advanced towards each other. In the first few moments of the fight they kept a wary distance between them, circling around the middle of the ring. There was a big contrast in their styles. Nelson presented his gloves in the proper way and moved on springy legs, making as if to dart forward to strike, but then changing direction and dancing sideways. Carani shuffled on stiff legs and held his arms out as if they bore some heavy but invisible load. Nelson's face gave nothing away. It wore his usual almost-smirk. Carani's expression was one of ferocious concentration, his lips pouting and the muscles of his jaw sticking out.

When Nelson finally skipped forward and planted a punch on Carani's cheek, Carani was taken by surprise. He shook his head impatiently, lowered it and frowned. He swung at Nelson but Nelson leaned coolly back and the fist swished harmlessly past his chin. So it was for the whole of Round One. Nelson landed four or five clean blows, not very hard, either to Carani's body or neck. Carani swung and swung but connected with nothing. Carani was looking out-classed.

I had brought a towel from the Castle, which I'd wetted in the stream that ran along the edge of the Rookery. While waiting for Skinner to call the next round I flapped it in front of Carani's face, which had become very red, and said,

'You've got to duck more,' I said. 'You're letting him hit you.'

'I don't care. I'm going to get him anyway. He can hit me as much as he likes but I'll knock him out.'

By the end of the second round Carani's left eye looked swollen and there was blood coming from his lower lip. He had landed two or three stomach blows, and got satisfying oofs out of Nelson, but his own head had been jolted by at least twice as many punches. He had tried at one point to get close and pummel, but Nelson just twisted out of the way, hitting Carani with a crisp punch on the ear and getting out of his reach again. It was quite obvious who was ahead on points.

'You've got to hit him a lot more,' I said during the second break, flapping frantically with my towel. I turned and glanced at Nelson who was sitting calmly, elbows on knees, and not looking at all as if he needed Romero's towel to cool him.

'Only once,' Carani said in a low voice.

'What?' I said, bending towards him.

'I only need to hit him once.'

'SECONDS OUT!' yelled Skinner.

Carani's strategy changed in Round Three. He blundered forward, a bit like Brian London against Henry Cooper, and wrapped one of his arms around Nelson while getting some ungainly punches into the body with the other. Nelson really hated this.

'Hey!' he shouted at one point.

He appealed to Collinshaw.

'Stop him doing this! Stop him holding!'

'Break!' shouted Collinshaw. 'Break! Break! Break!'

But Carani took no notice. He would only break in his own time, and when he did it looked as if he had hurt Nelson around the ribs. Nelson was less nimble now, and blowing hard. But he was still landing punches and, as Round Three was coming towards its climax, he was still well ahead by any reckoning of the points. Then in a single instant everything changed.

It wasn't quite clear whether Carani really meant to do it. He looked as if he aimed to close in again and Nelson, seeing this, crouched and covered his face with his gloves, while forcing his elbows forward. Quite unexpectedly Carani now swung his body all the way around, turning his back on Nelson, who uncovered his face in surprise. But Carani didn't stay turned away. He kept on pivoting until he'd swung through the full three hundred and sixty degrees, while moving his right arm in an underarm bowler's action. At the very point at which he and Nelson were face to face again, Carani's fist smashed into Nelson's chin at an upward angle. There was a snap of Nelson's teeth and his legs crumpled. For a moment he tottered, before he collapsed, without uttering a sound. He seemed to spiral to the ground, for the first time looking ungainly. He was already fully down when the side of his head thudded into the earth, and he lay still. He lay perfectly still. Collinshaw jumped forward. It was his moment: the one he'd been longing for.

'One ... two ... three ... four,' he called, while chopping the air in time with his arm. 'Five ... six ... seven ... eight ... nine ... and TEN! Counted out. Nelson's been knocked out. Carani wins. Hurray! Carani's the champ!'

The next moment Romero was kneeling beside the prone boxer, shaking him.

'Nelson,' he kept saying. 'Nelson! Wake up. Cripes, he really has been knocked out. He won't come round. Nelson! Nelson!'

Everybody could see that Nelson's eyes were open, but mostly showed white. His pupils had almost disappeared beneath his upper eyelids. Two boys raced off at a gallop to find Father Kentigern.

Extreme Unction

Nelson had not woken up by the time Father Kentigern came. And he didn't awake after Father K had carried him in his arms back to the Castle. He was taken straight into the Sick Room and, when Nurse Horgan saw the look of him, she telephoned the doctor.

The sensational news that went around the Refectory at tea was that Nelson had still not come round, and Father Sigbert had administered Extreme Unction.

'What's that?' said Corcoran at our table.

'It's for when you're dying, you loon,' said Collinshaw. 'They anoint you with an ointment and Holy Oil and say prayers for your soul.'

'I think the ointment's called chrism which is made out of myrrh,' said Deuchar, as well informed as ever in matters of liturgy. 'The three kings brought some of that at Christmas, which is why it's called chrism.'

'So that means Nelson's dying,' said Collinshaw. 'Cripes.'

We all looked at Carani. He had turned as white as lard. After tea in the Gallery he pulled me aside.

'Conroy, will you get those boxing gloves back to Old Tyler? They're in my locker. I don't think I can possibly touch them.'

I said I would, and fetching the gloves, took them straight down to the basement. Mr Tyler was fiddling with an electric fire.

'Element went phut,' he told me. 'I cannibalized one from another old fire I got. It's for Matron's Sitting Room. She says she's getting chilblains, which I cannot allow. A fine-grained woman, is Matron. High class. Not like that Nurse Gorgon that's straight out of the bog.'

'I thought you were a Communist, Mr Tyler. I thought you didn't like High-Class people.'

'I ain't talking politics, young feller. I'm talking about women: men and women. I'm talking about biology.'

He winked, giving the exchange an extra touch of mystery. Unable to think how to continue the conversation I showed him the boxing gloves.

'I brought these back.'

'Oh yurr, them things. I heard about the mischief. The boy's in a coma.'

'Couldn't it be that thing you said? Low Grade Something?'

'Vitality. Yurr. Possibility. The boy's not done for yet, say I. Fine boy that.'

He took the gloves and returned them to the box in which he'd found them, then sat down in his armchair.

'Come here,' he said.

I approached cautiously and, when I was near enough, Tyler grabbed my ear, squeezing it until it hurt.

'Ow!' I said

'Never mind "Ow!"' he said. 'Just cop this. You don't want to say nothing about where you got them gloves. You keep me out of it. You keep the name Tyler well to leeward when they start the inquisition.'

He twisted his hand and I felt my ear burn. He let go.

'What do you say about them gloves, then?' Tyler said.

'Nothing,' I said rubbing the ear. 'But I don't see how I can keep quiet, if I'm asked.'

'Did the monk see the gloves?'

'I don't think so. We got them off and out of the way before he came.'

'There's your answer, then. He won't ask. So you say nothing. Tell your friends to do the same. There was no boxing match. There was no fight, if you like. Nelson got hurt some other way.'

Inquisition

An ambulance came during the night and took Nelson away to hospital in York. Then Father Sigbert wanted to see all those who had been in the clearing at the time when Father Kentigern came up. Word had already gone around that no one was to say anything about the fight and, as boys came out one by one from Father Sigbert's room, the bond of silence seemed to be holding. People were simply saying they didn't know what happened. When Skinner went in I was next in line.

Skinner emerged with a trace of a smile on his lips.

'Father Sigbert wants to see you and Carani together,' he told me, 'and also Romero and Collinshaw. Hey, Collinshaw. Carani. Romero. He wants to see you three and Conroy all at the same time.'

We filed into the headmaster's room.

'I have just been told,' Father Sigbert said when we were standing before him, 'that when it happened Nelson was fighting and that you were all involved.'

Nobody said anything. A hollow space developed inside my belly, my face felt hot and my legs felt weak.

'We had our suspicions,' Father Sigbert went on, 'because Nelson had signs of a cut on his lip, and a possible black eye. Well? Has any of you got the guts to own up to this?'

Carani took a step forward. He was looking into empty space rather than at Father Sigbert. He spoke in a quiet but steady voice.

'Yes, Sir, it was me, Sir. We were boxing, that is, me and Nelson were. Then I punched him on the jaw and he went unconscious.'

'You think you hit him that hard?'

'Yes Sir. As hard as I could.'

Father Sigbert cleared his throat. His eye looked at each of us in turn. It was a severe look.

'Well you didn't, you know. And it is important that you didn't because, if you had, this could be a charge of manslaughter. Or grievous bodily harm, anyway. But the fact is that you didn't hit him as hard as you could.'

Carani frowned and now looked directly at Father Sigbert, unable to understand.

'But Sir. I meant to knock him out, and that's what I did.'

'Show me your hands.'

Carani extended his hands and Father Sigbert inspected the knuckles,' he said.

'You may have knocked him *down*, Carani. But not *out*. That happened when he hit his head on a sharp stone lying under the covering of dead leaves. He sustained a serious skull fracture and is now in quite a bad way, unfortunately.'

'But I knocked him out, Sir, I did. With a punch on the jaw.'

'No, Carani, you *didn't*. I will tell you what happened. All of you listen. You were playing at having a boxing match, or maybe a wrestling match. You tussled and Nelson went down. Perhaps he tripped. Anyway he fell and struck his head on the stone I mentioned, that sharp stone. There. That was all there was to it. A terrible unforeseeable accident, but an innocent one.'

'No, Sir! If Nelson … well, if he dies, I'm the one to blame, Sir. I know I am.'

'No, Carani, you are not, and you will not be punished. None of you will. The best thing we can do is all go into the Chapel together and offer some prayers for the full recovery of Timothy Nelson. Shall we go now?'

Religious Knowledge

The end of term came quite soon after that and I, probably in common with most of us, forgot all about Nelson in the joy of the Easter holidays. But coming back for summer term we remembered again, because Nelson was nowhere to be seen. No one spoke of it at first, but everybody wondered: what had happened to Nelson in the holidays?

Father Kentigern gave us the bare minimum of information.

'He's all right,' he said. 'Recovering. We're not sure whether he'll be back this term. We remember him at Mass every day. You must all keep praying for him.'

After that, any discussion with a master about Nelson would be quickly closed down and the whole term passed without further news. No one was surprised that Carani was especially shy of talking about Nelson, and we were careful not to raise the subject if he was in the room. It was Mr Dunn who, within a few days of the start of the summer holidays, finally let the truth slip. We were doing Religious Knowledge and he told us the legend of the Seven Sleepers of Ephesus. They were early Christians who hid from their persecutors in a cave, and the entrance of the cave got sealed up by a rock fall. Two hundred years later the Emperor Theodosius found them perfectly alive but sleeping, and woke them up. They were made saints and their feast day would be in a couple of weeks' time: 27 July.

I stuck up my hand.

'Sir, there's a scientific explanation for that,' I said.

'Oh really, Conroy, and what might that be?'

'Its called Low Grade Vitality, Sir, and Mr Tyler said it happened to one of his shipmates in the War.'

'I suggest you take Mr Tyler's tales with a large fistful of salt, Conroy, richly and fascinatingly embroidered though they be.'

'But I was just wondering if that's what happened to Nelson, Sir.'

'Nelson? Ah yes. Very sad. The doctors didn't think he would ever wake up from the coma, but he did, praise God. And you can forget science, it's the power of prayer that did it. A great many very devout people made a great many novenas. Who can tell me how long it takes to complete a novena?'

Deuchar shot up his hand.

'Nine weeks, Sir?'

'Exactly. And guess what, boys? After nine weeks of being in a coma, at the exact end of the *exact* ninth week, Nelson woke up. If that isn't prayers answered I don't know what is. It's a miracle, in its way. Not perhaps as great as that of the Seven Sleepers, but a

72

miracle certainly. But all the same, very sad. Very sad indeed.'

'Why hasn't he come back to school, Sir?' asked Collinshaw.

'Ah, well, having a coma for nine weeks will have its effects.'

'But is he ever coming back?'

'Oh, I would have to say I doubt it. I rather doubt he could cope with the lessons, you see. Or the sports. Not now. Not any more.'

He would not elaborate but — judging by the way he slowly shook his huge head, like a grim and doubtful dinosaur — he let us all know that Nelson's life, from now on, would not be very easy. It would not be very easy at all.

Confession

1961

It was some time around the middle of the night. I lay asleep in the dormitory at Lower House, floating on the inflated lilo of a dream. To sleep at school was always a yearned-for release from reality but now, at the age of twelve, I could never have enough of it. Being wrenched away from green-blanketed bliss by Father Gerald's furious hand-bell was every morning a torture.

In this particular dream there was soft sunlight, warmth, the sound of wind in the woods near at hand, a cake in the oven, the taste of raspberry jam, quiet music from the kitchen radio. But where was I? It seems I was not in the kitchen. It seems I was lying in the arms of Clara, hugging her, being hugged by her, and snuggling my face into her breasts. Some sort of heightened rapture slowly gripped me. Her flesh rose and fell as she breathed and I was lying on her, drowning between her breasts until I struggled up again, my mouth now seeking a nipple. Finding one, I closed my lips around it in luxurious kissing or sucking, quite suddenly a tingle of deliquescence rippled through me. Down through me, and out of me.

I awoke gasping. I was wet. My pyjamas and the sheet were wet. Oh God, no. I'd pissed in the bed.

But further cautious investigation inside my pyjamas revealed something a good deal stranger. The wetness wasn't a bit like pee. It was oozy and sticky. What had happened? It was somehow connected to my dream of Clara's breasts, and sucking her nipple, which I had certainly never actually done in any possible version of real life.

A Sin of the Flesh

Lower House was the half way stage between the Castle and College. It had its own building on the north, or College side of the valley, but it stood a judicious distance from the rest of the monastic and College complex. Boys between the ages of eleven and thirteen lived and studied at Lower House and, compared with life at the Castle, extraordinary new freedoms were on offer. At Lower House we wore long trousers. We could bring our own jams and bottled sauces into the refectory. We could keep bikes, and certain pets (such as gerbils, guinea pigs and pigeons, but not cats or dogs) and we could have our own money in an account at the Post Office, which stood beside the public road that ran through the site.

In our studies we began to develop some knowledge of trigonometry, and the beginnings of Greek. Some of us, as our second year progressed, developed newly creaking voices and the vestiges of pubic hair. Most of us also, in that time, learned the vestiges of masturbation.

After a day of taut anxiety over what had happened to me during the previous night in the dormitory, I confided in Romero.

'I pissed in the bed, only I didn't. It was nothing like piss. I think I must have a disease. Should I go to the Nurse?'

'Don't be thick, Conroy. I suppose you had a dream. Something sexy, was it?'

'Well actually yes, I think so. I can't possibly tell you the details.'

'Don't bother. It's normal. It's called having a wet dream. My step dad Henry explained it all. That was spunk that came out, not pee. Did your willy get big?'

'I don't know. Maybe.'

'If you rub it you can make it do that anytime you want. It's super fun, but it's a Mortal Sin, so you have to confess it afterwards.'

*

75

'Bless me Father, for I have sinned. It's three weeks since my last confession.'

Fifteen seconds of silence.

'Tell me your sins, child.'

'I lied I talked in Chapel during Mass swore took Our Lady's name in vain punched a boy on the—.'

'You did what?'

'I had a sort of fight with another boy.'

'Not that. The one before.'

'I took Our Lady's name in vain, Father.'

'That is a very serious sin. How did you abuse the Blessed Virgin?'

'I said "bloody". That's "by Our Lady", isn't it?'

'Indeed it is. How often did you say it?'

'Two or three times, I think. When I got angry.'

'Well I know you hear the word all around you these days, but remember every time is a stab in the beautiful heart of Our Blessed Lady. What else?'

'I, er, um, had unclean thoughts.'

'What sort of unclean thoughts?'

'About girls. About them having no clothes on, and things.'

'And I suppose you spilled the seed?'

'Yes.'

'Aren't you bit young for that yet?'

'No, Father.'

'Well the seed is provided by Almighty God for the generation of souls, not to be just spilled out into your pyjamas while you have filthy thoughts. So cut it out. A decade of the Rosary for your penance. Now say your Act of Contrition.'

I said the prayer while he muttered in Latin, ending with him sketching a cross in the air with his hand and uttering the words: *Ego te absolvo a peccatis tuis in nomine Patris et Filii et Spiritus Sancti. Amen.* Go and sin no more.'

In this, our second year at Lower House, we began Greek, for which we had Mr Costello. He had metallic red hair and no discernable neck. There was hardly the width of a matchstick between the collar of his Tattersall shirt and his chin.

'What do you boys think Greek studies are?' he said, handing out a text book, *Elementary Greek*.

'Myths, Sir.'

'Jason and the Argonauts, Sir.'

'Sir! Sir! The Labours of Hercules.'

'The Siege of Troy.'

'Leonidas at Thermopylae.'

The last suggestion was Carani's.

'All right, all right,' growled Mr Costello. 'None of that's wrong, but you're jumping the gun. Before you get to the gory fun, there's an awful lot of dry-as-dust learning to apply yourselves to.'

Everybody groaned.

'Groan away. But just to start with, you have to come to grips with a new alphabet. You will see it in *Elementary Greek*, entabled on the very first page strangely enough. So, you will have learned the names and symbols of the letters by the time we meet again. And don't think you'll not be tested, exhaustively.'

'Leonee-something. Who was he?' I asked Carani after the lesson. 'He wasn't in the siege of Troy.'

'Leonidas. No. The Persian War. He commanded three hundred Spartans defending a narrow pass that was the only way over the mountains into Greece. The Persian army was coming, thousands and thousands of them, and what happened was that two Athenians were watching the three hundred Spartans from a distance while they got ready for the battle. "What are they doing?" said one. The other one said, "Oh, they're just combing their hair."'

Carani laughed. It was not a scoff, but a laugh of profound admiration.

Father Syl

Father Sylvester, known as Syl and sometimes the Cat, had just joined Lower House to take charge of our Year. He was young and had not been long ordained a priest. There was something more modern, something more direct and unfussy about him than the other monks around us. He would hand out his ordination card, which showed his priestly name on one side (Sylvester Prewitt O.S.B.) with the date of the ordination and a simple prayer. On the other side was Salvador Dali's super-naturalistic painting *Christ of St John of the Cross* — a view of Jesus on the cross from the viewpoint of a bird hovering directly above the space between the top of the cross and his forward- and down-hanging head. You see only the crown of his head, the nape of his neck, his arms and shoulders and his tapering body in a steep downward perspective. Below lay a screen of clouds and, far below these, a tiny fishing boat grounded on the shore of a cadmium blue lake. We put the card with numerous others as place-finders in our missals.

'I showed it to my brother,' said Carani. 'He said it's a deeply weird crucifixion, but it's modern art, so it's sort of all right.'

We all agreed it was sort of all right.

The Cat's room was in a corner tower of the building, which we reached by climbing a spiral stair. We could sit here during any leisure time, playing chess or Risk, reading his books, and listening to his music. The room was hung with framed black and white photographs of objects in extreme close up: a snail, a human eye, the twist of a steel screw, the stem of an apple. The photographs had been taken and processed by Syl himself, in the dark room across in College. He also had a record player and a collection of modern jazz and folk records. Before he joined the monastery he had spent some time in New York City. He occasionally said "dig this" and "that's cool" in a voice with traces of an American twang. He taught us to distinguish bebop from cool jazz from hard bop: Parker from Brubeck from Coltrane. Syl taught us the significance of Woody Guthrie and the Seegers. Once we came back from the holiday to find he had a new LP with a picture on the cover of a beautiful singer and guitarist. She had long black hair and was called Joan Baez.

'I think this is how the Virgin Mary must have sung,' he murmured as he lowered the stylus onto the groove.

I can't now hear the liquid purity of Baez's voice without thinking of The Cat's tower room, and the Virgin Mary.

The Pet Place

Extract from *The Lower House Chronicle* January 1961: 'Hobbies Corner'.

THE PET PLACE During this last term the Pet Place has undergone considerable change and reconstruction and is a tribute to the constructive energy of the boys. The pigeon loft has been upgraded, with Mr Geraldo providing a new felted roof. A fine new run for rabbits and guinea pigs has also appeared, thanks again to the untiring efforts of Mr Geraldo. Some accidents occurred. A breeding programme for mice got somewhat out of control, but corrective measures were taken and important lessons were thereby learned about rodent husbandry. Some boys acquired young pigeons from nearby farms and the pigeon flight today approaches squadron strength. The aerobatics of two or three tumblers make for a most impressive display. Sylvester Prewitt O.S.B.

Most mornings those of us with business in the Pet Place would hurry down to it at eleven, when Break started, to provide food and water, remove droppings and refresh the bedding. Like most of the school and monastery buildings Lower House stood up on the valley's side, so that its garden and grounds were laid out along a quite steep, terraced slope below the building. The Pet Place was enclosed in a small copse of yew and Scotch pine away to the right.

The pigeons lived together in the Loft — a hut in which a boy could stand upright, recently re-roofed by the handyman Geraldo. Smaller beasts were kept in their own hutches inside the wired enclosure also made by Geraldo. The hutches were of plywood, some with legs but most standing on bricks, and were usually fronted by a pair of hinged doors, one covered with chicken wire, the other solid for privacy. These were usually fastened by a toggle. Sawdust and shavings for their floors was collected from the carpentry shop. Feed and straw — and many of the animals themselves — were brought by bike from the pet shop in our market town, three miles away.

All sorts of varieties of breeding pigeon, from racing types to tumblers and white fantail doves, dwelt in lofts above the local farms' barns. They offered variation to the farming family's diet, but there were always plenty of surplus squabs — "squeakers" as they were known locally — which the farmers were happy to sell to us for a shilling.

We gave our pigeons heroic names, derived from myth and the roll call of war: Venus, Apollo, Persephone, Hannibal, Napoleon, Nelson, Douglas Bader. The small animals were christened less exaltedly. Warren the rabbit. Dracula the rat. Caramac the hamster. Omo the albino hamster. One boy, Nugent, had called his mouse Bucephalos and was widely ridiculed.

Horror

For a couple or three weeks in the run-up to the end of Christmas term we would tell horror stories after lights out. Most of the boys' efforts were short and feeble. Carani's, though, was different. He gave us a story his brother had told him about a boy who lived with his aunt but they hated each other. In the garden there was a potting shed where the boy kept a ferret, which he worshipped as a god.

'Was it his pet?'

'No, because it was a god and you can't keep a god as a pet.'

'How did he get it? Did the aunt buy it for him?'

'She didn't even know about it. And when the boy went to feed it with meat he'd stolen from the kitchen he'd say: "Oh Sredni Vashtar".'

'What's Sredni Vashtar?'

'The animal's name, obviously. And he'd pray to it, saying "Oh great and beautiful avenger, there is just one thing I ask."'

'What does he want?' whispered Corcoran.

'Wait and see. Anyway one day the aunt secretly followed him to the shed and just as he got to the shed door she grabbed him by his collar and ordered him back to the house. On his way back he looked behind and saw the aunt opening the door of the shed.'

'I think I know what he was praying for,' whispered Corcoran. 'He was asking—.'

'Shut up, Porky,' said Biggins. 'Go on, Carani. What happened next?'

'It was just teatime and tea was waiting on a trolley with strawberry jam and toasted tea-cakes. The boy could just see the shed from the window. He buttered a tea-cake and watched. The aunt never came out. And then, after several minutes, he saw the long, low body of Sredni Vashtar creeping out and disappearing into the onion bed. And when one of the servants went to look for the aunt all the boy heard through the window was a terrible scream from inside the shed.'

'What did the boy do?'

'He just smiled and buttered himself another tea cake.'

Extra-curricular

Broad Field Farm lay up the valley, about two miles away. It was a good source of young pigeons, produced in the loft above the big stone barn that occupied one side of the farmyard. There was a boy on the farm of about our age and it was he who would go and fetch down any juvenile birds that were ready to leave the nest, and get a shilling in payment. His name was Walter.

Carani took to hanging around the farm on the Wednesday half-holiday. He would have long talks with Walter, who was a raw, scranky boy, not as tall as most of us, with close cut hair and sticking out cheekbones. His mouth had a curl to it, like a secret smile, as if to let us know that he knew things that we Lower House boys would never understand. Not just a thing or two. A *lot* of things.

Walter fascinated Carani. He heard from him about poaching and how to tickle trout, and the right way to set a snare, the use of long nets, and how to kill a pheasant with an air gun. Walter knew everything about the birds and wild animals living in the valley.

Once we went to the farm and found Walter walking stiffly and feeling sore. He said his Dad had given him a leathering for going out at night poaching. He felt no ill-will towards his father because he *had* gone out, so there was no harm in it as he deserved it, like.

When I woke the luminous hands of my watch told me it was half past two. Beyond the breathing and snoring of the other boys I could hear scattered sounds from the outside, from the woods that covered the escarpment behind the building: an owls's screech; yowling foxes; the hoarse rasp of a corncrake. I propped myself on an elbow and looked around. By the dim nightlight I could see Carani's bed was empty. Assuming he had gone to the bogs I lay there unable to get back to sleep, wondering why it was taking him so long to return to the dorm.

At last he came in wearing outside clothes. He began undressing.

'Hey Carani!' I hissed. 'Where've you been?'

'Out,' he whispered.

'Out? What've you been doing?'

'Shh! It's a secret.'

'Tell me.'

'Not now. I'm fagged out. Got to sleep.'

'Tell me in the morning. Promise.'

'All right. But you've got to not tell anyone else. If you do I'll beat you up.'

'All right.'

He kicked his outside clothes under the bed and put on his pyjamas. Within a couple of minutes he was asleep.

'We all know who the greatest English novelist is, don't we?' said Mr Costello, the next morning.

We nodded our heads. Mr Costello cupped his ear with his hand.

'Sir! Sir!'

We all knew the one answer that would satisfy him.

'And the answer is, Boulton?'

'Dickens, Sir.'

Mr Costello was besotted by Dickens.

'Quite right,' he said. 'There's a witless chap at Cambridge who reckons he knows the Big Four novelists, but makes nary a mention of Charles Dickens. Incredible. A Communist, probably. In actual *fact*, Dickens is one to whom no other novelist can hold a candle. *No other*. How many of you sorry mudlarks and chimneysweeps can name three of his incomparable works? '

Stubbings put up his hand.

'Yes, boy!

'*Great Expectations*, *Oliver Twist* and *A Tale of Two Cities*, Sir.'

'That's correct but a trite answer. All three have been made as films. Let's have some that haven't been meretriciously reprocessed for mass consumption. Books that you might have actually read, rather than merely goggled at on the screen.'

We called out various names.

'*A Christmas Carol* ... *David Copperfield* ... *The Old Curiosity Shop* ... *Martin Chuzzlewit* ... *One Pair of Hands*.'

'What did you say?' interrupted Mr Costello, pointing at Romero. 'Stand up boy.'

Romero stood up, his face wearing a faint smirk.

'I said *One Pair of Hands*, Sir. It's by Dickens.'

Mr Costello advanced menacingly between desks until he reached Romero. He grasped the meat of Romero's right ear and lowered his mouth to speak into it.

'I know it is, you pilchard.'

He yanked and twisted the ear. Romero's smirk was replaced by staring eyes and a painful grimace.

'But not the *same* Dickens, is it, clever-dick?'

'No, Sir.'

'Who is it by then? Give us the benefit of your vast literary expertise.'

Romero had now been forced downwards by the teacher's grip on his ear into a bent, cringing posture.

'Monica Dickens, Sir.'

'Who, I believe,' snarled Mr Costello.

He yanked Romero's ear for emphasis.

'Is some sort of de*scen*dant.'

He yanked again producing a yelp from Romero.

'Of the *real* Dickens.'

Mr Costello let go of Romero and returned to the front of the class.

'But the said Monica is a feeble and simpering purveyor of girly romances, not worthy to be mentioned in the same breath as the sublime author of *Bleak House* and *Our Mutual Friend*. I hope that is quite clear, Romero?'

'Yes, Sir.'

'Never try to be a smart-Alec with me, boy, or you'll re-*gret* it. What will you do?'

'Regret it, Sir.'

'Right. Sit down.'

'So what *were* you doing out last night? And, actually, how did you get out? Every door's locked at night.'

I had not been able to get him to talk about it at breakfast. He just said, 'Not now. Later. Pet place at Break.'

It was Break now and we were in the pigeon loft — which was in fact more like a hut — cleaning out the pigeons' nesting box, renewing the sawdust and filling the drinking bowl. I had two pigeons. One was a fantail, mostly white, which I had called Venus. The other was named Hector, after my favourite character in *The Iliad*. He was a magpie pigeon, one of a pair that Carani and I had got from the president of the British Magpie Pigeon Association. We'd written to him where he lived in Scotland to ask where you could get these aristocratic birds, which had caught my attention in *The Pigeon Fancier*, a magazine I bought at the bookstall on York Station on the way to school. In his kindness, or perhaps zeal to spread the word about his favourite breed, the president of the British Magpie Pigeon Association had sent us the pair as a free gift. They were striking, superior, long-necked pigeons, half as large again as any others in our loft. Carani's bird, the female, was called Andromache. The two were spectacular flyers, soaring high then tumbling downwards, over and over in vertiginous delight.

'So how did you escape?' I asked.

'There's a window in the boiler room,' he said. 'It gets you out to the back of the building.'

We caught the magpie pigeons and went outside.

'You mean where the bins are?'

'Yes. It's a bit of a drop.'

He stroked Andromache's crop, holding her as fancier's do cupped in his hand with his fingers trapping her wings and legs .

'But where did you go in the middle of the night?'

'I met Walter. We went to Monks Wood. Poaching.'

I stared at him.

'Did you catch anything?'

He tossed Andromache into the air and tracked her as she climbed in an irregular spiral through the air. I sent Hector up in pursuit, soaring on strong wings.

'Course we did. Three rabbits in Walter's snares. He might take me out with his ferret some time.'

'He's got a ferret?'

'Yes. Called Donny.'

'Does he worship it like Sredni Vashtar?'

'Of course not. It's a working ferret. But at the moment we're after pheasants, which we don't need him for. We're waiting for full moon, which in winter Walter says is a Poacher's Moon.'

'Why?'

'Because the pheasants roost in the trees and when moonlight's strong you can see them through the bare branches. Walter picks them off with his air rifle and they fall to the ground but not dead. So then we've got run and fall on them and wring their necks.'

'Gosh. Can I come with you when you next go?'

'I doubt it but I'll ask him. He prefers to work alone. It's his rule.'

'He's not alone if you're there.'

'If I'm there, that's different.'

This was how Carani increasingly thought. Rules applied to everybody except him.

Confessing to the Cat

On weekdays lessons finished at six and we had a break until supper at seven. On Saturdays this break was replaced by Benediction followed by silent study, during which boys sat in their classrooms doing STs – Study Tasks that had been assigned by the teachers. It was during this time that Confessions were heard and boys would leave their desks and go either to the priest sitting in the Chapel confessional, who came for the purpose from the monastery every week, or to one of LH's own priests in their rooms.

It was Romero who popularised the idea of confessing to The Cat.

'I never thought I would enjoy Confession — ever. The Cat gives you absolution all right, but he talks straight and most of the time he tells you your sins aren't serious.'

'What does he says about wanking?' said Brokowsky.

'You filthy beast, Brok! Trust you to want to know about that.'

'Shut up. I'm serious.'

'Well, he just says it's normal.'

'Did he say it wasn't a sin, though?'

'Not exactly. But he thinks it's no big deal and he couldn't care less about it. He just gives you three Hail Maries for penance.'

So some of us started confessing to Father Sylvester, in his room. It was a different Cat from the one who played Joan Baez records, who tied up his scapular and took on all comers at table tennis, who took crazy close-up photographs which he developed and printed himself. This was the Cat who put on the crisp, clean priestly robes and, by rotation, said Mass in the morning and, if it was Sunday, gave a sermon. Then he was deadly serious. He would take a subject from the Epistle or Gospel such as what St Paul meant by the word love, or Our Lord's parable of the talents, and talked about how they looked from every possible angle.

Equally in Confession he cracked no jokes. He sat in his room on an upright chair wearing his silk confessor's stole, and I had to kneel in front of him but a little to one side, at right angles, facing across him. He told me not to look at him as I recited my sins, but to turn my head his way when it was time for the absolution. He never spoke harshly but used a soft voice, making the odd remark about what I'd confessed to, asking if I had any questions and answering them factually. Then he would put one hand on my head and use the other to trace a cross with his thumb on my forehead while he said the words.

There was something that felt good about this, something straightforward but also caring and special. Something not like a Father but, in a way, like an older brother.

Poacher's Moon

Once, daringly, Walter appeared in person at Lower House. He was lurking in the Pet Place when we went down at morning break to fly the pigeons. He had brought a mouse that he'd promised to Mulligan for only sixpence. It was unheard of for any local boy to turn up in school grounds like that, but Walter, as Carani said, was fearless.

'Go on,' said Carani after Walter had handed Mulligan a battered toffee tin, punched with air-holes, inside which the mouse cowered. 'Let's see Donny. We all want to.'

Walter wore a bulgy and very greasy raincoat tied by a cracked old leather belt around his waist. He pulled the coat open above the belt and the whiskery head of his ferret poked out. The markings on his face were those of a cartoon bank-robber, a black mask through whose eyeholes a pair of alert, beady eyes gleamed. A powerful acrid smell, like a farmyard midden, reached our nostrils. Walter brought him out into full view.

'He takes Donny everywhere,' said Carani.

'I do,' said Walter. 'You gotter handle him alt time. Else he'll go wild.'

I touched Donny's head. I could feel the skull beneath his silky fur.

'Look sharp,' said Walter. 'If he bites you'll know it. His teeth are razors.'

When the full moon came — the Poacher's Moon — Carani slipped out of the dormitory around eleven. He'd told me I couldn't go as well, because Walter had said no. In this game a second was a help, but a third was a nuisance.

Lying there I pictured the two of them picking their way through the winter woods, Walter with his air rifle on his arm, their eyes scanning the branches for a roosting pheasant. It would be Walter's part to shoot and Carani's to run at the fallen bird and grab it before it recovered. An air rifle would knock a bird down, but not kill it.

I drifted to sleep. Then, faintly roused, I became aware of various noises. A telephone ringing for a long time, footstep running downstairs, the voice of Father Gerald. I looked at my watch — three-thirty — and then across at Carani's bed. He was not in it. I listened again. I heard the front door of the building slamming. Striding footsteps outside. Then nothing for three quarters of an hour.

The slam of a car door woke me once more. There were further noises in the hall, the stairs, and Father Gerald's raised voice, tight with anger.

'I don't want to hear it. Go to bed. I'll see you in the morning.'

Carani came in quietly. Several questions were whispered, but he said nothing. Father Gerald at the dormitory door heard us and called out in a low voice.

'Go back to sleep. All of you.'

There were more whispered questions after Father Gerald had gone, but Carani gave no answer. I saw him get under the bedclothes and curl up in a tight foetal ball.

Carani was banned from the Wednesday film for the rest of term and gated until further notice, being allowed outside only for rugger and to go to the Pet Place. More painfully his exploit earned him two canings, seven days apart, which were administered by Father Gerald. The Housemaster of Lower House had very sharp eye. In his younger days he played first-class cricket for Surrey and once, it was rumoured, he'd bowled Bradman out around his legs.

Such accuracy was of considerable use when giving a caning and Father Gerald could do it in such a way that a boy's bottom was entirely covered with weals without the skin being broken since no part of it was ever struck more than once. Carani, who tested this skill as it had never before been tested, claimed afterwards that the beating only hurt a little. Everyone knew that was a lie.

A week after his second caning Carani came in a few minutes late for tea. He looked grim.

'I've been talking to Walter,' he said. 'I found him waiting for me at the Pet Place. He told me he's got to go away tomorrow.'

'Where to?'

'Reform School. The court sentenced him to six months. It's like prison but it's also a school with lessons and gym.'

'What's he got to go there for?' said Nugent.

Carani gave him a pitying look.

'For him and me getting caught poaching by the gamekeeper, obviously. He says his parents aren't happy though. They think I should be sent to jug too.'

'You were lucky you weren't, Carani.'

'I might've been, though, if it hadn't been for Father Gerald having a word with the police and telling them he'd punish me himself. But it's still not fair on Walter.'

'Well this place is just as bad as any Reform School,' said Romero. 'So it makes no difference.'

'It does,' said Carani. 'Walter's not used to being locked up. He's a free spirit. Six months will seem like forever to him.'

'Why did he come over here to tell you?'

'Because of Donny. Walter's brought him over with a cage to keep him in. I have to look after him until Walter comes out.'

Sailing

The Big Lake was more or less reserved for the use of Sea Scouts, of which there was a College section and a Lower House section. LH only had access to the lake on one afternoon a week, whereas the older boys seemed to use it at any other time.

Floating inside a wooden boathouse there were a rowing boat and two Firefly sailing dinghies, a red boat and a white.

We would spend some of the time cleaning the boathouse, practising knots and rigging the boats, as well as learning technical terms such as forestay, backstay, halyard, and kicking-strap, and the difference between the tiller and the rudder, or gybing and luffing. Then in bright yellow life-jackets we went out in pairs, sailing around the triangular course indicated by three floating markers. Anyone who got dumped in the lake by a capsize was supposed to swim ashore while Syl used the rowing boat to salvage the dinghy. After stripping and towelling down they'd get hot chocolate from a massive thermos flask, while their clothes dried by the flames of the open log fire next to the boathouse .

One breezy afternoon, just as Syl blew the whistle to bring sailing to an end, Corcoran and Mulligan capsized the white boat. It wasn't clear whose fault it was as they both blamed each other, but Corcoran, a poor swimmer, got detached from his life-saver and couldn't get to shore. He had to be rescued by the rowing boat.

There was still half an hour before time to set off back to school for tea so, as soon as he'd towelled himself dry, Mulligan borrowed the dry shirt and shorts that The Cat always had with him for the purpose and went haring off around the lake to where the rest of us were having a game of stalking. Corcoran, though, had swallowed lake water and was complaining of not feeling well, so he sat on a dead tree trunk in front of the boathouse, naked under the big towel he was wrapped in, while Father Syl built up the fire to a blaze.

On the far side of the lake Collinshaw came up to me.

'Let's stalk The Cat and Porky. Let's creep up and surprise them.'

Protected from sight by the lakeside bullrushes, we left the others and made our way around the lake shore until we were able to creep behind the boat house. The wind made it impossible to hear what was happening at the front so we poked our heads around the corner of the building to check the state of things in the camp.

The two of them sat side by side on the tree trunk, with their backs to us. They were looking out across the water and Syl was speaking in a low voice. He had his arm draped across the boy's shoulders, which had now stopped shivering. Then the monk turned his head towards Corcoran and reached with his free hand to take the boy's chin between his finger and thumb. He turned Corcoran's face towards his face. We could see them in profile, looking at each other. Still murmuring Syl leaned towards Corcoran and put his lips on Corcoran's lips. It took me a moment to realise what was happening, but there was only one possible construction to it. The Cat was kissing Corcoran. He was kissing him avidly like someone eating.

I looked at Collinshaw. His mouth had dropped open in surprise. Then he snapped it shut and jerked his head backwards. Silently we crawled away and, as soon as we could, pelted back around the lake to the others. We agreed to say nothing of what we had seen

Berserk

Corcoran had always been a timid boy and even a bit of a sad case, who stammered and blushed a lot. He kept two framed photographs of his mother and father on his bedside table. In one his father, pipe in mouth, had just completed a professional-looking golf swing and in the other his mother was sitting forward on an armchair with a cup of tea and a Yorkshire Terrier at her feet. Alongside these memorabilia lay Corcoran's rosary in a little plastic pill-box, which had a blue medallion of the Blessed Virgin glued to the lid. Romero, who slept in the neighbouring bed, told me Corcoran recited the rosary every night in the dark to guard against self-abuse.

He used to be known, casually, as Corky but, as he was a few pounds fatter than the rest of us, his nickname evolved into Porky. Whether he objected to this he never said. Anyway, no one thought Porky was of much account until that day, that day shortly after the incident at the lake, when he went berserk at teatime in the refectory. Mulligan, who had been sitting beside him, claimed it started after someone had helped himself to Porky's personal tomato sauce bottle. This theory made some sort of sense, as the bottle played a leading role in what followed.

The chatter in the room was silenced by something between a high-pitched shriek and a drawn out howl. Everybody turned. Corcoran had started up, causing his chair to tumble backwards behind him. His eyes bulged and looked hot, with tears beginning to form. He started yelling incoherent sounds, then got hold of the sauce bottle. It was uncapped. He jerked the bottle back and forth above his head in such a way that the red sauce was ejaculated out of it, flying through the air in gobs. He stumbled into the middle of the aisle between the tables, still shouting and brandishing the bottle. Tomato sauce flew around him, onto the tables, into the food and onto the clothing and the hair of the boys sitting anywhere near. No one could understand what he was shouting. The words were lost in a torrent of fury, snot and tears.

Father Syl got up and went towards Corcoran with hands outstretched, patting the air in a calming gesture. This provoked the boy, with a new, more guttural scream, to hurl the bottle at him. It bounced off Syl's face, drawing blood from the nose. Then Corcoran turned and bolted from the refectory. The Cat picked up a napkin and applied it to his bleeding nostrils while Father Gerald, gathering up the scapular of his habit, strode out in pursuit of the boy. We learned later that he had found him in the Chapel, kneeling and sobbing in front of the statue of Our Lady.

Corcoran spent the night in the Infirmary and the next day his parents came and took him home. He did not return.

Retribution

Hector and Andromache, a devoted couple, had just produced a clutch of eggs and were sitting on them when, like a Homeric god's act of retribution, disaster came to the pet place. The first boy down there at break on that particular day was Stebbings, the owner of the rat Dracula. Before any of the rest of us arrived at the small fir wood he came running back towards us, with something in his hands. His hands were bloody and they held the remains of a black and white rat whose head had been ripped off.

'Look,' he said. 'Look what's happened.'

Stebbings's voice shook, his eyes were watery with unshed tears.

'God! What's that?' said Mulligan. 'That's not Dracula?'

Stebbings nodded miserably.

'I don't know what happened. I just found him like this. He was on the ground outside his cage.'

'Well how did he get out?'

'I don't know. But the point is, it's not just Dracula. It's all the other pets. Come and look. It's horrible.'

The scene at the Pet Place was carnage. The small animal's enclosure was littered with corpses. Some had been eviscerated and apparently fed on. Others lay inert with no apparent wounds, but limp and dead all the same. The first word that came into our heads was both an explanation and an accusation: Donny. Of Walter's ferret there was no sign.

In the loft the massacre had had the thoroughness of an SS reprisal operation. There were blood and feathers everywhere. Two or three pigeons, including Carani's magpie Andromache, had somehow survived but the rest were slaughtered, and their nests and eggs despoiled. With no means of escape the birds had been easy prey. Easy meat.

I caught Andromache and brought her out, tucking her into my hand and looked for Carani to show him that his pigeon was alive. I found him standing beside Donny's cage, looking around with surprise on his face, but it was not a painful or distressed surprise.

'My God,' he said. 'Bloody marvellous, isn't it? '

'Are you mad Carani?,' I said. 'It's bloody, all right, but *marvellous*? That ferret's destroyed the entire pet place. He's killed nearly everything in sight.'

'No, I'm not mad and nor is Donny.'

'Then why did he?'

'He was doing what nature dictates. And bloody marvellously, if you want my opinion.'

'Some people want to find him and kill him. They want revenge.'

'There's not much hope of that. When they feed like this, ferrets go to ground and sleep and sleep for days. I doubt Donny will actually ever come back.'

I offered him the pigeon.

'Hector's had his head ripped off but he didn't get Andromache. Here. '

I bundled the pigeon into Carani's hands. Without hesitation he tossed it into the air.

'If she's not too scared to come home, you can have her,' he said, watching as Andromache gained height. 'I've had enough of pigeons. I'm going to get a hawk now.'

He walked away from the pet place, and was never seen to go down there again.

The Christmas Play

Extract from *The Lower House Chronicle* January 1961:

THIS YEAR'S PLAY was 'King Henry at Agincourt', expertly extracted from Shakespeare's play by Mr Hugh Kerridge of the Upper School English Department, and directed by him with some rehearsals taken by Father Sylvester. The part of Henry was played with considerable commitment and aplomb by Richard Carani, ably supported by John Romero as the Herald, a splendidly splenetic Pistol from Simon Plumb and Nigel Deuchar, who spoke the words of the Chorus with spirit. The whole cast acquitted themselves well and we left the school theatre with our patriotism much uplifted and the words ringing in our ears "We few, we happy few, we band of brothers." Special mention should go to Mrs Kerridge for designing and making the costumes and to Mrs E. Jerrold of the Music Dept for her splendid "entre-acte" oboe-playing.

Stalking

1964

Oloroso

'D'your parents allow you to drink?' barked Colonel Collinshaw. He was sitting in a wing chair, all tarnished brass tacks and leprous leather, with a whisky-and-ginger-ale in his hand.

'Oh yes. They do,' I said. 'I mean, they don't mind.'

The Colonel wafted his glass vaguely towards the other end of the room.

'There's sherry, then. Over there. Duncan, do the honours.'

It was a few days after the beginning of August and I had come to the hunting lodge beside the shores of Loch Rannoch that had been taken by the Collinshaws for deer stalking. I had never been here before, or met Duncan Collinshaw's parents. I was to stay five days.

Duncan led me to a trolley by the wall, which seemed to be loosening at the joints so it leaned out of true and became trapezoid. Glasses and decanters were ranged on the top deck while bottles, many grimed with sticky dust, were crammed together on the lower like tired passengers on a crowded bus. He poured me a glass of Oloroso, whose caramel sweetness reminded me of cough medicine.

Colonel Collinshaw planted his whisky on the chair-arm and rose. He strode to the mantelpiece above the crackling log fire and took an untipped cigarette from a silver box. This he hung from his lips while, standing with legs apart, he fished in a waistcoat pocket for his lighter. It was only as he thumbed up the lighter's hinged cover, flicked the wheel to light it and sucked the flame into his cigarette that I saw he had done the entire operation using only his right hand. The sleeve of his left arm was empty and tucked up. Collinshaw's father had only one arm.

As he returned to his chair and sat back, drawing deeply on his cigarette, I remembered our form master at the Castle. I hadn't thought of Mr Dunn for years but now I saw that Colonel Collinshaw provided a sharply contrasting case. Neither clumsy nor lop-sided as Mr Dunn was, the Colonel acted as if being one-armed was quite the thing and, actually, more natural than to have two. Later I asked Collinshaw how it happened.

'He was a beachmaster at Dunkirk. They were strafed by Messerschmidts and his arm was shot off. He picked it up and carried it to the dressing station, but they couldn't re-attach it.'

'God. That's terrible.'

'He doesn't think so. He claims there are only three things he can't do.'

'What are they?'

'Tying flies is one and tying a shoelace is another.'

'What's the third?'

'He'll never say. He does that thing, tapping the side of his nose. '

'Can he shoot?'

'He's famous for it. He's supposed to be the best one-arm shot in the country with a twelve-bore, and he's better than anyone here with a rifle except the ghillies. You may see tomorrow when we go deer stalking. He uses a crutch.'

'A crutch?'

'For the gun, stupid.'

Fishing

Tomorrow proved to be too bright, and the air too still, so the stalk was postponed to the following day and fishing was decreed instead. Duncan and I were allotted one of the two rowing boats that were tied up to a rickety wooden jetty, while his parents took the other. Mrs Collinshaw rowed sturdily away along the lake shore, while her husband sat in the stern with a tattered Panama hat on his head, holding a rod over the stern with a trailing line. Duncan and I headed in the opposite direction, pulling an oar apiece and watching until the senior Collinshaws were lost to sight around a spit of land. Immediately we shipped the oars and he took from his shirt pocket two of several cigarettes that he'd pilfered from the mantelpiece cigarette box.

'If we can't see them, they can't see us,' he said.

We lit up.

'Well it's a beautiful day,' I said.

I couldn't think of anything less banal to say. Duncan was not a boy who inspired imaginative conversation.

'Worse luck,' he said. 'Let's hope we get some bad weather tomorrow. For the deer stalk.'

'That's what I don't understand,' I said. 'What's wrong with this weather?'

'You don't know much about deer stalking, do you? We need some cloud cover and a bit of a breeze, obviously. The deer are less likely to spot us and even less likely to smell us. We've got to be down wind of course.'

'Do you like deer stalking?'

'Oh yes. And anyway it's just what I need at the moment, to keep my mind off everything.'

'What everything?'

'Well, if you must know, I think I'm in love, actually.'

He dragged on the cigarette, inhaling and breathing out smoke in very much the same way as his father.

'Don't you know if you are?'

'Actually it's quite hard to know when you're our age. At something like twenty-five you *would* know. It's just that I've never felt like this before. About a girl, I mean.'

'Who is it?'

He reddened.

'She's called Ailish MacKenzie.'

'Ailish? What sort of name is that?'

'A Scottish name, obviously. See that house there?'

He pointed to a headland some further distance along the shore. On it I could see a substantial residence above a lakeside stand of firs. Smoke from one of its chimneys rose lazily into the shimmering blue air. A lawn sloped steeply down from the house towards the lake.

'That's where she lives. Her father's a doctor. I've known her for ages because our parents play bridge. But she was always just a kid before. A bit of a tomboy, actually. But this year she's got rather grown up, if you see what I'm getting at. So when I saw her I just, um, *you* know…'

I didn't know. What knowledge I had of love was mostly literary.

'So what did it feel like exactly? What are the symptoms? Is it a bolt of lightning, or more of a sudden fever, like in Shakespeare?'

'No, actually. If you must know it's more like a stomach-ache. It's as if your guts were knotted up. I can't stop thinking about her.'

'And what exactly do you think? '

'Oh, what it would feel like to kiss her. Stuff like that.'

'Kiss her! Excuse me while I throw up, Collie!'

'Well, you asked. '

A wounded defensive tone was in his voice.

'Just wait till you see her,' he went on. 'Then you'll understand. They're coming over for dinner, so let's see what you think then. You'll probably fall in love with her yourself.'

Aunt Cyril

We had taken a sandwich lunch with us and didn't return until late in the afternoon when Duncan said we had to take tea with Aunt Cyril. She inhabited a self-contained suite of rooms under the roof of the lodge.

'You've got to meet her. She's a hell of a character. She's my mother's aunt.'

'Why's she called Cyril?'

'She's really Sybil. Everyone's always called her Cyril. I don't know why. I suppose she likes it.'

He led the way up the main stairs. They had a curious steel rail running up the side of them, at the level of the steps. I had been meaning to ask about it.

'What 's that exactly?'

'Aunt Cyril's railway chair. She can't manage the stairs.'

'Why not?'

'Mainly because she's so fat.'

A second staircase rose to the attic floor, with no rail in place.

'How does she manage these then?'

'With difficulty. It was once used as the servants' quarters. Aunt Cyril prefers it up here because it's like a flat. She can have it all to herself and doesn't have to mix with everybody else unless she wants to. And because of the views.'

'Does she live here all the time?'

'Of course not, stupid. Nobody lives here all the time. It's a hunting lodge. People just come for the summer. The rest of the time she lives in Cambridge. She's a don, or something.'

We found Aunt Cyril smoking a cheroot and reading a thick book which, as I saw when she put it down, was a volume of *The Works of Edmund Spenser*. She wore a very large check shirt and thick corduroy trousers. Her heavily swollen ankles, warmed by a two-bar electric fire, showed below the turn-ups.

'Hello Duncan. Who's your friend?'

Her voice was throaty, and she wheezed.

'This is Christopher, Aunt Cyril. From school.'

'Sit down, Christopher from school, and tell me all about yourself while Duncan makes tea. You know where everything is, dear. There are some biscuits in the tin. I hope you like fig rolls, Christopher. I am a slave to them.'

I said I did, which was not entirely true but, at least, polite. Duncan disappeared into a small kitchen off Aunt Cyril's sitting room.

'I'm glad to have been relieved from my duty to Spenser. A pretty versifier, admittedly, but in every other way an absolute fright. Real conversation is the perfect antidote, I find. Where do your people live?'

I told her.

'Horrid part of the world. How can you stand it? All mill chimneys and red brick.'

I said no, actually, I lived in the countryside, surrounded by farms.

'Girlfriend of mine was a farmer. Well, a land girl, actually. She looked topping on a tractor in boots and gaiters. But I really do prefer the moors to farmland when push comes to shove.'

'Why is that?'

'You get a better class of animal up here. Domestic animals are so — *domestic*. Not to mention the birds. And I grant you Scots men are hairy beasts but the women are true as a billiards table. No people truer. One I knew walked twenty miles through the heather to bring me a hatful of plover's eggs. Or I suppose that should be a bonnet-full. Years ago, but still: was there ever a finer tribute?'

'She must have been in love with you, Auntie,' said Duncan, bringing in the biscuit tin.

'Duncan, please! It was far more complicated than that. But where was I?'

'Tell him about the time you were a chauffeur for the Savoy Hotel,' said Duncan on his way back to the kitchen.

'Were you really?' I said.

'Oh yes. I worked for an outfit called X Garage. Highly fashionable we were. We drove Fairbanks and Pickford and all the stars around town. We had Daimlers. Wonderful cars to drive. They were called landaulettes because the back seats could be opened to the skies. The Fairbanks adored that. They loved being seen, you know.'

She mentioned other Hollywood celebrities she had driven. I showed polite interest but they were names from the silent screen, and meant nothing to me. Then Duncan brought in a teapot and china cups on a japanned tray and the conversation turned to the next day's stalk.

Stalking

In the morning we assembled outside at the back of the lodge: it was six in the morning. There were five of us in the Land Rover: Duncan and me, Colonel and Mrs Collinshaw and someone called Wim Windt, who was staying at a hotel at Kinloch Rannoch and had arrived at the lodge in a large chauffeur-driven car. He had a round belly and a foreign accent, which I couldn't quite place.

We drove five miles up and into the heather above the lake where we met the ghillies, four of them, headed by one bearing the title of Head Stalker. They carried wicker baskets, guns and lidded leather tubes slung on straps from their shoulders. I soon realised that Head Stalker, whose name was Young, enjoyed plenipotentiary powers. Even Colonel Collinshaw was in awe of Old-Young, so-called to differentiate him from his son Young-Young who was also with us. Old-Young wielded the sort of authority that I would later observe in College porters. Nominally servants, they called you "Sir" in a tone of voice indistinguishable from how they would have called you a cunt.

Old-Young's absolute authority was brought home to me in the question of dress. Each of the ghillies wore brogues, ribbed stockings, tweed knee-breeches and thick tweed jackets. The Collinshaws wore hiking boots, tweeds, waxed gabardine coats and tweed caps, the peaks of which were buttoned, while Wim Windt was kitted out in a Jermyn Street version of the ghillies' attire, with every leather button gleaming new, fore-and-aft creases in his breeches and a pristine Sherlock Holmes deerstalker hat. My own outfit was some way out of line. Duncan had lent me a cap, but otherwise I wore jeans, plimsolls and a grey parka. I had a red woollen scarf around my neck. As soon as he saw it Old-Young took the scarf off me.

'You'll keep it in your pocket, laddie,' he said. 'You wouldna want to spook oor deer wi' that.'

We had walked for miles and Duncan and I were faint with hunger, before Old-Young at last declared that the wicker food basket could be opened. Duncan and I were sitting in the heather getting started on some chicken wings and hard-boiled eggs when Colonel Collinshaw came over to ask if I'd ever fired a rifle. I couldn't honestly say that I had.

'We may be giving Duncan a shot. Depends on the situation, range and so on.'

He winked and cocked his head towards his son.

'We've got to blood the boy at some point. Thing is, if he doesn't shoot straight and kill the beast outright we're obliged to track it and finish the job. Not done to leave a wounded stag to die, you see?'

This exchange got me thinking for the first time about what we were doing. The job, Duncan's father had called it. Not done to leave, and so on.

'Why are we doing this?' I asked Duncan. 'What's the point of it?'

'It's hunting,' he said. 'People have always done it.'

'But why?'

'To get meat. In this case, venison. And, of course, it's fun.'

'Is it?'

After lunch, and back on the march, I was feeling distinctly cold, footsore and several hours away from the comfortable chairs and the log fires back at the lodge. For a while I walked alongside Mr Windt, who was puffing, heavily sweating and from time to time stumbling over the stones on the track underfoot.

'How're you doing?' I said. 'I'm knackered.'

He turned his head fractionally in my direction but not far enough to actually look at me.

'Uh!' he said, whatever that meant.

He turned his head to face front again and we pressed on. A few minutes later I trod on a loose stone, and turned my ankle, yelping at the pain, which Windt appeared not to notice. I hopped off the track and leaned against a rock. After a few moments I was able to go on after the others, but now with a limp that I did my best to disguise.

Less than an hour later we were traversing the side of a glen, following a narrow trodden path in single file, when Old-Young pointed across to the other side.

'There,' he said, sinking to one knee. 'Get doun.'

I was only too glad to obey the command. Shifting onto his rump, Old-Young unslung the leather tube from his shoulder and undid the fastening. With a show of deliberation he withdrew a leather-and-brass-bound telescope a yard long, of a kind I more usually associated with The Ancient Mariner or Long John Silver. He lay back in the heather, rested the boot of one leg on the drawn-up knickerbockered knee of the other to make a stable support for the telescope and, with the instrument in position, he raked the opposing slope. He soon found what he was looking for: apparently a herd of red deer, though quite invisible to my own naked eye.

'Small herd,' he murmured. 'Five, six, seven, eight … nine of 'em. Mostly switches, but one good stag, a ten-pointer maybe. We'll try for him.'

Old-Young issued some terse orders, most of which I did not catch. I did gather that I was not going to be part of the execution squad, or "detail" as Colonel Collinshaw called it: that was to consist of the Colonel, Wim Windt, Duncan and Old-Young and the third ghillie. Young-Young and the fourth ghillie were to remain where we were with Mrs Collinshaw and myself .

'We'll get a lovely view of the excitement from here,' Duncan's mother told me. 'And in the meantime we can have a nice chat.'

The detail (of stag murderers, as I was beginning to think of them) set off diagonally down the slope towards a position downwind of their prey. They adopted a furtive crouching gait reminiscent of tommies in the Great War moving along a shallow trench.

Mrs Collinshaw was a bright-eyed woman with pepper and salt hair.

'Don't *you* shoot?' I asked her.

'Oh no, not me. A woman's place, you know.'

She laughed.

'When you're married to Douglas…'

'But you do fish.'

'Oh yes, that's allowed, you see.'

'I'm afraid I don't.'

She laughed again. She was a frequent laugher.

'I suppose it's because I never do catch anything. It suits me actually. The truth is I don't much want to. Killing things is men's fun and I'm perfectly happy to leave them to it. I like sitting in the boat on the lake, of course. It's sort of … like a meditation. It takes you out of yourself. Now, that's enough about me. Tell me about yourself, Christopher.'

For the next ten minutes she teased a few autobiographical notes out of me, and even seemed interested, which I liked in her.

'Oh look,' she said then, pointing down into the glen. 'They're in position, I do believe.'

She had a pair of binoculars, which she now raised to her eyes.

'I wonder if Duncan will get a shot. Oh good! It looks like he will. Oh, Young-Young. Would you let Christopher have a go with your spyglass?'

Young-Young handed me his telescope and I used it rather as I had seen his father do, balancing the far end in the notch of my drawn-up knees. I pointed it in the direction Mrs Collinshaw had indicated and after some time I located the shooting detail. They were grouped together with a large boulder between themselves and the stag. Swinging the telescope I saw him obliviously grazing at a range of perhaps seventy yards. Duncan had started crawling inch by inch up the boulder, presumably so that he could shoot from the top of it. Behind him, and I guessed unknown to him, Old-Young took up a firing position of his own. He was not, I supposed, a man to take a chance on the Young Master's shooting ability.

Duncan splayed himself out on the rock and took the rifle from his father. He tucked the stock into his shoulder and squinted through the telescopic sights. His right hand went to the trigger.

'Oh my goodness!' said Mrs Collinshaw in sudden exclamation. 'Who on earth?'

We heard a faint thudding of hooves and saw a horse and rider coming over the skyline on the far side of the glen. I swung my telescope towards them. The rider was female. Her hair blew around and it was a tangle of intense ginger. She took one hand off the reins and waved it signal-wise in the air and gave a whooping cry. The deer, difficult to spot while they were standing, could now be clearly seen walking and then quickly enough running together, skipping up the side of the glen, away from the rider and also away from the guns.

There was a cracking sound. Duncan had fired after the deer and immediately we heard his father shouting angrily at him. I heard the word 'Never' very emphatically. Old-Young meanwhile had held his fire and the deer, quite unscathed, disappeared from view.

I swung the telescope back towards the horse. I could see now that its fiery-haired rider was not only female but young. She wore no hard hat, and appeared at first glance, and to my astonishment and momentary excitement, to be riding topless. But then I realised she had on a close-fitting sleeveless shirt, pink in colour. She was laughing as she pulled her horse up and coolly began schooling it in circles.

The Colonel turned his wrath away from his son and towards the equestrian, waving his arm at her and issuing volleys of furious oaths, which reached us muffled by the contrary wind.

'Good God!' said Mrs Collinshaw beside me, peering through her binoculars. 'I do believe it's the MacKenzie girl. Well, I mean, it could hardly be anyone else, with that hair. What a thing to do! It looked quite deliberate. It looked as if she knew exactly what she was doing.'

'Do you mean that's Ailish MacKenzie?,' I said. 'Duncan mentioned her.'

'Yes. The daughter of the local doctor. About your age, I think. But what a minx. I mean to say! Scattering the herd like that, just when Duncan was about to take his shot.'

I looked at Susan Collinshaw. She did not appear at all angry or even indignant. If anything she was enjoying herself.

'Douglas is beside himself, look. Oh dear! Well, the child's got spunk, I'll give her that.'

She slapped her palm to her mouth.

'Oh God I've just remembered!' she said. 'The MacKenzies are all coming to dinner on Saturday. Well, well! That should be interesting.'

The detail was making its way back towards us. Colonel Collinshaw was snorting and beetroot veins bulged in his cheeks. Duncan also looked put out, his own face literally so, since it seemed to have fractionally dropped on one side, with that side of his mouth also turned down, giving him a lop-sided and petulant look. He was undoubtedly chastened by the ticking off he'd got from his father for shooting at the retreating deer. But even more complicated feelings had by now prevailed. His *inamorata* had just ruined his chances of getting his first stag, and a ten-points antler trophy.

Later that night Mrs Collinshaw had great difficulty in dissuading the Colonel from telephoning Dr MacKenzie immediately and telling him that, next time he saw Ailish in the glen, he'd shoot her in the head.

Daughters of the Tsar

Next day at breakfast I showed Duncan my ankle. It seemed to have swollen to almost twice its normal circumference. He called his mother to look.

'Can you wiggle it?' she said.

I wiggled it minutely but enough to make me grimace.

'I shouldn't risk going on the stalk today, Christopher. It's probably just sprained but you'd better lie up. We'll find you a good book to keep you happy.'

There was obviously no question of Duncan missing the stalk. I didn't much mind.

'Actually I brought books to read for my holiday history essay,' I said, 'and I've not really got started yet. So I can do that.'

'Oh?' said Mrs Collinshaw. 'What's it about?'

'It's on Rasputin and the Romanovs.'

'He was the mad monk, wasn't he? With strange powers?'

'I'm not sure about the powers. Maybe it was all just tricks. In the book I read it's not clear.'

Colonel Collinshaw snorted over his kipper.

'Bloody fool, the Tsar. Wife led him by the nose, and the monk led her by the nose. Effing her, shouldn't be surprised, the monk.'

'Darling! Not in front of the boys!'

'End result: a total balls-up of the Russian war effort, open door to communism and blood all over the cobblestones. '

He was dissecting the fish with dextrous twists of his fork.

'And the poor young children terribly slaughtered with their parents,' said Mrs Collinshaw.

'Isn't there some connection with Aunt Cyril?' the Colonel said.

'Yes, I can't quite remember what, exactly,' said Mrs Collinshaw, pushing away her empty plate and standing. 'It was when she worked for that couturier in Paris, I think. Now, Christopher dear, I'll see if I can find you some aspirins for the pain.'

Wim Windt arrived as we were leaving the breakfast table and, soon, the stalkers had all packed, with guns and haversacks, into the Land Rover. I stood in the yard and waved as they drove off to their rendezvous with the ghillies. Limping inside I brought down the books that I had borrowed from the public library at home. I had read one of them on the train coming up. It had a photograph on the cover showing Rasputin full-face, with long greasy dark hair, centre-parted, and an unimpressive straggly beard. He stared intensely with the eyes of a hypnotist and I wondered if that was the secret of his power. Whether or not Duncan's father was right about him and the Tsarina, Rasputin appeared to be particularly adept at holding women in thrall and many of these he blatantly and frequently effed, as the Colonel would have put it.

I was sitting in a sagging armchair in what they called the library, though to my mind it was too small to be called that. Still, it had hundreds of books with decayed leather bindings, many in series and all behind glass. I picked up my own second book, a life of Nicholas II, opened it near the end and started reading about the Tsar and his family at the Ipatiev House in Ekaterinburg. The countdown to their deaths had a strong physical effect on me. I was very sorry for the sickly Tsarevitch in his wheelchair, of course, but it was his four beautiful sisters (they looked to me beautiful in the photographs, sad eyed and dressed in white linen) whose fate formed a hollow pit of nausea inside me. I tried to imagine what the execution squad felt as they opened fire in the confined space of the house's cellar: what they would later remember of the bullets ripping into the girls' bodies; the air full of choking clouds of cordite smoke and sickening screams; the crumpled bodies and the blood. With those memories, I wondered how they could ever have slept again.

I heard a mechanical noise, a clanking and a whirring, that came from the hall. I pinched the book closed over my finger and went out to investigate. Aunt Cyril was riding down the stairs on her railway chair. She yelped when she saw me.

'It's you! Why aren't you out slaughtering dumb animals?'

'I sprained my ankle yesterday. I'm resting it.'

She reached the bottom and climbed with some effort out of the chair.

'You nearly did *me* an injury appearing like that. I thought I had the place to myself. Have they abandoned you then? That's typical. They'd rather kill a healthy animal than sympathise with a wounded human being.'

'I don't mind. Mrs Collinshaw left me some sandwiches.'

'You won't starve then.'

She padded across the hall towards the lakeside door, her vast body swathed in a silken gown with a dragon rampant on the back.

'I'm going for a swim. Care to join me?'

'All right.'

I hobbled up the stairs and put on my trunks. When I caught up with Aunt Cyril she had arrived at the shore end of the jetty and cast aside the dragon robe. I saw that she had crammed her great bulk into a green woollen bathing suit. The thick fat around her jowls, arms and legs was loose, lumpy and unstable, while the tight contained areas within the costume bulged roundly with all the solidity of a bag crammed with suet. She had pulled a black rubber bathing cap over her hair, which seemed to shrink her head out of proportion to the rest of her. Together with the

111

swimming goggles that she tightened over her eyes, this gave her the appearance of one of those pre-war pilots, such as Amy Johnson.

Hearing my approach she turned and I saw on her face what seemed to me an expression of pure happiness. Then she fixed her eyes on the end of the wooden jetty, spread her arms wide and, launching herself forward, started to run or rather to galumph in bounding strides along the board-walk. A bird sitting further along squawked and flew up in alarm as the pier began to quake and undulate beneath her. I was reminded of a loaded bomber plane labouring along the runway to take off. As she reached the end, and only for a moment, actual flight was attained as she hurled herself into the air, before crash-diving into the water and going under in a cloud of foam and bubbles.

I got to the pier's end in time to see Aunt Cyril's head as it rose from the depths like a seal, her face appearing first. The eyes behind the goggles were shining.

'Come on in, Christopher! It's bliss. Nothing like it. Nothing in the world.'

I did an immediate header and the shock of icy water made me forget myself entirely for at least half a minute.

Later when we had towelled off and gone back into the hall she said,

'I always have coffee after a swim. Come and join me when you're dressed, if you like. You know where I am.'

Scoop

'Do you swim every day?' I said.

I was back in the chair I'd sat in when Duncan and I had tea with her, but now sipping a cup of double strength instant coffee.

'Oh yes. One of the few pleasures I have left apart from whisky and teaching. It may be hard for you to

112

imagine but when you're as fat as me everything is a perfectly ghastly effort. You drag yourself about in a never-ending and exhausting fight against gravity. Terrible thing, gravity. How I hate Isaac Newton for inventing the stuff.'

Her laugh wheezed, like pulling open a damaged concertina.

'Anyway, the point is the only time I'm in equilibrium is in the water, see?'

She lit a cheroot.

'So tell me, Christopher, how are you going to kill the time between now and the return of the deer's execution squad? '

'I've got a school essay to write. I'm reading up on it.'

'On what subject, may I ask?'

'It's Russian history. It's about Rasputin.'

'Ha! That's wonderful! You've got a stroke of luck, my boy. You've got a scoop.'

'How do you mean?'

'Do you know where Rasputin was killed ?'

'In house of Prince Yusupov in St Petersburg. Yusupov himself shot him.'

'Exactly. Felix Yusupov. I knew him once upon a time. Worked for him, actually.'

'You *worked* for Prince Yusupov?'

'Yes. But we were sort of friends too. Well, mainly his wife Irina. She was the Tsar's niece. A most beautiful girl. She would be a model now. In fact, she was a model *then*. She modelled their own designs. She and Felix had a fashion house in Paris called Maison Irfé. It was in the twenties.'

'You mean the man who shot Rasputin had a dress shop?'

Again, that punctured-squeeze-box laugh.

'Yes, if you want to put it like that.'

'How on earth did you meet?'

'Remember I told you I drove for that outfit X-Garage? I took the Yusupovs all over the south of England one summer. 1927, I think it was. Irina took a fancy to me and offered me a job chauffeuring for them in Paris.'

She lay back in her chair, with her eyes resting on the ceiling. She dragged on her cheroot and sent a stream of smoke upwards.

'I wasn't sure whether to accept, until she mentioned they lived just near the Renault factory at Boulogne-Billancourt and had just bought themselves a Renault Vivasix. Well, I couldn't resist after that. It turned out to be an absolutely brilliant car, though you don't hear so much it nowadays. Six-cylinder. Lovely long nose. Beautiful to drive once you got used to the gear-change. I lasted six months in France until I had to come home and do cramming for Cambridge.'

'Did the Prince ever talk about how he killed Rasputin?'

'Oh yes, often. People were always asking, you know, and he was quite at ease about it. According to his version of events they fed him cakes they'd supposedly laced with cyanide, but mysteriously this had no effect. Rasputin kept on laughing and joking and quaffing vodka. Then Felix went and got a gun and shot him in the chest. Believe it or not the frightful man still wouldn't die.'

'Until one of the others shot him in the head, I think.'

Aunt Cyril sighed.

'Probably. The details of the story did vary somewhat every time Felix told it. I think in the end, they dumped the bloody man through a hole in the river ice.'

She'd told me nothing that wasn't in the book I'd read, but I felt almost dizzy at this unexpected contact, albeit second-hand, with a world-changing historical event.

'I expect he knew the Tsar's daughters too.' I said. 'Did he talk about them?'

'Oh yes. They were such spoiled bitches, according to Felix.'

'Oh! Were they?'

That buzz of pleasure abruptly disappeared. Aunt Cyril noticed my face registering disappointment.

'Does that upset you, Christopher? Remember these girls were born Grand Duchesses. They were bound to be hideously spoiled. They didn't think about other people, except as a lower form of life.'

'But they couldn't help being spoiled,' I said. 'I think it's a bit much of you to call them bitches, when they were basically innocent. It says in the book they did volunteer nursing of troops wounded in the war.'

'They did. It must have a bit of a reality check. You know, they got paid a wage in cash and had no idea what to do with it. Imagine being eighteen and not having the first idea how to use money. So perhaps you're right and they *were* innocents.'

She tapped her volume of *The Faerie Queene*.

'One of Spenser's themes is of the beautiful innocent girl trying to put right the wrongs done to her father the King. It's romantic tosh but certain lines are rather apposite to more recent times. '

She picked up the book and leafed through it until she found the passage she wanted.

> *'Their sceptres stretched*
> *   from East to Western shore,*
> *And all the world in their subjection held;*
> *Till that infernal fiend with foul uproar*
> *For-wasted all their land, and them expelled.*

It's a pretty good description of the Russian Revolution, don't you think?'

Ailish

A few minutes later I drained my cup and excused myself on the grounds of needing to work. I went downstairs deflated. Aunt Cyril clearly thought my feelings about the Tsar's girls was equally romantic tosh, shallow and transient, while I wanted to have feelings that lasted forever.

By now the thought of going back to my reading lacked allure, so I went outside, and started limping southwards along the lakeside path. After twenty minutes the MacKenzie house came into view. My ankle was hurting and I sat on a rock to rest, looking at the house.

I suppose I was three hundred yards away. A girl came out onto the lawn that stretched down between house and lake. She wore jeans and a thick white jumper and had a mass of uncontained red hair. It was Ailish MacKenzie. I slid off the rock and continued towards the house until I reached the pine copse that edged the shore. Moving to the far side of the little wood I found I was no more than a hundred yards from Ailish, but I was confident she hadn't seen me. She was messing about with a dog, a black Labrador, throwing a ball for it. Every now and then she would crouch and put her arms around it, or fondle its ears and let it lick her face. Then she would be up and running around and laughing while the dog chased her, yelping and leaping to get the ball. Finally she hurled the ball hard and sat down on the grass. The ball came bouncing down in my direction, with the dog in pursuit. I flinched behind a tree. I was wondering what I would do if the dog found me and started barking.

The danger passed and the dog was on its way back to Ailish with the ball in its drooling mouth. She patted it and lay down to signal the end of the game.

I could see her clearly. I tried to imagine what it was like to be her. To be a girl. She looked my age. What she was doing in her garden was just the sort of thing I might have been doing in mine. Yet there was a great un-jumpable canyon between us. Not just the physical differences, extraordinary though they were, but the whole outlook on everything. That's what people talked about: the battle of the sexes. The French said 'Vive la différence!' with a hefty exclamation mark. It was a fashionable enough trope, a seam that cartoonists mined endlessly. But as for me, I wished I understood *la différence*.

I heard a car crunching gravel and the dog took off towards the sound, barking insanely. A few moments later a man who I soon realised was her father appeared at the side of the house carrying a bulging leather case in one hand, and a smouldering cherrywood pipe in the other.

'Ailish! Are you out there?'

He walked to the top edge of the sloping lawn and looked around. He spotted her, went down the slope and stood above her. He said something. Ailish jumped up and answered him. They began to have an argument.

'That's not fair!' she said, her voice reaching me on the wind.

He spoke again.

'Why do I have to?' I heard her say.

Her father brought the discussion to an end, jammed the pipe back between his teeth and turned to walk crisply up to the house. She slumped onto the grass again and the dog joined her wagging its tail. She fondled its ears for a bit, then lay down. She was lying on her back, hidden from the house by the slope of the lawn. But I could see her clearly, lying star-shaped. I saw her wriggling for a moment as if to get comfortable. Then I saw her shove a hand under the front of her jeans, and its rubbing movement.

For a moment I didn't twig, but then I did and a blush flooded into my face. She had no idea I was watching, but I felt engulfed in shame at what she was doing, and that I had seen it. I began to stumble back by the way I had come. Sticks cracked under my feet but I didn't care. My heart stopped pounding only when I knew I was out of sight of the MacKenzie house.

Flaying

The hunting party came back, having at last made a kill .

'Eight-pointer,' said Colonel Collinshaw. 'Bloody Windt took the shot and almost cocked it up but luckily Old-Young had the beast covered.'

'Come and see,' Duncan said to me. 'They're going to skin it and that's not to be missed.'

I hopped and limped as best I could after him, across the yard and into the skinning shed. The carcase of a stag, looking much bigger than I imagined, lay on a table in the centre. Its mild brown eyes were open in death. Duncan pointed to the antlers.

'They're not much to boast about, but Mr Windt is as pleased as Punch. Eight points, you see?'

He touched each tip with his finger and counted them off.

Young-Young was in charge of the business, with the other two ghillies to assist.

'Stand by the wall you two and keep your selves still,' he said to Duncan and me. 'These knives are sharp so stay out of the way.'

'Look at your watch,' said Duncan quietly. 'Time him.'

The two helpers were stationed one at each end of the deer, pulling the legs hard to keep the corpse rigid. Young-Young began by making a circular cut around both hind legs just above the rear hooves, and then ran the knife up the front side of the legs. He pulled the skin away from the leg flesh and tore it off like sellotape all the way to the haunches. Working with the knife to shave away the connecting tissue he peeled the skin from the haunches until he had all the separated skin in one handful just under the animal's tail. He made a deep nick under the tail then yanked hard, and the tail came away within the skin. Making another seam all the way up the deer's belly he unpeeled the skin from its body, shaving connecting tissue with a flashing blade to left and right. The flesh beneath gleamed like wet marble, with indistinct striations and formations showing beneath the surface in pinks, reds, blues and purples.

'Turn,' he said.

The body was swivelled onto its flayed belly. Young-Young now got hold of the skin at the base of the spine and simply unpeeled it all the way to the neck. He took the skin off the forelegs, just as he had off the hind legs, and now the whole of the hide was removed. The assistants slid the corpse so that the antlered head rested in the middle of the table. Young Young severed it at the top of the neck, and lifted away the head and the whole skin. Duncan nudged me and I looked at my watch. It had all been done in less than two minutes.

'Let's go,' said Duncan. 'There's nothing but the guts to come out now, and the smell's horrible.'

Before dinner we assembled as usual for sherry in the drawing room.

'How's the ankle, Christopher?' asked Duncan's mother.

'It's hurting a lot.'

'Have you rested it?'

I said nothing of my walk along the shore. Instead I just said,

'Well, I did go swimming with Aunt Cyril.'

'Did you indeed?'

She laughed but, immediately reverting to seriousness, put on the glasses that hung on a chain around her neck and asked to see the damaged joint.

'Oh dear, it doesn't appear to be any better, does it? Worse, if anything. We'd better call Dr MacKenzie to have a look.'

She went down to the hall to telephone and I exchanged a glance with Duncan. He tipped his head, obviously wanting to talk privately.

'Just going out on the terrace with Christopher,' he said to his father, who merely grunted.

The terrace was reached from the house through French windows. As we went down Duncan let me lean my hand on his shoulder to take the pressure off my ankle. Passing Mrs Collinshaw on the phone in the hall I heard her saying,

'It's about Duncan's friend who's been staying. He's made a bit of a mess of his ankle I'm afraid ... Yes, could you possibly?'

We sat in wrought iron chairs at a wrought iron table.

'When you see Dr MacKenzie, I want you to find out what you can about Ailish,' said Duncan. 'I want to know if she's coming with her parents tomorrow night for dinner, which I bloody hope she isn't.'

I hadn't told him about my earlier sighting of Ailish.

'Why? Don't you want to see her?'

'Of course I don't, idiot. Not after what she did yesterday on her horse. I'm hoping she'll be so ashamed she'll stay at home. Or her parents will make her stay.'

'But I thought you were crazy about her. If you are, you should want to see her.'

'Well I'm not. Not any bloody more. It'll be bad enough having to entertain the horrible Archie, without her being there too.'

'Who's Archie?'

'Her brother.'

'Why's he horrible?

'He's eleven.'

'Ah!'

His mother put her head around the door.

'He's coming over right away, Christopher. About ten minutes I should think. Why don't you come through to the library? He can see you in there.'

'Remember what I said,' whispered Duncan fiercely as I was again leaning on his arm to go back inside.

The doctor was probably fifty, with wavy grey-streaked hair, a frontal lock of which fell youthfully across his forehead. He questioned me about how the injury had happened, pressed the swollen tissue here and there and asked me to try to move my foot around, which was now more or less impossible.

'You'd better go for an X-Ray,' he said. 'I'll take you over to the hospital in Pitlochry tomorrow morning. I've got to go anyway. Here.'

He opened his medical bag and stirred the contents around until he found two small brown pill bottles. He shook three from one, and a single pill from the other.

'Some painkillers and a sleeping tablet to get you through the night. I'll pick you up at eight-thirty and in the meantime keep the leg up. No weight on it, OK?'

His eye caught the library books on the table beside my chair.

'Yours?' he said, picking up *The Romanovs* and flicking through the pages. 'Not the best advertisement for the system of monarchy, but what happened to the children was unforgiveable.'

I liked him for that.

Sadly Inexperienced

Sitting beside Dr MacKenzie in his Vauxhall, heavy-headed from the sleeping pill and dull from the pain-killers, I thought I'd better save the conversation about Ailish for the return journey. I did not calculate that the doctor would not be bringing me back at all, and that it would be Mrs Collinshaw who came to collect and drive me back to the lodge, now with my foot and ankle tightly encased in a plaster cast. On the way she said that she would telephone my parents and tell them what's happened, and that I must talk to them myself.

'It's just a question of how, or if, you're going to get home tomorrow, Christopher. I really think it's out of the question for you to travel by train on your own.'

We got through on the phone and my father said he would come for me in the car. The rest of the day passed quietly. The hospital had lent me a pair of crutches and I was able to get around clumsily with these, though I spent most of the day lying on a sofa, playing cards and Scrabble with Duncan, and even a game of chess which, when I play it, becomes little more than a game of chance. I beat him nevertheless. His mind was elsewhere.

'I can't believe you never asked the doctor about Ailish,' he said.

'What difference does it make? She'll either come, or she won't.'

'My mother refuses to phone and ask about it. She says as far as she's concerned Ailish is coming. I daren't ask my pa. He'd go off like a rocket at the bare mention of Ailish.'

'So what will he do when he sees her?'

'I don't know. The real point is, what will *I* say to her.'

'Don't say anything.'

'You don't understand.'

'Is there something you're not telling me?'

'When we went over there to tea, just after we arrived. I haven't told you about that.'

'I think you did mention it.'

'Not what happened.'

'What did happen?'

'OK. This is the thing. They've got a ping-pong table in a room above the garage. We were sent off, her and me, to have a game while they played cards. And when we got there, well, she ... This is embarrassing.'

'She what? Come on, Duncan!'

'She didn't want to play ping-pong. She had something quite different in mind.'

'You mean she—?'

'There was a record player in there. She put on a record and said why don't we dance? So we did and she put her arms around me and we danced for a bit and then she, well, she kissed me on the lips, and stuck her tongue in, and started sort of rubbing herself against me.'

'God, Duncan! You said you only imagined what kissing her would be like. Now you're saying you actually did kiss her.'

'No. She kissed me, as a matter of fact.'

'Yes, and you kissed her back.'

'I don't know. I mean, yes I did, or tried to. But I'd hardly got started when she just pushed me away and said I was sadly inexperienced. Those are the words she said. Sadly inexperienced.'

'Well you're a bit more experienced now.'

'Guess what the record was, though.'

'I Wanna Be Your Lover Baby?'

He gave a rueful smile.

'No. It was You're No Good — the Swinging Blue Jeans.'

I laughed so hard I jarred my ankle inside its plaster.

The Foolishness of Youth

The Rover arrived and the four MacKenzies stepped out. Apart from Aunt Cyril we were all waiting for them at the front door. Ailish wore pale yellow tights under a dress of brown velvet. The hem of the dress ended half way down her thighs and, at the top, a bib was buttoned to broad straps that went over her shoulders and down her back. Beneath the dress she wore a yellow ribbed jumper, and a bag made of some kind of oriental carpet material hung from her shoulder. She was slim, and tall for her age, and had used a little make-up: a suggestion of mascara and a very pale lipstick. This was minimal, but the effect was surprising. Walking ahead of her parents and Archie to the wide open front door she looked to me like a young woman.

It was an illusion, of course. All the time Dr MacKenzie was in control of her, holding his hand flat

123

against the small of her back. Fractionally ahead of him, she stopped short at the threshold where the womanly impression vanished and she was a child again. Her father pressed her forward and she came hesitantly in, with him and her mother just behind.

'Hello Douglas,' said her father. 'Ailish has something she would like to say to you. Ailish?'

He gave her another gentle shove and she took half a step towards Colonel Collinshaw. She met the Colonel's eye for a moment then looked down. Her hands went behind her back.

'What I did in the glen, on Wednesday,' she said towards the floor. Her voice was wispy, submissive. 'Well, I'm sorry Colonel Collinshaw. I'm sorry about it. I shouldn't have.'

She looked at her father, who was almost by her side, as if to check that this was enough. Dr MacKenzie motioned towards the Colonel, who cleared his throat.

'All right, young lady. Apology accepted. We shall put it down to the foolishness of youth. But mind you, if I ever see you up there during a stalk again, I'll—.'

'Douglas, dear!' warned his wife. 'Shall we go up to the drawing room for a drink? There's a lovely fire.'

Going upstairs on crutches is extremely laborious and I was behind the others. Ailish went round the turn of the stair just ahead of me so that my eyes were level with her bottom. She was still holding her hands behind her and I saw through the banister that the fingers on both of them were so tightly crossed they were white.

Slaughter of the Innocents

It was a dull dinner during which the adults spoke about the idiocy of the County Council, the state of the fishing and other matters of local interest while the rest of us remained almost silent. Then, as Mrs Collinshaw unfolded a green baize-covered table for bridge, it was light enough for Duncan, Ailish and

124

Archie to go into the garden for what she called 'a little run-around'. Meanwhile I crutched my way to the library, which I was beginning to consider my own personal territory.

I sat in the deep, sagging armchair, sleepy after two glasses of oloroso before dinner. I picked up *Rasputin and the Romanovs* but did not read. I laid the book on my knee, shut my eyes and thought about Ailish. If she could kiss Duncan then she might kiss me. If she could kiss me, then we might well ... After a while, though lightly dozing, I realised that I had given myself an erection. I heard the door open and close, and Ailish's voice.

'Did you see me rub my cunt?'

I came awake and blinked

'What? What did you say?'

She stared at me with unnerving steadiness.

'On Wednesday. I robbed the hunt of its prey. Did you see it?'

Coming to my senses I quickly moved *Rasputin and the Romanovs* to cover the bulge under my fly.

'Oh! I must have dropped off. Sorry. Yes. Yes, I did. I was up on the side of the valley.'

'The glen.'

'I mean the glen.'

'So?'

'I wasn't with the shooters. I was looking down on them, about three or four hundred yards away. But I had a telescope and I watched you. It thought what you did was —.'

What did I think it was? Brave? Rash? Magnificent? Stupid? All of the above?

'I thought it was very daring. You might have got shot. Have you all come in now? Where are the others?'

'Still outside. They're kicking a football.'

She was fishing in her bag and drew out a printed leaflet, which she handed across.

'Look at this. It explains why I did it.'

It was a single page folded leaflet with a logo and the heading *Hunt Saboteurs Association*. The front was mainly taken up with a press photograph of a pack of hounds tearing a fox to pieces, with STOP THE SLAUGHTER OF THE INNOCENTS! in gory lettering that appeared to drip with blood. I realised that a kiss, if it had ever been on the cards, was definitely off them now. I opened the leaflet up to look at the text inside. This was big on slogans, which took a markedly aggressive tone.

TAKE DIRECT ACTION! TO HELL WITH BLOODY HUNTING! SPIKE THE GROUSE-GUNS!

These were interspersed with facts and figures: how long it typically took a hunted fox to die; the cruelties of the hind-cull; the average number of grouse that meet their deaths on the 'inglorious twelfth'.

'My God!' I said. 'You'd better not show this to Colonel Collinshaw. He's the best one-armed grouse shooter in the country, if not in the world.'

'It's not just him. Since I got interested in this I've had the whole of this area against me. They're all absolutely addicted to blood sports. I can't even speak to my riding friends any more. All anyone wants to do around here is massacre foxes, deer and grouse. It's a bloodbath and it bloody sickens me. And I *hate* myself for apologising. Daddy told me he'd sell my poor horse if I didn't.'

I looked into her eyes. They were burning so intensely it seemed impossible to look at them for long. Mine flinched down to my lap and found themselves staring instead into the fanatic eyes of Rasputin on the cover of the book.

She took the leaflet back and showed me the application form on the reverse side.

'Here, you *have* to join. It's only two and six, look.'

'Oh, thanks. Yes. But ... I tell you what. Have you met Aunt Cyril?'

'Aunt who?'

126

'Cyril. Duncan's mother's aunt. I say that because I think she might really agree with you. About blood sports, that is. So she could be a genuine recruit for you. I'll take you up to meet her, if you like. She's a professor or something.'

I rode up on the railway and we found Aunt Cyril writing in a notebook, which rested on a board that she'd stretched across the arms of her chair.

'Aunt Cyril, this is Ailish,' I said. 'She's Dr MacKenzie's daughter.'

'Of *course* she is,' said Aunt Cyril, beaming at us. 'Your father's attended me once or twice, my dear, and told me of his children. But I had no idea you were so grown up. Come in, come in. Take a seat. I'm having whisky which is a bit strong for you but I can stretch to a glass of sherry.'

'Actually I don't drink,' said Ailish. 'Christopher says you're anti-bloodsports, like us. Do you want to join the Hunt Saboteurs' Association?'

'Straight to the point. I like that.'

Ailish pulled another the leaflet out of her bag and handed it over. Aunt Cyril studied the picture on the front. She put it on her writing board and laid her index-finger near the stricken fox's head describing a circle around it.

'Daun Russel,' she said quietly, as if to herself. 'A cole-fox full of sly iniquity.'

'No,' said Ailish, much more loudly and with a shocked upward inflection. 'No, he's not! He's not! That's the point. It's what we're fighting against.'

She stood up and seized back the leaflet. Aunt Cyril put out a hand to stop her but too late

'Ailish, dear, I was just quoting—.'

'He's an innocent wild animal with every right to his life,' said Ailish.

'Of course he is, I was only—.'

'I don't think you're pro-animals and anti-blood sports at all. I think you're just like all the others.'

She marched to the door that led to the stairs. She turned.

'I'm going down. I think they're calling.'

We listened to her feet thumping on the treads as she ran down.

'What a fierce child,' said Aunt Cyril.

'She took what you said wrongly,' I said. 'She didn't know it was Chaucer.'

'But you did, young Christopher. Good for you.'

'I like Chaucer. And we've read the *Nun's Priest's Tale* at school. Look, I'd better go down too.'

'All right then. Tell her, will you? I'm too bound up in my books, that's my trouble. Tell her to send or bring me that leaflet and I'll subscribe to her dreadful association.'

In the drawing room bridge was over and the MacKenzies were getting ready to leave. Ailish looked at me, aggrieved. As everyone was going out, I said in a whisper.

'You misunderstood. She was quoting Geoffrey Chaucer. She loves wild animals, really she does.'

Ailish gave a quick, incredulous laugh.

'Geoffrey Chaucer? What's he got to do with anything?'

'Anyway, look, she'll join the Association if you get that leaflet back to her. And so will I, Ailish. As soon as I get home I'll send off a postal order. I promise.'

'You make sure you do that or I'll hate you for ever.'

She poked me in the chest with her finger. It was the only physical contact of any kind I had with her.

Go in Peace

The next morning, Sunday, Mrs Collinshaw took Duncan and me to Mass at Pitlochry. From the outside it looked more like a dance hall than a church but I was drawn to the wooden crucifix behind the altar. It was evidently directly carved and showed the body of Christ hanging in a sinuous S-shape, but with his head tilted counter to the body's flow. It was the form of a beautiful adolescent, not of a man of thirty-three. And, while there was nothing of torture in it, there seemed to me a good deal of sexuality. I was so preoccupied looking at it that I paid little attention to the sermon, which was something about the hardships of working on the land, delivered by the ruddy complexioned priest in a thick braying Donegal accent.

He raced through the rest of Mass at breakneck speed, delivering the closing words — *Ite Missa est* — with what sounded like a sigh of relief. Driving home, Mrs Collinshaw was scornful of the man.

'He's a relief priest, as Father Murdoch's on holiday. Gone fishing. This fellow will be over here from Ireland on his own holiday. That's what they do in August — they parish-swap. What a terrible sermon, didn't you think? All that stuff about the potato famine and the cruel landlords. Do we really have to hear that kind of thing? At one point I thought he was about to launch into a full-scale attack on Oliver Cromwell. And all that stuff about the potato! Ha! What's that got to do with God, I'd like to know.'

'I thought the carved crucifix was really good,' I said.

'You have good taste, Christopher. It's a Gill, apparently. Must be quite valuable. Heaven knows how a tiny church like that got hold of a piece by him. Some rich patron I suppose.'

When we got back my father had arrived in the car to take me home. He had got up at four-thirty to drive the two hundred and fifty miles. He didn't seem to mind.

'See you in September back at Shed,' said Duncan, using the school's slang name.

'Worse luck,' I said. 'I mean Shed, not you. Thanks for having me anyway.'

As soon as we set off, the balloon of tension began to deflate inside me.

'How was it?' my father asked. 'Shoot any deer?'

'They wouldn't even let me near a rifle on the first day, and then I broke my ankle. I didn't see them shoot a deer, but I saw them skin one.'

I told him how Young-Young had peeled the hide from the deer as if he were removing a banana skin.

'It's always a pleasure to watch experts working with their hands,' my father said. 'I've never forgotten the men I used to watch in Kendal, where I was sent to learn foundry-work. They could chase a screw to a hundredth of an inch solely on a hand-lathe. Hand and eye, that was all it was.'

I had always found it calming to be alone with him. The time would come, and soon enough, when all his ideas would seem to me reactionary and bigoted, and he would think me smug and supercilious in my sleeve-worn idealism. But, now, he made few demands. He liked to tell stories, which I liked listening to, about his life, the war and the eccentricities of his family.

Gradually, sitting beside him, and with the road home stretching ahead of us, I began to forget Ailish, Duncan and my broken ankle, and to feel at ease.

Forgetful Snow

1965

The snow began to fall at some point south of Rugby. In general the north is expected to be colder than the south but in that January expectations were reversed and a transparent curtain of snowflakes began to whip and whirl past the train window, thinly at first and then more thickly until somewhere in Buckinghamshire they appeared as a silent storm of cotton flocks. Looking through this turbulence, however, I saw that the underlying theme was different. There was a calm, a near stasis, about the newly laid snowscape. Forgetful snow as T. S. Eliot called it in *The Waste Land*, my favourite poem at the time. I supposed he meant that to cover something entirely is a way of forgetting it and, looking out of the train, I saw how assiduously the snow was now forgetting the fields, the trees and housetops, obliterating the colours, crusting and reshaping everything. A visible forgetfulness was falling over the land and it made all the stronger my feeling of travelling from home into an entirely different scene.

Johnny Romero had phoned me on the day after Boxing Day and asked me if I could possibly get to Sussex in a week's time, and stay two or three nights with his family. On one of those evenings he would be throwing a party.

'All very sudden,' I said. 'You didn't mention it at school.'

'Didn't I? Oh well, I just thought you might like to come. There'll be the cream of Sussex society, with actual honourables. Also you'll meet a host of beautiful girls.'

'Who else from school is coming?'

'No one. Just you, if you can. '

I thought he was being somehow cagey on this point but thinking about it I rather liked the idea of travelling across country, seeing a bit of London on the way, and ending up in a county I had never been to. So I entered into negotiations with my parents, who agreed the financing and logistics of the trip. A week later I picked up a long distance train to London where I would arrive around lunchtime.

By the time I reached Euston if was evident that snow in the extreme south had been even heavier than what I had seen from the train, and it was still falling thickly. The pavements of London were canyons of grimed snow, where walkers dodged the side-wash of buses and cars and hopped over dirty pools of slush-water. I took the Northern Line to Embankment and changed to the Circle and District for Victoria. When I got there all the departures boards were telling the same story. Every line across the Downs was blocked. All trains were cancelled.

I had never been in London on my own before. I knew nobody there and with limited cash in my pocket I had no option but to go to one of the concourse call-boxes and telephone home. My mother listened to my tale and then I heard her summoning my father. I dimly made out their brief conference, with her as I imagined holding the phone up and away from her ear. Then she was talking to me again.

'Christopher, don't worry darling. We've got an idea. Go to the station café and have a cup of coffee and a sandwich and then call us back in half an hour.'

While I toyed with a thin slice of watery ham between slightly thicker slices of cardboard, more cross-country phone calls were made until it was arranged that I would be put up for the night by a daughter of some friends of my parents, Romy Nardge and her husband Peter. I later learned they were really the Nagys, and that he was Pieter.

'They're frightfully nice and young,' my mother said on the phone. 'Only just married. You'll like them. They're musicians.'

She gave me an address and told me to take a taxi. The Nagys would let me phone Johnny from there.

Romy

It was a Kensington mansion-flat on an upper floor, not far off the High Street. A tall woman in her mid-twenties, with shimmering yellow hair, came in answer to my ring and ushered me into the warmth of her central-heating.

'Welcome Christopher!' said Romy Nagy. 'This is marvellous. I am so fond of your parents. I remember my mum and me staying with them one summer years ago when I was a little girl. Before you were born.'

'I hope I'm not being an inconvenience.'

She took my hold-all bag from me.

'Not at all. I'm delighted and so will Pieter be. Let's get this out of the way and then we can talk properly.'

Romy led me along a short corridor and into a small spare bedroom papered with scenes from Peter Rabbit, which was where I'd be sleeping. There was a single bed and also a child's cot with wooden bars, and a mobile of yellow ducks hanging over it. It was exactly like the cot I myself had slept in until I was three.

'It'll be baby's room, with luck,' Romy said, putting my case on the bed. 'Although baby's showing no urgent inclination to turn up so far — not for want of trying on our part I might add.'

I looked at her fully for the first time. Romy possessed a small nose and a wide and generous mouth. Her bare feet had crimson-varnished toenails. She wore close-fitting slacks and a voluminous woollen sweater, and gave off a hint of some subtle and perhaps expensive perfume. Her blonde hair with its soft sheen like brushed gold, and the intense blue of her eyes, dazzled me. Her voice — pure, musical and articulating a sense of fun never far from laughter — was no less charming. And yet I couldn't stop myself from imagining the process of her and her new husband 'trying' for their baby. Romy might have read my thought. She laughed.

'Sorry Christopher. Too much information. Look, make yourself comfortable. Bathroom's next door. I'm putting the kettle on. Come through to the sitting room for a cuppa when you like.'

A few minutes later we were sitting in easy chairs of minimalist Nordic design and sipping tea from mugs. The flat was furnished in a spare contemporary style. Framed posters for art exhibitions at the Tate and the I.C.A hung on the walls. Druggets and rag-rugs in various strong colours lay on the pinewood floors and, in the furniture, white wood and glass predominated. The only object more than a few years old was the grand piano, which stood in the corner of the room beside a curtained window. I talked about my journey, feeling quite easy in her company now. The tension and uncertainty that built up around my cancelled train had cleared away and Romy's intimidating radiance had been softened by her natural friendliness.

'As a matter of fact your turning up like this is rather perfect,' she said. 'We have tickets for Olivier in *Othello* this evening, but now Peter's been asked at the last minute to sit in for a player who's got the 'flu. He's out there rehearsing now, in fact. So how lucky am I? I've got a substitute of my own and won't have to sit in the stalls lonely as a cloud. Would you care to squire me to the Old Vic, kind sir?'

I said I would, very much.

'I expect the trains will be running normally tomorrow,' she went on. 'In the mean time you have the chance to see the Great Actor strutting his stuff. I hope you're not missing anything even more interesting down in Sussex tonight.'

'I don't think so. The party isn't until Monday. And I really do want to see *Othello*. It's one of our set books at school as it happens.'

'Well then, what could be better?'

Pieter

We heard a key in the lock and Pieter Nagy strode energetically in. He was laughing at a remark made by someone he'd met on the stairs.

'Do you know what that bloody communist Jim Simpson just said to me? Harold Wilson is no better than a Tory, said he. Ha! I told him. I said not even Ted Heath's what *I* call a Tory, never mind bloody Harold.'

He pulled up short and noticed me.

'Well, who have we here catching flies?'

I snapped my mouth shut. It must have fallen open involuntarily when Pieter Nagy appeared. He wore an old duffle coat, a baggy shirt and corduroys, and had an undeniably handsome and intelligent face, with dark alert eyes and abundant floppy black hair. His hands were long and expressive, as I reckoned they would have to be since he was a professional pianist. He gesticulated a good deal with them as he talked, so that they became part of his equally undeniable verbal eloquence.

The dissonant chord that his appearance struck lay in the parts of Pieter's body that his clothing concealed. He stood no more than a little over five foot high, with thin bandy legs and large narrow feet, below an unusually wide pelvis. His torso was almost square when you saw him full on, for his shoulders were by no means narrow. It was only when he turned sideways that you could see the full extent of the bodily distortion for at the top of his back, slightly off centre, a mound rose almost like an extra shoulder. Pieter was what is called, in Victor Hugo's novel, a *bossu*. I knew no better word for his condition in English than the usual translation of that term.

'Darling, this is Christopher Conroy,' said Romy. 'You know. Joe and Monica's boy? He's on his way through London to some friends in Sussex but all trains out of Victoria have been cancelled because of the snow. So Monica phoned here and I said of course, there's room at the inn.'

Pieter bounded forward and put out his hand, which I shook.

'Delighted to see you old chap and glad to be a port in a storm.'

'And the marvellous thing is,' Romy followed up, 'Christopher can have your ticket for Olivier at the Old Vic. So it won't go to waste after all.'

'Splendid. The great Thespis of our age doing his bus conductor act. Strange business, but worth seeing I'm sure. I look forward to hearing your review, Christopher.'

Bus Conductor Act

Olivier had opened in *Othello* a year earlier but the sell-out production continued in rep, and would run for at least a year more. Arriving at the Old Vic that evening we found the foyer, the bars, even the toilets humming with expectation as the audience readied itself to witness a theatrical legend.

Romy gave me a couple of pounds and sent me to the bar to get a gin for herself and an orange juice for me. I came back to find her sitting at a table reviewing her make up in a compact mirror. She had changed for the evening into a short yellow dress that I thought modern and exciting. It revealed her knees and even a little of her thighs, which were sheathed in the palest of pink stockings.

'I've been meaning to ask,' I said attempting nonchalance as I sat down opposite her. 'What did Pieter mean by Laurence Olivier's bus conductor act?'

'It's rather insulting really,' she said snapping the compact shut. 'It's what one of the critics unkindly said about his performance.'

'What did they say?'

'That he portrays the noble Moor as a West Indian bus conductor.'

We had stalls seats about ten rows back. As the first scenes rolled by — business between a Venetian nobleman and Iago, talk of love and war, rumours in the wind of a Senator's virginal young daughter being tupped by a black ram — the audience was tense with impatience for Olivier's entrance. When at last it came there was a feeling that now the real play had begun, for this staging was in truth not a simple retelling of a well-known tale of interracial marriage, professional envy and sexual jealousy. The real burden and drama of it was the transformation of one of the world's most recognisable and feted white actors into the illusion of an African. Olivier's rolling eyes, growly voice, rocking gait and ever-spreading fingers all told of an intense effort of the will on the actor's part not just to act but to *be* the part; not just to have Othello's identity but to eat it whole. This cultural appropriation, as I would much later learn to call it, was breathtaking. You waited for a chink to show, a flaw to reveal itself, a stitch to be dropped.

In the interval I was sent to fetch more drinks while Romy disappeared to the 'Powder Room'. I waited my turn at the bar behind two young men, one of whom was black and the other perhaps Indian. Both spoke in impeccable R.P., the tones of one or other of the heavyweight public schools.

'They do say,' the black one was explaining, 'that every inch of his body is boot polished. Does he even blacken his balls I wonder?'

'You know what I'd like to see? A production in which every role is played by a coloured person *except* the lead.'

'Good idea, Ramesh, but I think we should introduce a refinement, just to reinforce the point. The white guy playing Othello is in blackface as usual, but every one of the blacks must equally be painted white.'

'You really should copyright that, Charles. *Black Skin, White Masks*, isn't that the book? Now, what're you drinking?'

When I found Romy again she was talking to a couple dressed in evening wear.

'This is Wim and Magda Windt,' Romy said. 'They are great supporters of the arts here in London.'

It took a moment for me to recognize the dinner-jacketed man — square-set, hair *en brosse*, pockmarked face — who was inspecting me with the kind of puzzled expression that someone might adopt when looking at a plate of unknown food.

'Don't you remember me, Mr Windt?' I said. 'We were together last summer in Scotland, at Colonel Collinshaw's deer stalking party.'

Windt, whose nationality I had never determined, gave a grunt that could have meant anything, but most likely indicated that he had no idea who I was. His wife gave me a vaguely pained smile such as the Royal Family adopts when mingling with the unwashed.

'You got a stag,' I persisted.

Windt's eyes bulged a little.

'Yes, that is so,' he said. 'Eight points.'

'Have you got it mounted? The head, I mean.'

'Mounted?'

For a moment it seemed he didn't understand and it occurred to me he may have read my enquiry as some kind of sexual reference.

'On the wall,' I said.

'On the wall. Yes. So I have.'

For some reason I desperately wanted to know more about Windt's trophy. I wondered if he prized it, boasted about it.

'Where? I mean, which wall have you put it on? Your study? Your hall?'

'No, no. Not in the Hall. On the wall of the toilet I have put it.'

There was no time for any further acquaintance as the Windts hurried off, no doubt to their box and their chilled champagne.

'He is astoundingly rich,' said Romy. 'But nobody seems to know how he made it. *You* don't I suppose, having met him before?'

'Not a clue. I never really talked to him. He's a friend of my friend's father, Colonel Collinshaw, who is the world's greatest one-armed grouse shot. '

Romy laughed and drained her gin in one swig.

'Right. Let's go back in,' she said.

Intermezzo

We heard the piano sounding softly even before Romy put the key into the flat door.

'It's a Brahms intermezzo, the E Flat,' she murmured as we slipped inside. 'Doesn't he do it just perfectly?'

We took off our coats and crept into the sitting room where we stood listening. Romy's face assumed a look not far short of ecstasy as the short piece unfolded. It was played as an exercise in stealthy hesitance, as if Pieter were feeling his way towards the gentlest sound the piano was capable of. As the last soft note dwindled away Romy began applauding with a rapid fluttering of her hands together, which I followed with a slower more solid clap. Pieter lowered the piano lid and slid off the stool.

'That was quite marvellous, darling,' she said.

'No it wasn't,' he said. 'I have no beef with the bombastic Brahms. It's the spooky sensitive Brahms I can't get alongside.'

'Don't be silly Pieter!' said his wife. 'You play it perfectly, doesn't he Christopher?'

'Yes, he does,' I said.

'Well, I cocked it up towards the end. Wrong tempo. Wrong emphasis. Wrong something. How was Olivier?'

'*Maestoso con fuoco*,' Romy said. 'But also a little *troppo* from time to time. The supporting cast weren't bad, but the audience was only there for him really. They went mad at the curtain call.'

'*Troppo*? So he over-cooked it. He normally does.'

'Well, sometimes it was just a teeny bit like a dictator addressing his people, or maybe his army. There was just the suggestion of ranting here and there.'

Romy had said nothing in the taxi on the way home about dictators giving speeches. I wondered if she had produced the idea now only because she didn't want to contradict Pieter's expectations. Yet on reflection the greatest actor had undeniably strayed perilously close to the borders of ranting at times.

'Did you see anyone there?'

'Only the Windts. God they're stuck-up. He was telling me about his latest act of philanthropy – something to do with keeping D'Oyly Carte afloat by bringing the Bolshoi Ballet over. I didn't follow the details.'

'He does love to boast of his contacts on the Central Committee,' Pieter said. 'Apparently he played a key role in smoothing over Nureyev's defection in sixty-one. So what did *you* think of Olivier, Christopher? Did I miss a treat?'

'He was incredible,' I said.

'That's likely. Credibility is beyond the powers of the old ham by now, I should think.'

He made a harsh chuckling sound, partly nasal, which was his characteristic way of laughing.

'So how was your evening darling?' Romy asked.

He wafted the air with his hand as if at a fly.

'Janet sang like a goddess, as ever. I stumbled along in her wake. Shall we have beans on toast? I'm starving.'

Later, lying in the bed and trying to think who Mr MacGregor on the wallpaper reminded me of, I could hear Pieter and Romy in the next room. I had gone to bed hoping above all I would not hear them 'trying for a baby', but in a way this was equally disturbing: Pieter's voice going on and on, largely indecipherably except for a few words — 'Nonsense!' at one point and 'That's as may be.' I could hear her replying, or perhaps protesting, but none of the words. It was clear that some sort of marital disagreement was in progress and that Pieter was angry. But for what reason? Was it, for instance, about me, whose arrival in the flat he had not been consulted on? Taking one last look at Mr MacGregor, I snapped off the bedside light and put my head under the pillow to block the sounds. Of course! I thought. He was the spit of Old-Young, the Collinshaws' Head Stalker.

Aggiornamento

In the morning Romy phoned enquiries and found that rail services to Sussex were restored.

'You'll be able to take a one twenty-three train,' she said. 'Why don't you phone your friend and tell him? We can come back here for brunch after Mass, and then we'll drive you to Victoria.'

Mass was at the Brompton Oratory 'where they pull out all the stops', as Pieter put it in the car on the way down. He was so low in the driver's seat that I worried whether he could properly see the road ahead.

'It'll be sung,' he went on, 'and partly in English, which I personally detest. It's the thin end of a wedge, because mark my words there's much worse to come. Some of those left-wing cardinals have been plotting the end of Latin for years. They'll get their way now that the Council's coming to a long overdue conclusion, no doubt of it.'

'Don't listen to Pieter's grumbling, Christopher,' said Romy. 'He's a terrible old curmudgeon where modernising the Church is concerned.'

'Darling!' said Pieter. 'As you perfectly well know, Our Lord said the Church was built on a rock. Not a bowl of jelly. A rock. You can't change that. You can't modernise a rock.'

Romy changed the subject, pointing out for me the Natural History Museum and then the V and A as we

141

passed them by. Moments later Pieter had found a parking space on the Brompton Road.

Coming away more than an hour later he was once more agitated about the modernisation of the Church. From the pulpit the priest had become almost rhapsodic about the 'momentous changes in the way we worship that will come as the Second Vatican Council draws to a close'.

'Well, that preacher was properly toeing the Vatican Two party line,' Pieter said as he gunned the engine and juddered off the kerb. 'What do your monks at school think, Christopher? I suppose they too have swallowed it in one greedy gulp.'

I said that they appeared to be rather in favour of change, as far as I could tell. Pieter flung the car across the Brompton Road in a screeching U-turn, provoking a volley of horns from the oncoming traffic.

'Doesn't surprise me,' Pieter said, settling the car in the inside lane. 'From what I've heard most of the younger ones are Marxists anyway. And the old stagers are probably too terrified to raise an eyebrow, let alone open their mouths in protest. *Aggiornamento*. It sounds grand in Italian, doesn't it? But it just means getting trendy.'

'It means getting up to date, Pieter,' said Romy.

'What date precisely? The day before yesterday? Yesterday? Today, tomorrow? This time next Thursday fortnight? It's a farce. It makes the Church no better than the House of Dior with the Pope as peddler of fashions and fads.'

'Darling,' said Romy, laying her hand on her husband's back exactly at the summit of his deformity, 'don't you think the Holy Father's guided by the Holy Spirit? Is it for us to question him?'

We were at a red light. Pieter brought the car to a stop, sank his head down to the steering wheel and banged his forehead on it with a deep groan.

'You don't understand. You don't understand how terrible this makes me feel. They're going to take everything away. The Mass. Latin. Plainsong. Who

142

knows what else? All my life I've worshipped this way. All my life.'

Romy glanced back at me, in the rear seat, as if unsure whether to say anything in my hearing. She decided to speak anyway.

'Why don't you go and see Father Pearson at Farm Street? He's sensible.'

'No, not the Jesuits. I've got to talk to someone who realises how much this hurts.'

'Who, then?'

'Someone who can give me hope.'

Chez Webster

On the down train to Sussex I had much to think about. First of all there was Romy Nagy. At Victoria she'd bought a platform ticket and walked me to the train. Just before I boarded, and to my intense surprise and confusion, she had suddenly gripped my shoulders and kissed me. I could still sense the pressure of her lips on my cheek, and her scent in my nose. As we trundled through the south London suburbs I shut my eyes and tried to reconstruct exactly how she'd been when I first really looked at her, standing in the spare room and speaking of 'trying' for a baby. I could clearly picture her parts: the clarity of her eyes, the length of her eyelashes, the softness of her breasts under the sweater. I visualised her ears, her hair, her wrists and hands, her knees and her red-painted toenails. But now that she was no longer in front of me I couldn't integrate any of it or see her as a whole, though we had parted only twenty minutes before.

Secondly, her husband. Pieter was a difficult case, there was no denying it. He was by turns charming, articulate, angry, and sardonic, then despairing, and joking, until he got round to being angry again. I thought he should see a head-shrinker as much as a priest. My friends and I had reached that age of fascination with psychological states and the noun 'complex' was frequently heard among us. Well, Pieter Nagy had a complex all right, although what kind of a complex was hard to say. Something to do with his deformity, or so I supposed.

At the station Johnny Romero was waiting with his stepfather, Henry Webster, in what they called the shooting brake. Henry was a tall and handsome man with a good head of black hair shot with grey, and a calming, competent manner. He drove for about ten minutes to a well-groomed village, with a stone church of ancient foundation, and thatched cottages in various pastel shades. A pink painted inn called the Dick Turpin advertised a menu of Wholesome British Grub on a blackboard by the door. Next to this stood a Village Store and nearby a shop selling Antiques and Curios. Take away these modern accidentals and the whole place would have looked like a Christmas card picture of the mail coach age, just as the inn's name was itself intended to evoke.

Romero's conversation at school had tended to give the loose impression that his people's social circle consisted largely of millionaires and the hereditary nobility. If so, they themselves lived more modestly. The wisteria-clad house, going by the dated hoppers crowning its downspouts, had been built in 1904. Its windows and tiled roof belonged to the domestic arm of the Queen Anne revival, while the furnishings and pictures inside spoke of a comfortable and cultured affluence rather than a magnate's millions. Johnny's mother Phyllis Webster received me warmly and I was inspected, with guarded solemnity, by his younger sister Harriet. Johnny showed me up to an attic bedroom with its dormer window and sharply angled ceiling, where I was to sleep.

Back in the sitting room I started looking at the pictures. These were mostly landscape watercolours with a few modernist drawings and artistic photographs. One of these was an extreme close-up of an apple stem plunging into what had seemed, when I first knew the image in Fr Sylvester's room at Lower

144

House, like an astronomical black hole. On the white strip below the print a title was written in freehand, 'Stalk', with a signature 'Sylvester Prewitt'.

'He's made quite a name for himself in photography since he left the monastery,' said Johnny. 'Watch your back, David Bailey.'

Considering it carefully, I now saw the photograph differently than I had before.

'It looks like an arsehole.'

'I know,' said Johnny. 'But that's not the obscenest thing Chez Webster. Have a look here.'

He went to the mantelpiece and took down a glazed ceramic bowl. Its outside showed a creature, a hoofed and naked man but with a bull's head, running in hot pursuit. He held his arms out ready to grasp while his penis preceded the rest of him, rampantly erect. Johnny revolved the bowl and showed me the object of his lust, a woman in a shift dress but with her breasts bared, looking fearfully behind her as she fled. Johnny then tipped the bowl and pointed to the figures on the inside. The Minotaur had caught up with his prey after all and was here depicted enjoying her to the full.

'It's a Picasso original,' Johnny said. 'My parents were given it by Magda Windt, who's pals with him. She used to be a notorious artist's model in Paris.'

'Was she really?'

'Yes, and probably Picasso's mistress before the war, just one of the many. She never talks about it.'

'Funnily enough I met her only last night. We were at the Old Vic and she knows the person I was with. She doesn't look anything like an artist's model now.'

'I know,' said Johnny, returning the bowl to its place. 'Respectability has crushed her libido, according to Henry, like a hippopotamus sitting on a bird of paradise.'

Autograph Hunter

That evening we all went down to the Dick Turpin to sample the Wholesome Grub. There was a mix-up in the kitchen and the wrong dishes were delivered, leaving us with a long wait for the right ones. Then the wine was judged to be corked, although on this point the waiter, a spotty youth, and after him the pub landlord, both wanted to argue the toss. Henry Webster handled these problems with firmness laced with easy courtesy, but there was never any question that a replacement bottle must come by return, and that any possible tip for good service was under review.

I was sitting next to him and as the waiter and manager retreated he turned his attention to me.

'Good of you to step into the breach,' he said.

'What breach?'

'The one made when Richard Carani dropped out.'

'Carani? Was he coming?'

'Couldn't in the end. Some family thing. '

I glanced at Johnny, who was teasing his sister about ponies, or ballet. So. I was Carani's last minute substitute. I suddenly despised him for not telling me the truth.

Although I said nothing about it, Henry sensed my discomfort and took trouble to put me at my ease. He asked me about myself and listened carefully to what I had to say. From time to time he came back with a follow-up question, an observation or a light anecdote of soldiering in India, that was triggered by my description of my father's war service, and another, prompted by what I'd told him of my mother's family, of how he had sneaked a bottle of Mooney's Whiskey into a monastery guesthouse once in County Clare. But he didn't, as so many adults do, launch into a string of highlights from his own autobiography or, worse still, deliver a lengthy lecture with advice for my own future career.

When he asked about the snow-cancelled train and where I had stayed in London, I mentioned how I'd been taken to see *Othello* by Romy Nagy on the previous night.

'She's a singer,' I said, 'but she uses her original name, Romy Purvis. Her parents know my parents.'

Henry called across to Phyllis.

'Did you hear that, darling? Christopher here was on a date last night with Romy Purvis.'

'Wow. Lucky boy,' she said.

'Do you know her?' I said.

'*Of* her,' said Henry. 'She must be London's whizziest soprano under thirty. A star in the making. I hope she is spoiled and petulant, and everything a diva should be.'

'Oh no, she's not like that. The complete opposite. I thought she was—. Well, really nice. But I didn't know she was famous. I had the idea her husband Pieter was, though. He's a pianist.'

'The hunchback, yes? Actually, the poor fellow's not a famous concert pianist, more of a reasonably well-known accompanist. So what did you make of Olivier? We saw him during the first run. Phyllis thinks the man's a Titan, but I find it all a bit studied. There's a lot to be said for an actor to appear to be making it up as he or she goes along, even when they're not.'

By now, I was not so sure about Olivier either, but I hardly had the chance to say so as we were now both gathered into the talk at the other end of the table, which had turned to next day's party preparations. The dining table was to be dismantled to make space for dancing, with music provided by a hired D.J. from Brighton. A bar was to be set up in the sitting room, to be manned and regulated by Henry. Buffet food would also be laid out nearby. All sofas and chairs were to be shifted to the walls. How the right kind of subdued lighting was to be achieved was still on the agenda.

147

Various jobs were allocated along the usual gender lines. Food preparation was in the hands of Phyllis and her daily help 'from the village', whose name was Barbara. Drinks and glasses were to be collected by Henry from the wine merchant, in the shooting brake. He had taken the afternoon off at his office for the purpose, he said. Johnny and I were to deal with the furniture and help the disc jockey set up, and settle the difficult matter of the lighting. Harriet was to give Mavis, the bull terrier, a long walk to tire her out, in the hope she would obediently sleep through the entire evening.

A man stopped in the act of walking past our table, doing a double take as he noticed Henry Webster. He was a scrawny, bald fellow in a cheap suit, whose thin strands of combed-over hair glistened with Brilliantine

'It isn't?' he said. 'Yes, it is, by golly! Kenneth More. You're Kenneth More, ain't you? Of course you are! Of *course* you are! Well, well!'

Henry looked startled. After a moment, he shook his head.

'No,' he said. 'You're quite mistaken.'

'I quite understand that you'll say that, but look here. By chance, I happen to be reading this.'

He produced a copy of *The Thirty-Nine Steps* from his pocket, and showed it to Henry, tapped the image on the cover showing the book's hero. The paperback had been issued following the release of a film version a few years before, in which Kenneth More had starred. The artwork was reasonably like the actor. It was also reasonably like Henry.

'That's you, don't deny it.'

'I do deny it.'

The man produced a fountain pen from the inside pocket of his jacket.

'I wonder if I might I trouble you to autograph the book, Kenneth? May I call you Kenneth?'

'No,' said Henry, 'because actually it isn't my name. I'm not Kenneth More. I never have been

148

Kenneth More. And I am not an actor, not of any kind.'

The stranger wasn't listening. He opened the novel at the title page and placed it in front of Henry while offering him the pen with an ingratiating smile.

'If you would be good enough, let it say "to Charlie Ware with fond memories of our coincidental meeting at the Dick Turpin pub" or something of that order. My friends won't half be impressed.'

Henry took the pen and wrote something. Charlie Ware picked the book up and read it, his smile fading to disappointment.

'Well there's no call for that,' he said. 'That's what I call jolly rude. Spoilt my book, that has.'

Henry pushed his chair back from the table and stood up. Gripping Charlie Ware by the arm he walked him firmly out of the dining room, all the time speaking to the autograph hunter in a low voice, with his mouth close to the other man's ear.

Meanwhile the family were laughing.

'What an egregious little man,' said Phyllis. 'It's not the first time this has happened, though. I remember someone thinking Henry was John Gregson once. Or was it Dirk Bogarde? No matter. There was something indefinably matinee idol about him in those days, which is why I married him, of course.'

After no more than two minutes Henry rejoined us.

'What did you say to him, darling?' said Phyllis.

'I was telling him where to shove his pen and his book.'

But the encounter with Charlie Ware seemed to have unsettled Henry and he remained quiet and pensive for the rest of the evening.

Expected Guest

Next morning, the day of the party, I was coming down the stairs into the parquet-floored hall when I

149

heard a raised voice speaking in what sounded to me like Russian. The door of one of the rooms off the hall — Henry's study, apparently — was slightly ajar and it was from here the voice came. With half a dozen stairs still to go I stopped to listen. Yes, it was definitely Russian. I heard the word "spasseeba", which I knew means "please". Although a voice can sound different when speaking a foreign language, it was obviously Henry's, and I wondered why he sounded so angry.

As I continued my descent the conversation abruptly ended and I heard the sound of the telephone landing on its cradle with a *ting*. The door opened and Johnny's stepfather came out just as I set foot on the parquet. I could see into the room behind him — a desk, a blotter, pens, numerous books and papers and a typewriter.

'Morning Christopher!' he said. 'Sleep well?'

If Henry Webster had been angry in Russian, he was all smiles in English. He didn't wait for a reply to his question, but spread his arms and shepherded me towards the dining room.

'Breakfast. I hope you're hungry.'

'I am rather.'

'Good man. The inner being must be built up for the rigours of party preparations, not to speak of the party itself. My nose tells me we are having grilled bacon and possibly mushrooms. Yum-yum.'

In the dining room Johnny was already in his place alongside Harriet, a freckled child who wore long plaits and looked about ten. I knew her to be the offspring of Phyllis's marriage to Henry, rather than her earlier one to Johnny's father Colonel Anthony L. Romero of the U.S. Marine Corp.

Henry and I went to the sideboard, where Johnny's mother had laid out the elements of a cooked breakfast, and began to help ourselves. Phyllis, looking up from *The Times*, said,

'Oh by the way chaps! I heard it on the radio in the bath. T. S. Eliot has died. Apparently quite suddenly. A stroke or something, I suppose.'

Henry reached his place at the table and deposited his plate, then intoned.

> *'I Tiresias, old man with wrinkled dugs*
> *Perceived the scene, and foretold the rest —*
> *I too awaited the expected guest.*

The expected guest,' he repeated as he sat down. 'That must be you, young Christopher.'

Even though I was very keen on Eliot's verse, to hear that he was dead didn't feel like an occasion for actual grief. You might mourn for a person, a relative, but you don't for a distant monument. At the same time I was rather pleased that Henry had found a quotation that, by making it refer to me, had somehow brought me closer to the spirit of the great poet. Without further remark Henry opened a second copy of *The Times* that lay next to his plate. He took a biro from his pocket, clicked it and began to do the crossword. He had finished most of it by the time I'd finished eating.

45 rpm

By eight-thirty Henry had left for London, promising he would be back in time to do his bit. Johnny and I disassembled the dining table then set about pushing chairs to the wall and rolling up rugs to make a dancing area.

'Your stepfather's a whizz at the crossword,' I said.

'The one in the *Times* is child's play to him. He also does *The Listener* crossword which is the hardest there is.'

'He speaks Russian, doesn't he?'

'Probably. He knows endless languages. I've lost count of how many.'

'I overheard him speaking Russian on the phone when I was coming down to breakfast. What does he do exactly?'

'Oh, he's in the Foreign Office.'

'Doing what?'

'How should I know? Diplomatic stuff.'

Barbara, a plump youngish woman, arrived to help with the food. Johnny and I, having got the room satisfactorily arranged and settled on an acceptably soft lighting scheme, went to his bedroom to play some records. There were sandwiches for lunch. Harriet reneged on her only real task for the day and disappeared down the lane to her friend's house where she would be spending the night. So Johnny and I, protesting at having to take unscheduled exercise in the snow, took Mavis out. When we returned, having thrown numerous snowballs at each other, a green Mini van was parked in the drive. Henry had still not turned up from London.

'I can't think where he is,' said Phyllis. 'I phoned the office and they said he'd left at midday. I suppose he must have had a lunch appointment, but it's bloody inconvenient letting it overrun like this. Oh, by the way boys, Rod Rashley's here. He's setting up in the sitting room. Go and see if he needs any help.'

Rod Rashley was the disc jockey, and driver of the Mini van. His hair was cut to collar length with a straight fringe and he wore numerous rings on his fingers, a roll-neck shirt and closely fitting purple velvet trousers. He cannot have been more than twenty, but he had an impressive pair of amplifiers, a panel with knobs and sliders that he called his 'mixing desk', and two turntables, all of which was set up in an array in front of the fireplace. He also had a pair of heavy cabin trunks filled with seven inch, 45 rpm records.

'Your party is it?' he asked me.

'No, mine,' said Johnny. 'I hope you've got Where Did Our Love Go?'

152

Rod looked at Johnny as if he had asked whether giraffes had long necks.

'Never fear, sonny. I got all the Motown groups. And I got all the top ten records of the last twelve months. Obviously except for the Jim Reeves and Val Doonican crap.'

He nodded at the two cabin trunks.

'Take a look, if you like.'

We did. The cases were crammed, with all the records card-indexed by the groups' names. I checked for You Really Got Me and The House of the Rising Sun and found them easily. I told him it was a good system, enabling him to find any requests and have them on the turntable in seconds.

'Requests? Who d'you think I am, mate, *Family Favourites*? I decide what I spin and don't worry it'll be nothing but the best, to coin a phrase. I like to do a bit of dancing too so I hope the crumpet'll be nicely toasted and there's enough strawberry jam, know what I mean to say?'

But despite his lascivious wink, neither of us could honestly have put into words precisely what he did mean to say.

As soon as the system was installed Rod put on a couple of songs as a test, but he wouldn't play any more.

'I'm contracted for the night, not the day. Anyway I'm off home now. Got a bird waiting, and the shortness of her skirt you would not believe. I'll be back at seven thirty as per. And meantime you *don't* touch the equipment.'

Carbuncular

'This is terrible,' said Phyllis coming through from the kitchen after Rod Rashley had left. 'Henry's phoned. Apparently there's a flap and he can't get back for the moment. I'll have to leave Barbara to get on in the kitchen while I collect the drink.'

We went with her to help lift and carry, coming back from the shop with several seven-pint cans of Watney's, bottles of wine (Blue Nun, Hirondelle) and a great many fizzy soft drinks.

'I know some guys who only drink spirits,' Johnny confided as we were setting the bar up. 'But mother won't let us have any. Expect they'll bring their own though.'

'What if your stepfather doesn't get back in time? Who's going to run the bar?'

I was finding that the nearer Johnny's party approached the more I dreaded it. I had not originally foreseen this, but I realised now I was in a funk about meeting all these beautiful and no doubt sophisticated girls Johnny had promised me. I didn't think it likely they'd be much impressed by my northern provenance, or my provincial idea of men's fashion. So, seeing a way of avoiding total humiliation, I went to Phyllis in the kitchen and applied for the job of barman.

'No, Christopher,' she said. 'You must dance and charm the girls. Anyway it needs an adult, so I've got Barbara's husband Keith on stand-by, in case Henry doesn't get here in time. He's an ambulance driver so he'll be perfect.'

Although it was unclear why this was an ideal qualification, Keith was certainly the better choice, so I trudged upstairs glumly to change into the clothes that would certainly humiliate me all evening. My chance of charming the elite teenagers of West Sussex was as remote a possibility as watching a flock of pigs fly in formation across the setting sun.

On the landing outside my room was a bookcase, in which I noticed a copy of Eliot's poems. I took it in with me, to look up Henry's quotation. I knew it to be from *The Waste Land* but I couldn't remember the continuation. I found the place and read:

I Tiresias, old man with wrinkled dugs
Perceived the scene, and foretold the rest —

I too awaited the expected guest.
He, the young man carbuncular, arrives.

Carbuncular? My fingertip went to my chin to feel the tender makings of a new red spot that was still in formation. I was more of a Prufrock than Tiresias's young man.

There will be time, there will be time
To prepare a face to meet the faces that you meet…

All too little time, I thought, as I glumly opened my case to take out my party-going clothes.

Mods and Rockers

'You're from the *North*? You poor sod. You live on the other side of the moon.'

We were an hour or more into the party and the speaker was a thick-eared boy with a fleshy nose and a voice baying to rise above the pumping volume of the Swinging Blue Jeans. He was standing beside me at the buffet table loading his plate with Phyllis's, or perhaps Barbara's, Coronation Chicken.

'What do you mean by that?' I said.

'Darkness against light, boy. Coal mines and moors against white horses cut into the Downs. North against south, see? I suppose your girlfriend's more like Cilla Black, while my bird Virginia's the actual spit of Marianne Faithful. Beautiful blonde — get it?'

I didn't, quite. Was he trying to be funny? It was safer to assume he wasn't.

'Good for her. I haven't got a girlfriend myself. Is Virginia here with you?'

'Oh no, she lives in London. Hampstead. I only see her in town. We have a flat off the King's Road.'

Later with food and a couple more drinks inside me I tried talking to a girl who wore a miniskirt of large black and white squares and a red shirt that might have been satin. Around her waist was a shiny wide white PVC belt and her finger ends gleamed with pale pink nail varnish. We spoke in the unnatural loud voices that were necessary to be heard above the pounding music.

'Are you a mod or a rocker?' she said.

The running fights between the two youth groups, which were staged on many of the beaches of southern England, had been a news story for much of the previous year.

'I don't know,' I said. 'Do I have to be one or the other?'

'You do, actually, if you want to be in any way hip.'

'The thing is, I don't know much about them. I've just seen them on the news fighting on the beaches and the landing-grounds.'

'There's a lot more to it than that,' she said sternly. Her tone implied that she had studied the deep roots of the mod-rocker wars with anthropological rigour.

'Tell me, then.'

'Well the point is they're actually total opposites. Mods believe in modern things like fashion and scooters. Rockers are hairy and very dirty under their fingernails. They wear leather and don't care about fashion and stuff. They literally worship their motorbikes.'

A picture came to my mind of crazed druid-like figures appeasing their machines with blood-offerings.

'Do they make sacrifices?'

'I'm sorry?'

'Do they carry out holocausts to their bikes — burnt offerings and all that?'

'What are you actually on about?'

'Never mind. If I really have to choose, I don't much like the sound of the rockers so I suppose that would make me a mod.'

'You're not actually being very *committed*. And you haven't got the right clothes. Have you actually been to Carnaby Street?'

'No I haven't.'

'Where are you actually from then?'

'A long way from Carnaby Street.'

She lost interest in me at this point and caught the arm of a boy who was drifting past.

'Simon!' she shouted. 'I thought I'd never find you. Come and dance.'

A bit later I stood with Romero watching the dancing and listening to a punchy track by The Kinks, 'All Day and All of the Night'. I pointed to the girl with the checkerboard skirt, now jumping energetically from one leg to the other while working her arms like pistons.

'I was talking to her. I think I bored her.'

'What did you talk about?'

'She was explaining the difference between the mods and the rockers. It all sounded a bit theological. The mods have faith in fashion and the rockers pray to their motorbikes. What's her name?'

'She's called Annabel Darcy. Her father's Chief Constable of Sussex and her older brother's lead singer in The Chosen Fugue.'

'You mean the beat group?'

'Of course I mean the beat group. They were all set to play tonight, but then it turned out they had to go on tour to Australia. So we have to make do with the delightful Rodney Rashley.'

The Chosen Fugue had had a hit called 'I Don't Exist' a few months ago. I'd seen them more than once on Top of the Pops, fronted by the tall and willowy Rick Darcy, who sang in a deep voice, with occasional breaks into falsetto. Their sound was driven by a chiming lead guitar riff over the usual thumping bass line, and the beat from a drummer who always performed in a pork pie hat.

As we stood watching the dancing a girl came up and slid an arm around Johnny's waist. He responded at once, turning his face towards her and kissing her on the mouth. I felt both acute envy at his easy social manner, and embarrassment at the sucking

157

lasciviousness of his kiss. Their mouths parted and she bent her head to whisper something into his ear, then moved away from us.

'I've got to go and dance with her in a minute,' he said. 'She probably wants to snog me some more. Why don't you find someone to have a dance with yourself? My mother says I've got to encourage everyone to dance all the time.'

'But who?'

'That girl over there, standing by herself. Her name's Theresa. She goes to a convent school but you can't have everything. Go on.'

I didn't fully understand what Johnny meant by his remark about the convent school, but I couldn't shirk the challenge. I headed towards the girl just as Rod Rashley, crouching over his turntables, was setting up a segue into a track by the Rolling Stones. I noticed as I passed him that he was using the Picasso bowl from the mantelpiece as an ashtray, and that an unusually large roll-up lay smouldering in it.

'Would you like to dance?' I said.

Close to her I could see that, while she was no Twiggy, she was slim and had striking looks. Her nose with just the suggestion of the hawk about it, her black hair and intensely dark eyes, gave her a Mediterranean look. To better frame her eyes she wore thick black mascara and eye-liner, while the eyes themselves were dark, lively and with a hint of humour.

'I don't mind,' she said.

So far, so non-committal: but my dance with Theresa was surprising. At first she wriggled about nimbly but conventionally in time to the Stones, and then the Yardbirds, shaking her shoulders and snaking her arms. I joggled my body this way and that in sympathy. But then the music changed, and the next track was Marianne Faithfull's slower 'As Tears Go By'. Smoothly and as if by the tacit agreement of us both she moved into my arms, pressing herself to me while laying her head against my shoulder. I was a

158

little fuzzy from alcohol and this, in combination with the softness of her body against me, now felt infinitely more pleasant than anything I had experienced that evening, not to say in the whole of my previous life. I fell into a kind of trance, and was thinking that this was one of those moments that shouldn't ever be allowed to end — until suddenly it did. The police had arrived.

Pooped

It must have been after eleven o'clock at this point. Henry had still not appeared, so presumably the flap we thought he'd been attending to was still on. This was in fact true, but the flap was far different from anything we could have imagined. Looking up from Theresa's embrace I noticed a uniformed constable, capped not helmeted, standing in the doorway of the dancing room. Even above the decibels delivered by Rodney's system, doors could be heard slamming in other rooms, Mavis barking furiously and then Phyllis's voice, almost in a shriek.

'What the *hell's* going on?'

Theresa detached herself from me and looked around. The music stopped. Someone other than Rod must have lifted the stylus from the groove because there was now no sign of the disc jockey. Mavis continued to bark. We could hear feet on the stairs and tramping around in the rooms above us, while there were also lights flashing outside and men calling to each other. It seemed the house and grounds were being searched. Then a moustached and middle-aged officer joined the constable in the doorway. He wore leather gloves and a cap with a silver motif running across the peak. He was looking this way and that around the room.

'Daddy! What in *God's* name are you doing here?'

It was Annabel Darcy. She pushed through the crowd of paused dancers and confronted her father, hands on hips.

'This is bloody typical of you,' she said shrilly, 'always spoiling everything that I bloody do.'

Theresa and I exchanged looks. She compressed her lips and shook her head and we laughed together, which felt almost as intimate as when we'd held each other close minutes before.

Looking back I don't think I have ever been to a party so thoroughly pooped. The last period before midnight — during which parents started arriving to convey their teenagers home — was not like a party at all, more like one of those funereal gatherings following a cremation. Rod the D.J. never reappeared so the music stopped completely. This didn't make much difference as we were all too conscious of the continued police presence to get back into the dancing spirit. Going to fetch a Coke for Theresa, I looked around for Johnny. He was not in either the dancing room or the drawing room.

'Do *you* know what the police are here for?' I asked Keith behind the drinks table.

'Not a notion, sonny,' he said. 'But I'll tell you one thing. I never saw anyone scarper faster than that Rod when he saw the coppers coming through the door. Talk about Rod the Rocket. He was through the French windows and out into the snow like a dog with its tail on fire.'

My way back took me through the hall. The door of Henry's study was slightly ajar and I heard adult voices inside, but not what they were saying, and the slam of a metal drawer being closed. The door between the hall and dancing room was blocked by people. As they made way for me to go through, one of them, a tousled youth in blue jeans, voiced a different theory to that suggested by Keith.

'Apparently they're looking for Mr Webster, though search me why they need to turn his own house over.'

Someone else laughed.

'They will probably search you, Giles. I hope you're clean.'

To make matters worse, when I got back to where I'd left Theresa, she was no longer there. I found her in the middle of a group of girls whispering into each other's ears, bending their knees and laughing. I handed her the drink and backed off, accepting that our brief encounter was over.

I hung around watching the police coming and going for a while then went to find Johnny. He was in the kitchen, sitting at the table with his mother while behind them Barbara was at the sink washing dishes. Phyllis looked bewildered and I thought she might have been crying. Johnny sat beside her and was patting her hand as it lay on the table. He snatched it away when he saw me coming in.

'What on earth's happening?' I said.

Johnny looked at his mother. She sighed in a juddering exhalation then groped for her packet of Senior Service.

'You may as well tell him,' she said, having fumbled a cigarette out, lit it and inhaled ferociously. 'It'll probably be all over the papers tomorrow morning anyway.'

Johnny got up and moved to the kitchen door where he jerked his head at me. I went out with him. Most of the police had gone by now. The study was empty and we went inside and Johnny shut the door. One of the drawers of a filing cabinet was half open, with papers spilling out.

'Henry's disappeared,' he said. 'He went to the office this morning, then left after a couple of hours, and now nobody knows where he is.'

'But he phoned here this afternoon, didn't he?'

'Yes, but he didn't say where he was, or what he was doing.'

'Your mother said there's a flap at his office.'

'Exactly. The flap's actually about him going AWOL. Or being kidnapped. Or whatever it is.'

'Kidnapped? That's a bit extreme. Perhaps he just couldn't face having to give out drinks at your party all evening.'

161

'No, Henry's not like that. Normally he absolutely loves doing this sort of thing.'

'What if he's got ill? Or had an accident?'

'All the hospitals have been checked. He's not there.'

'So why did the police descend on the house?'

'To see if his passport was here, my mother says. In case he's gone abroad.'

'Really? A bobby on a bike could have checked on that. This was ten Z-cars and the actual Chief Constable. '

'I know. That's what's so weird. I think my mother knows a bit more than she's saying.'

'She thinks it'll be in the papers.'

'Yes. Maybe Henry's more important than I ever thought he was.'

We heard people calling Johnny's name from the hall and went out. The guests were leaving in Jags, Rovers and the odd Bentley, driven by their impatient fathers. I saw Theresa with two other girls, now in winter coats and scarves, stalking across the snow to be transported home by the parent of one of them. For a moment in the doorway she had turned her head and looked back at me, twitching her lips in what may have been a smile, or perhaps (as I thought later lying in bed) a simulated kiss. Further analysis told me, if it *was* a kiss, it cost her nothing. She had no reason to think she would ever to see me again.

Broken China

In the morning *The Times* had a short paragraph saying that the police were concerned about the whereabouts of Henry Webster, a senior official at the Foreign Office, who had gone missing the previous day. Officers had visited his Sussex home, while enquiries at all hospitals had led to nothing. Airports and ferries were being watched. The police were keeping an open mind about what, if anything, may have happened to Mr Webster.

Not long after breakfast a black chauffeur-driven Daimler came and Roger, a work friend of Henry's, stepped out. He was a bland, smiling type, very much my idea of the standard civil servant, with a high forehead and heavy eyebrows. He was closeted in the study with Phyllis for almost an hour, then immediately left. Less tearful, but looking rather as if someone had whacked her on the top of her head, Phyllis took Johnny and me into the drawing room. It had not yet been cleared up and was littered with dirty plates, Coke cans and half-empty beer glasses.

'This is as much as I can tell you,' she said, her voice weak and shaky. 'Keep it to yourselves, will you? Roger says that Henry's probably out of the country. He says he may have been ... he may have been *spying*, for God's sake! How can that be? I know Henry. Or I thought I did. He's *good*. I mean, he's always been the stalwart type. But people in the office are now saying he's the next Philby. No! I just can't ... He knew Kim Philby a bit, of course, which doesn't much help his case. But really! Henry, a *spy*? Anyway, according to Roger, the story is they were about to take him in for questioning which he got wind of so he's gone. Gone! And he was supposed to be helping with the *party*! He was supposed to be ... a father and a husband. Didn't he love us at all? And what am I going to tell Harriet?'

'Where's he gone to, Mummy?' said Johnny.

'Oh! I don't know, darling. Roger says he could be heading for Moscow, but how he'd get there is anybody's guess. Some sort of roundabout route, probably.'

The phone, which stood on a table in the hall and had been ringing continuously, had been taken off the hook. But now Barbara, coming in to work, tidily replaced the receiver and it promptly rang again. Barbara picked it up.

'Hello,' we heard her say. 'Residence of Mr and Mrs Webster.'

Hearing her from the sitting room Phyllis clicked her tongue and had started towards the hall to prevent Barbara from selling the story to the *News of the World*. But the daily help had already laid the receiver down and come into the room.

'It's Christopher's Mum, Mrs Webster. Wants a quick word with him.'

I went to the phone.

'We read something in the paper, Christopher. Is it the same Henry Webster, Johnny's stepfather?'

'Yes.'

'Will you let me speak to Mrs Webster? I just want to make sure everything's all right for your journey home tomorrow.'

I passed the receiver to Phyllis and went back into the sitting room. Barbara was on her knees sweeping the fireplace and the area around Rodney Rashley's still undismantled equipment. She heaved to her feet and on her way out showed us what was in the dustpan: a large quantity of butt-ends and cigarette ash intermixed with some jumbled shards of broken china.

'Careless blighter,' she said. 'He's only gone and smashed that smutty ashtray.'

Dodgy Handshakes

It was a desultory afternoon and evening. Phyllis spent much of the time sitting by the phone, taking it off the hook every five minutes, then putting it back in the hope of speaking to someone other than the gutter press and ideally to Henry himself. There was a short item on the TV news, but the whereabouts of the absconded Henry was still unknown. Around five-thirty a Rolls-Royce arrived and two figures that I recognised climbed out of the rear: Wim and Magda Windt. I didn't make myself known.

While the Windts conferred with Phyllis, Johnny and I took Mavis for her evening walk. On our return we had a closer look at the Windts' Rolls, still parked in the drive. A young man with long blond hair was leaning against the radiator grille smoking.

'All right?' he said.

We nodded and went inside.

'That's their son, Serge,' said Johnny. 'His only function in life is to be his father's stooge.'

About twenty minutes later the Windts were driven off by Serge, leaving Phyllis in a disappointed mood. She'd hoped they would bring some positive news.

'They told me no word from Henry has been heard, not of any kind,' she said.

'How would those two know anything?' said Johnny.

'They very well might. The Windts have connections everywhere, including in Russia. But I had a horrid feeling while they were here. It was the look on his face.'

'What kind of look?' said Johnny.

'A kind of gloating look.'

After that and for the rest of the evening she lapsed back into despondency.

'I mean, what actually happened?' she kept saying. 'What happened to make him go off like that? He gave absolutely no indication of anything. Anything at all.'

The next morning Keith from the village turned up. It was his day off work, and he had been engaged to drive me to the station. I had rather hoped I'd be conveyed in an ambulance, but it was merely his own Ford Anglia.

'Very strange business, this,' he said driving with exaggerated caution although the roads having been salted and gritted were merely slushy now. 'It's in the paper this morning. 'Course Mr Webster was always nice enough to Barbara and me. Hell of a toff, though. Charterhouse and Oxford. You can't ever properly trust them, and now it turns out he's been spying for the Russians. But I mean to say, what does that make him — a Communist? Him? Living in that bloody great house, big government job and all that money!

165

Doesn't bloody make sense, does it? I wonder who tipped him off. One of his masonic friends, I reckon. Clubs in Pall Mall, dodgy handshakes, helping each other out. Can't trust them, can you?'

Sitting later in my northbound train I thought again about Keith's last question: who *had* warned Henry? Phyllis said that he'd been under suspicion, and was about to be questioned. So how did he hear of this in advance? It must have been at the eleventh hour, or his flight would never have been so sudden, so dramatic.

Then the intrusion of Charlie Ware into our dinner at the Dick Turpin came to me. That insistent and deluded autograph hunter had brandished a copy of John Buchan's *The Thirty-Nine Steps*, which was a spy story, and in the film adaptation Kenneth More had played Richard Hannay. And Richard Hannay had spent most of the story under suspicion and on the run.

The landscape through which the train passed gradually became more legible as we pushed on northwards. By the time we'd crossed the Manchester Ship Canal the snow was already a memory and home was only an hour away.

Soviet Relations

1966

Pilgrims

At Victoria I found the first of my fellow pilgrims gathering at the head of the platform, an hour before our departure time. We chatted in groups as Father Placid, Father Theodore and Mr Gilmore, the expedition's leaders, moved between us checking that we had our passports, and telling us which *couchette* compartments we would be sleeping in.

The previous night I had stayed with the Nagys in Kensington, where Pieter had been scathing about the stated aims and purposes of our trip. These had seemed straightforward enough to me: to be part of the group carrying a letter of greeting from Cardinal Heenan to Patriarch Alexis, and to take part ecumenically in Eastertide services at the monastery at Zagorsk and the vigil service in Moscow's patriarchal cathedral, all at the expense of our indulgent parents. Pieter Nagy scorned any idea that the contact would be ecumenical because, according to him, the Russian Orthodox hierarchy could hardy call themselves Christians at all, being (as he claimed) firmly lodged in the obsidian darkness of the Communist Party's pocket.

'They are lickspittles to a man. The idea of Heenan treating with them is ludicrous. Is this so-called pilgrimage led by some of your Marxist monks? From what I've heard the Dominicans are riddled with reds, so why not your lot?'

I was looking around the station for a sight of Johnny Romero, who had also signed up for the trip. I caught sight of a woman in dark glasses and a headscarf standing, or rather lurking, behind a pillar. She seemed to be trying to attract someone's attention, and it took me a few moments to twig that her object was me. She was beckoning sharply and I went with a degree of caution towards her. I had covered half the distance when I saw that she was Johnny's mother, Phyllis Webster.

'Hello Mrs Webster. I've been looking for Johnny.'

'Had to pull out. He's confined to bed with glandular fever, according to Dr Beckett. Raging temperature, sore throat, and a rash all over him, poor darling. The Kissing Disease supposedly, though I can't think who he's been kissing lately unless it's me.'

'You mean he's missing the whole journey?'

'Afraid so.'

'So are you taking his place, or something? I didn't see you in the original list of parents coming with us.'

'God, no. For reasons you can probably guess I've become a little allergic to Russia, even if they'd allow me in — or if they did, out again. I only came up to town to speak to you, Christopher, because I've got a favour to ask.'

'What kind of favour Mrs Webster?'

'It's just something for Henry.'

She brought out a parcel wrapped in brown paper and wound in sellotape. She put it into my hands.

'He left in such a hurry — well, you already know that, don't you? Anyway, he had no time for packing any of the things he might need, and now he's written to say he would dearly love to have this. Would you be a darling and give it to him?'

'When I'm in Russia?'

'Of course when you're in Russia. Russia's where he is.'

'How will I meet him?'

'He'll make contact, at your hotel in Moscow I should think. He's living near the city centre apparently. Don't worry. It's not dangerous. I gather Henry's quite the celebrity over there since his defection and has the powers-that-be eating out of his hand.'

I turned the package over. It was unmarked and unidentifiable.

168

'OK, if that's all there is to it, yes of course I will.'

'You're an angel, Christopher. I've been told it would be highly unlikely to get through if I posted it. The original courier was going to be Johnny, of course, but, as he's *hors de combat*, I was sure I could rely on you.'

She leaned forward and gave me a kiss on the cheek. It was not the fragrant, soft-lipped kiss with which Romy Nagy had anointed my forehead while seeing me out of her flat an hour before. Phyllis's kiss was a brisk, dry, cigarette-smelling kiss.

'Goodbye, then, and have a marvellous time. Get in touch when you're back. Oh! And it'd be so nice if you can take a snap of Henry for me, too. I do so worry about him.'

She moved off and I watched until I lost her in the continually shifting station crowd. I weighed the package in my hands. It felt like a book. What if it was a banned one? *Doctor Zhivago* or *Nineteen Eighty-Four*? Mr Gilmore had been quite explicit about the former in his briefing at the end of term.

'For Pete's sake don't pack *Doctor Zhivago* in your luggage,' he had told us. 'You could end up in the Lubyanka.'

I was seized by annoyance at my own sluggish thinking. I should have asked, when Mrs Webster passed it to me, what precisely it was. With no means of parcelling it up again, I could hardly now rip it open to find out. So I slipped Henry Webster's package into my travel bag and returned to the group, who were now filing through the ticket barrier and making towards the train.

Bogey Switch

On the rail journey between Berlin and Moscow there came a point as one entered Soviet Union territory where the carriages had to be hoisted off their bogies by hydraulic jacks. The sets of wheels were then run out of the way and a new set was substituted. This, as the railway enthusiast Father Theodore told us, was because Socialist trains ran on a wider railway gauge than Capitalist ones.

'It's symbolic of the entire cultural split,' he said. 'Another alphabet, variant dates for Easter, different rail gauges. Prepare yourselves to cross into another dimension.'

The changeover happened in the middle of the afternoon, at the Soviet-Poland border. Our party had been travelling more than two days by now, during which we had seen the sights of West Berlin, crossed the Wall by a local train and departed from Berlin Ostbahnhof late on the previous night.

'We're entering Mother Russia and guess what this place is called,' said Brokowsky, looking out of the carriage window as we drew at stealthy pace into the border station. Brokowsky was the only one of us at this point who could read Cyrillic script. 'It's Brest.'

He jutted out his lips as he spoke the name, while his hands cupped two invisible mounds in the area of his chest. One or two in the compartment cackled with laughter.

'Talking of which,' said Julian Parker-Fitch airily. 'Are you aware there's a girl's school on this train?'

'A what?' I said.

'A school party like us, although from London: Camden High School for Girls, to be exact. They've been on board since Berlin.'

'You're well-informed, Parks. How do you know?'

'Ear to the wall, dear boy. I was in the crapper when I heard them shrieking from the next carriage — in English. So I asked Father Theodore. He said they're either doing Russian language or history A level and have come to expose themselves to the culture at first hand.'

'Expose themselves?' said Brokowsky. 'Funny turn of phrase that monk has.'

'The point is, when are we going to get the chance to meet these fragrant nymphs?'

Our leaders' briefing had not prepared us for anything like this. It had concentrated on what our contacts with Soviet citizens would be like, and how careful we must be in that quarter.

'On visits to the Soviet Union, western tourists are attended at all times by one of more Intourist guides,' said Father Placid. 'We will be no different. These guides double as essentially our minders. Their job is simultaneously to look after our needs and to see that we don't get into trouble, such as going to any places deemed inappropriate or meeting inappropriate people.'

'What sort of people Sir?'

'We're talking about dissidents,' said Mr Gilmore. 'Writers, actors, teachers, some scientists. People who wish to publicise violations of human rights and to gain freedom of expression. That is in short supply in the USSR I'm sorry to say. Dissidents operate clandestinely because they're regarded as counter-revolutionaries, and lackeys of Capitalism. If they're caught engaging in so-called anti-Soviet activities they risk being sent to Siberia.'

'Is that the Salt Mines, Sir?' said Parker-Fitch.

'I'm talking about prisons and labour camps. If you've read *One Day in the Life of Ivan Denisovitch* you'll know what I'm talking about.'

It was one of only two books by contemporary Russians I had read, the other being Yevtushenko's *Precocious Autobiography*.

'So be careful. Should anyone approach you in Red Square with a request, say, to bring any sort of writings out of the country, say *nyet* and walk away. This would be as much for their good as for yours.'

'Mr Gilmore isn't joking,' Father Placid added. 'Our journey has the character of a Pilgrimage. We must be models of good behaviour, since we are carrying a message of friendship from Cardinal Heenan to the Patriarch. But more than that we are showing the Soviets the face of Western Christianity at Easter, the most sacred festival in both the Catholic and the Russian Orthodox calendars. Our two Easters coincide this year, as they occasionally do, and our — your — participation in their Easter liturgies will hopefully send a persuasive signal of Christian faith and solidarity.'

He'd handed out a sheet with a run-down of what we would be doing between the fourth and the twentieth of April. Glancing through it I could see that our scheduled trips to monasteries and cathedrals were assiduously balanced by museums of economic achievement or socialist friendship, and other materialist shrines. But nowhere in the itinerary had the Camden High School for Girls been envisaged.

The train had squealed to a halt and we heard the voice of Mr Gilmore in the corridor, calling out.

'Come on everyone. Coats and scarves on and prepare to disembark. Or, if you prefer, detrain. Get out onto the platform, anyway. Quickly now.'

Mr Gilmore was our head of modern languages. Russian was one of the languages he taught, albeit only to one pupil, Andy Brokowsky, whose mother was Russian.

An icy blast swept through the station. On the platform I watched as the girls of Camden School descended from their carriage, then danced and jiggled about in groups of three or four as they met the cold air. I was standing in a group of our own and every now and then we took a quick look towards the girls. No one wanted to be seen to stare but they were obviously curious about us, too. They were giving us sidelong glances and then convulsing into giggles. Soon contacts were being made between one or two of our lot and some of them

'We should go over and say hello,' said Parker-Fitch.

'Go on, then. I dare you,' said Brokowsky.

'All right, I will.'

Grinning back at Brokowsky and me over his shoulder, not entirely sure of himself, Parker-Fitch sauntered over to the nearest group of three. We couldn't hear what he said on reaching them, but a conversation had evidently started. I drifted across with Brokovsky and as nonchalantly as possible joined the group. Parker-Fitch was speaking to one who had brown curly hair and the shrewd bright eyes of a squirrel.

'So what school are you?' she said.

Parker-Fitch said the name.

'And who on earth are those two men in long black dresses?'

'They're monks, in their habits. They wear them all the time.'

'Even in bed?'

'How would I know? I don't go to bed with them.'

She looked at her friends, widening her eyes and giving a faint shake of the head.

'Anyway, say hello to my friends Christopher and Andy,' said Parker-Fitch

'Hello, Christopher and Andy'

'And what's your name?' I asked.

'I'm Patty. This is Ginny, and this is Miranda. We live in Hampstead.'

Ginny was white-skinned, Nordic, with blonde hair. The tip of her nose had reddened in the cold. Miranda had an Iberian look about her, though tall and with a hint of Moorish exoticism. She was the one I couldn't stop glancing at.

'So why of all things have you got two monks with you?' asked Ginny.

'They're our schoolmasters,' said Parker-Fitch. 'We're a monastery school.'

'So are you all going to become monks? Poor you!'

'Of course we're not. I'm going to be barrister, actually.'

'Bully for you,' said Patty. 'I'm going to be a brain surgeon. Or Prime Minister. I can't quite decide. Ginny will be running the Bank of England and Miranda, of course, will be a great concert pianist and conductor of the Berlin Philharmonic.'

Miranda smiled a little wanly and looked at her feet. Father Theodore bustled up to us.

'Come on. You'll want to see the bogey-switch. Walk up this way to the end of the platform and we'll get a good view of the operation across the tracks.'

With some reluctance we trailed after him, but the girls of Camden didn't follow.

'"I'm going to be a barrister, *actually*"', said Brokowsky, sniggering and capering.

'Fuck off, Brokowsky,' said Parker-Fitch. 'I didn't notice you contributing anything to the conversation.'

From the vantage point that Father Theodore led us to we could see that the six carriages of our train were now waiting to enter one by one into a bay between two close platforms, along which heavy lifting jacks were arranged in series. One carriage was already in position with boiler suited railway workers busy around it, shouting, some with shrill voices (half of them were women), as they manoeuvred the lifting gear into place. Then with an explosive release of steamy air the jacks worked in synchrony, lifting the entire carriage up by three or four feet. The narrow bogeys were then rolled backwards out of the way and the wider bogeys trundled into position from the front. With these in place the carriage was lowered and secured to the new set of wheels before being shunted forward to make room for the next carriage.

Father Theodore, who had been timing the exercise on his wristwatch, told us it had taken eleven minutes.

'It means we have an hour to wait for the whole train to be done so, to kill the time, we've taken over a waiting room for a choir practice. We have to sing in the service tomorrow afternoon let's not forget.'

The Tomb of Sergius

Our hotel, the Yaroslavskaya, was a gigantic barracks occupying half a dozen identical blocks that ranged along a wide Moscow street. The blocks had fourteen floors, and the guest rooms were arranged in straight corridors at least fifty yards in length. At the ends of each of them was a desk, behind which sat a formidable woman keeping a dragon's eye on all comings and goings. Universally these women had wire-wool hair drawn into a bun at the back.

The rooms were utilitarian, even Spartan. The one I shared with Brokowsky and Morrison had a couple of framed photographs as its only decoration. One was of the Soviet pavilion at the 1937 Paris Exhibition topped by its two monumental figures sculpted, according to the caption, by Vera Mukhina. The other was of a similarly colossal statue of a sword-brandishing woman entitled 'The Motherland Is Calling', the work of Yevgeny Vucetich.

'It's bound to be bugged,' said Brokowsky lowering his voice as we walked in. He lifted the phone and listened to the dialling signal, as if this might reveal the KGB's handiwork. It didn't. He hung up and pointed to a small vent near the ceiling, covered by a metal grill. 'It'll be in there.'

'You're paranoid,' said Morrison. 'Why would the secret police want to listen to your prattle?'

Next morning was our first official outing, a thirty-mile drive to Zagorsk, in a coach emblazoned with the logo of Intourist, the state travel agency. We left Moscow along generously proportioned boulevards flanked by huge apartment blocks. It was a city under snow, a clean white crust on the rooftops, ledges, and windowsills, and churned-up, yellow-brown, frozen sludge on the ground. We were warm inside the bus but outside the air stung the lining of our nostrils; the iced wind drove through our clothes and clung to us.

Father Theodore had said that people across the Iron Curtain lived in another dimension. To me, the more accurate parallel was with species differentiation. It was like chimps and bonobos, products of divergent evolution, looking at each other across the Congo River. We believed in individual

175

freedom, capitalism and God while they insisted on conformity, five years plans and atheism.

Material divergence was also evident. The appearance of the shops seemed designed to suppress rather than encourage consumption. Their windows were small, with scant and dusty displays. The signage was uniform and neon completely absent. Traffic in the streets consisted of many trams, buses and canvas-covered trucks, and a few taxis, but hardly any individual cars. Those that did appear were often long, and black, with six doors and thick chrome bumpers — Zils. According to Rudge, who was keenly attuned to the motoring culture of any society, these were used exclusively by party officials. The taxis were small Moskvitch saloons, the same model as might have conveyed the very few ordinary Muscovites who owned a private car.

'But I like the Spartan look of the city,' said Morrison, who was keen on socialism. 'The people have more important things to think about than shopping and flashy cars.'

'But the lack of cars is appalling,' protested Rudge. 'You call this a people's paradise. I see nothing but putrid poverty. I hate it. Do you know how much it costs a Russian to get a new car?'

We didn't know.

'Three years' wages, and you have to pay in cash. But there's a five year waiting list so in practice it's almost impossible to get one.'

'Why not buy second-hand?'

'There are no second-hand cars in Russia because a person who's got a car would have to be a lunatic to sell it, even if they allowed him to, which they don't. It's appalling.'

'What's appalling?' said Morrison. 'I'm not appalled. Anyway I don't call this a people's paradise, not yet, because they're still working on it — and it's hard work. The Revolution is not a dinner party, or an embroidery. Mao Tse Tung said that.'

'Good thing it's not a dinner party going by the crap they call food,' said Parker-Fitch. 'It's not the communism I object to — they can have that, if it's what they really want. It's their everyday habits. How can you buddy up to people who boil their tea, eat pickled gherkins for breakfast and smoke tobacco mixed with dried vulture dung?'

Our official guides were Valentina (grizzled and muscular in the face) and Lydia (bony and birdlike) who took turns to give a commentary on the passing scene relayed through speakers set in the coach's ceiling.

'Now we are passing Space Needle, monument to great achievements of all Soviet heroes of space,' said Lydia. 'You see Yuri Gagarin and other cosmonauts are portrayed around its base.'

'On your left,' cut in Valentina, 'you will see the Moscow University whose dimensions are 329 metres in the height with thirty-six storeys and so it is tallest building in Europe. This great University has thirty thousand students, covers four hundred and twenty acres and contains ninety-three miles of corridors. Its library has six million books. All courses here at the university are free.'

'But now,' said Lydia, 'we must inform you about Zagorsk, our tour destination for today, which lies seventy kilometres from Moscow. Zagorsk is big religious complex. It contains one of Soviet Union's official permitted monasteries. Soviet Union does not forbid the religion. Those wishing to practise it are free to do so. In Zagorsk there are two hundred and twenty seven monks and same number of trainees in Theological College. There is also here residence of Patriarch.'

Father Placid now stood up and faced the length of the coach. He reached for Lydia's microphone and, though she looked a shade put out, she ceded it to him.

'Thank you Lydia, thank you Valentina,' he said. 'May I just add a few words of my own on Zagorsk? If you like, you can see it as the equivalent of the Vatican City. Just as St Peter's contains the tomb of St Peter, Zagorsk boasts the tomb of St Sergius, who is Russia's patron saint. The entire place is surrounded by fortified walls. It was once besieged for over a year by a Polish army but held out. Now the Soviet Union bosses Poland. Such are the cycles of history. Immediately after the revolution the religious buildings were handed over to secular activities and one was even a museum of electrical and radio engineering, I believe. But since World War Two there has been a rapprochement. The Patriarch is allowed his official residence at Zagorsk once again. Various monasteries and cathedrals co-exist there, albeit leading a fairly precarious existence. They will be glad of our support and our prayers. Thank you, Lydia, for your forbearance.'

During Father Placid's address Valentina and Lydia, muttering together, and casting dark glances in his direction, had not looked at all forbearing. Now Lydia smiled coldly as she received back the microphone.

'Please to notice,' she told us, 'unlike the traffic jam in capitalist cities our traffic flows so freely here in Moscow. We are proud of the freedom of the vehicles in our streets. But now we are in the suburbs, where housing of the soviet workers is given freely to them by our government in these beautiful modern apartment blocks, as you see.'

'They love the word free, have you noticed?' said Brokowsky. 'According to them, everything is free here, except really nothing is.'

Having de-bussed and been conducted through a massive gatehouse into Zagorsk, we walked past innumerable onion domes and buildings with gigantic portals and slit windows. Bearded monks and priests in black robes and pillbox hats scurried across the open spaces between them.

'The main theological college is here,' said Father Placid, leading us towards one of the huge church doors. 'As Lydia told us on the bus there are over two hundred students. Did you know as a young man Stalin studied for five years for the priesthood ?'

'What, in Zagorsk?'

'Oh, I doubt it was here. Probably Georgia where he was born.'

'How would you say his studying for the priesthood prepared him for life as a brutal dictator, Sir?' said Brokovsky.

The monk had the grace to laugh.

As we entered the church we were met by a rotund and massively bearded figure in ornate gold robes. It was the Patriarch himself, preceded and followed by a small retinue. It was less of a meeting and more a standing in the same space, for the old man remained splendidly aloof smiling and nodding his head while his followers spoke for him. After making a short reciprocal speech, Father Placid presented a scroll and received a small icon in return. Then we followed the Russians to the tomb of St Sergius, which was surrounded by a knot of fervent and head-scarfed old women. The Patriarch intoned some prayers in a rich bass voice, to which the women returned lengthy and shrill ululations. We then delivered our Latin Litany of the Saints and the four-part hymn, which we had last practised in the waiting room at Brest station, singing this time in the parrot-learned dead language of Church Slavonic.

The people nodded and smiled at us. Critical judgement of our performance was suspended. It was not how well we had done that was amazing: it was, that we had done it at all.

Call Me Nik

Next morning at the Yaroslavskaya, I was coming out of my hotel room — Brokowsky and Morrison had gone to breakfast before me — when I noticed a young man standing beside our dragon's desk chatting with her. As soon as I appeared he broke away and hurried in my direction, gesturing.

'You are Mr Conrov?'

'I'm sorry?'

'Your name, I think it is Conrov?'

He stood in front of me, smiling.

'No, it's Conroy. Who are you?'

'I am friend of Mr Henry Webster. Well, I believe you have somethink for him from his wife in England. A package.'

I had suffered a few nervous moments crossing the frontier at Brest. A squad of armed customs officers, indistinguishable from police in their wide peaked caps and long grey leather-belted topcoats, entered our compartment. I imagined them rifling through our luggage before coming up with Henry Webster's parcel, demanding to know whose it was, then marching me off for interrogation. In fact, though each of our passports was scrutinised, and baleful eyes were cast over our persons and the compartment as a whole, there was no attempt to search the luggage.

'But what is your name?' I said.

'Ah, sorry! I am Nikolai Komarov. Please to call me Nik.'

He held out his hand and I shook it, but hesitantly and, noticing this, the Russian gripped my hand even harder. He had straight dark hair lying close to his skull, a sharp and boney nose, and eyes that darted here and there. He was short in stature, thin and in his mid- or late-twenties. He wore a dark olive-green overcoat.

I pulled my hand free, feeling I had done badly in the opening moves of this unexpected contact with a native Russian. I had been awkward and communicated uncertainty.

'So how do you know my name?' I said, trying a more authoritative tone. I glanced up and down the corridor. It was deserted.

'From Mr Henry Webster, of course. The package you carry from his wife in England. He asked me to bring to him this package. So now, if I come with you in your room, you can perhaps give it to me?'

Immediately after passing the scrutiny of the border guards, I'd felt more relaxed about the article —whatever it was — that I was the courier of. But, since we'd got to Moscow, the longer it continued in my possession, the more it weighed on me as an undischarged responsibility. Phyllis had told me Henry would appear at some point and I would give it to him. That sounded simple enough. But when would he? And how? And what if he never showed up and I was left with the damn thing?

I had not, in any case, been prepared for the appearance of an intermediary, though I could see the advantage of it. Nik was offering to lift the burden. Rid me of the problem. I simply had to give him the package and just like that would be relieved of it.

'Oh! All right,' I said.

I turned around and went back to the room. I keyed the lock and Nik followed me inside. He stood humming some tune to himself as I opened my case and brought out Phyllis's parcel. I held it for a moment in both hands, without turning back to Nik. I thought, what are you doing? Nik had produced no evidence that he was Henry's go-between. He might be KGB and mean harm to our pilgrimage or to Henry. I didn't wish harm on Henry. Traitor though he was to my country I couldn't help liking the man and was rather looking forward to meeting him again and handing over the 'little something', an act that Mrs Webster had surely intended to be in person. And equally surely, I thought, if this Nik was a genuine emissary, he would be carrying a note from Henry vouching for him.

'Actually, I'm not sure about this,' I said.

'It's OK, Mr Conrov.' Nik was wheedling now. 'I am his friend. It will be so much more easy this way for you.'

Nik was immediately behind me, reaching over my shoulder to grab the package. I snatched it away, took a step from him and swivelled about, keeping the package behind my back.

'I'm sorry. I must give it to Henry Webster personally.'

Nik spread his hands.

'Personally, yes of course, *personally*. I shall tell it to no one.'

He thinks "personally" is the same as "privately", I thought.

'That's not what I'm saying. I must give it to Henry, to Mr Webster, from my hands into his.'

'No! You must give it to me!'

Nik darted towards me and I stepped smartly back. He now clenched his boney fist and seemed about to raise it when a female voice was heard at the door behind us. Nik spun around. A woman was backing into the room drawing with her a trolley laden with cleaning equipment. She turned and addressed a question to us. Nik answered in three words, then turned back to me with a pained smile. He gave a rigid bow and, pushing past the cleaner, hurried out of the room.

International Friendship

Today we were invited to a buffet lunch at the Palace of International Friendship. The Palace's status and function in the structure of Soviet society was mysterious. We remained locked into a bitterly Cold War with the Soviets so, as Brokowsky pointed out, it was reasonable to wonder what kind of friendship this could be, exactly. On the evidence of this morning we were expected to forge relations with certain hand-picked English-speaking students, with whom we would listen to speeches on youthful cooperation, amicable understanding and the universality of youth. The speech from our side was delivered by Julian Parker-Fitch, who had the job because he was the captain of our inter-school debating team. He told the Russians just what they wanted to hear: there was in reality no Cold War because of the warmth generated by what we young people had in common. Brokowsky was standing beside me.

'This is pure crap,' he said in my ear.

'Yes, but diplomat's crap,' I said. 'Or in Parker-Fitch's case future barrister's crap. What on earth does universal youth really have in common?'

'Raging hormones,' he said. 'They generate warmth by rubbing together.'

'I wish.'

Soft drinks had been laid on. I was just opening a bottle of some kind of fruit juice when a dimple-cheeked, russet-haired female student came up to me.

'Welcome to Moscow Palace of Friendship,' she said. 'My name is Tatiana.'

'Oh! Like the Grand Duchess.'

'Like who?'

'Grand Duchess Tatiana. She was the prettiest of your Tsar Nicholas's four daughters. Well *I* think she was the prettiest.'

This other Tatiana lowered her eyes.

'We do not speak of Tsar. He was Nikolai Romanov, a very bad man. How do you know his daughters?'

'From a book. It had pictures of them. Last year I wrote an essay for my history teacher about Rasputin who was a friend of the Tsarina. I was doing a holiday task. You have heard of Rasputin?'

She simply shrugged, lifting her arms out from her sides.

'Now he was a *properly* bad man,' I said, 'with very long hair. He was a bad influence around the Tsar's, sorry, Nikolai Romanov's court.'

There was pause, then she said,

'We expected you English boys will have the long hair.'

'Really? Why?'

'Because Beatles also are English.'

'Are the Beatles popular here in the Soviet Union?'

Her dimples deepened as she smiled.

'Oh yes. John, Paul, George and Bingo. Bingo is my favourite.'

'Can you get their records here?'

'No. It is impossible.'

She lowered her voice.

'But my friend has some. Her father got them. He is diplomat. She loves you yeah, yeah, yeah!'

She giggled. Over her shoulder I saw a figure standing for a moment at the doorway, his eyes scanning the room. The hall or lobby behind him was shadowed and the door was half closed. But he looked familiar, which was perhaps because he rather resembled the actor John Gregson.

'I wish Beatles would make one concert here in Soviet Union,' said Tatiana.

'I'm afraid that's unlikely to happen. They've said they're not going to play in public any more. They got sick of Beatlemania.'

'Beatlemania? What is it?'

The figure was still hovering at the door, as if undecided whether to enter. I saw in that moment who he looked like: not John Gregson, but Henry Webster.

'Excuse me,' I said. 'There's a man over there I want to speak to. Wait for me. I'll come back and tell you about Beatlemania.'

I walked quickly across to the doorway but, by the time I got there, whoever it was had gone. I looked this way and that. Perhaps after all it was not Henry. I returned to the hall but by now Tatiana too had disappeared.

The Tomb of Lenin

Lydia gathered us up and together we took a short icy walk to Red Square to see the tomb of V.I. Lenin. A long line of people was ranged along the outside wall of the castle, which was coloured somewhere between rose-red and rust-red. Shuffling forward by inches in the freezing wind these were people's pilgrims, votaries of an atheist whose cult had already lasted nearly half a century.

'Come along, come along,' said Lydia, marshalling us as we came near. 'We not will have to wait. We will go to front of line.'

The pair of great-coated military entrance guards seemed to make no complaint, and nor did those foremost in the queue. They watched us patient and sheeplike as we were bustled past them and down the steps by Lydia and into the vestibule. Here we paused while she gave us her patter. Behind her as she spoke the infinite succession of pilgrims continued to descend the steps and pass into the Burial Chamber.

'This Mausoleum lies on the highest part of the Red Square,' she told us. 'It was designed in 1925, after death of Lenin, by architect Alexey Shchusev. It is one low pyramid of five steps high and is constructed of granite stone weighing ten thousand tons. As we shall in one moment see, embalmed body of V.I. Lenin lies within the Burial Hall. Hall is five-metre cube. Lenin's stone coffin rests on one black pedestal, and it is open for the visitor to see inside. So far, more than ten million people have visited this place to view body of our great revolutionary leader.'

She made an ushering gesture towards the Burial Hall, and shot out her arm to stem the shuffling line of visitants. In single file we walked ahead of them into the mausoleum chamber. The air was both stale and frigid. Passing the coffin I looked down at Lenin. His flesh was not flesh-like but waxy with a certain gloss, the lips tomato red. To look at the corpse was dispiriting. It gave something like the effect of mock joints of meat lying deep in the dust of a bankrupt butcher's window. Or an old and obsolete inmate of Madame Tussaud's, abandoned in a damp cellar deep below the exhibition halls.

The more accurate parallel might be with the 'uncorrupted' body of a Catholic saint. Many years later I would visit Cascia in central Italy, and the shrine to St Rita, patroness of unhappy wives. She lay on view in a side chapel — a decaying corpse on which not entirely successful attempts had been made to keep it presentable. The faithful came to Rita to have their troubled lives fixed and, looking at the faces of those paying their respects in Red Square, the same might have been true of Lenin.

The evening was given over to the Moscow State Circus, which along with the Bolshoi Ballet was a Soviet cultural institution we had all heard of. In the audience two rows below us were the Camden High School girls. At the interval a group of us went out to the Refreshment Bar, but the girls stayed put. I caught the eye of Miranda as I passed their row and jerked my head in invitation. She shook her head.

The circus acts were hardly different from those I used to see annually at Christmas at the Blackpool Tower: acrobats on horseback, tumblers on swings, lions tamed, seals balancing balls, educated chimps, bears on skates, clown cars with bent axles. Here it was all highly efficient, and yet in some way joyless. As act succeeded act, each was mechanically applauded exactly as I had once seen delegates on the television news applauding a speech by Leonid Brezhnev.

Going out with the crowd at the end I found myself shoulder-to-shoulder with Miranda.

'You should have come for an ice cream. Only twenty copeks and quite lascivious.'

She turned to me.

'What did you say?'

'Delicious. I said the ice creams here are delicious.'

'No you didn't. You said lascivious. Is that your idea of amusing?'

'So what if it is?'

'You're trying too hard. You're trying *much* too hard.'

She pushed ahead to join her friends.

Vigil

The climax of our activity as pilgrims to Russia was attendance at the only full-scale Easter Vigil service officially permitted in Moscow. The Intourist coach collected us on the evening of Holy Saturday and drove a short distance to Yelokhovsky Cathedral. Approaching in the dark, it was difficult to take in the huge domed building but it was immediately evident that a crowd was milling around outside. These were devotés, certainly, but not of Christianity. Many had placards whose iconography was typical, even stereotypical, of revolutionary atheism — cigar smoking priests arm-in-arm with cartoonish top-hatted capitalists, old women using the cross as a crutch. We also heard shouting and the possibly drunken singing of hymn-parodies.

As soon as our coach appeared, the people surged forward to surround it. They had apparently been waiting for us. The driver drove stiffly forward by inches through the crowd, while fists thumped the coach's side panels. Of the guides only Lydia was on duty tonight. She looked edgy, white-faced, but said nothing until Father Theodore spoke to her and she switched on the microphone.

'These are young communists,' she told us. 'They have come to show they don't like the religion, which Karl Marx called opium of the people. Don't worry. They will not hurt us.'

But she did not sound entirely sure, for now the demonstrators began to behave like a mob, waving fists and shouting with distorted faces close to the coach windows. When we eventually reached a parking spot Lydia opened the door at the front and leaned out. She beckoned to one of the policeman, who was standing at the edge of the crowd and eyeing the disorder with an air of dull complacency. He acknowledged her but made no move, merely shaking his finger towards her. Lydia reached out to close the coach door but, before she could, a man had forced his

187

way up the coach steps and dodged under her arm. He was in his early twenties and wore a green woollen coat and open neck shirt. Doing a double take, I realised he was Nik Komarov.

Having forced his way inside, Nik froze at the head of the coach, staring around. Staring at us. I was certainly shocked to see him, but he himself actually looked electrocuted. Wide-eyed, he was more prey than predator; he was like a deer in the forest at night, caught in head-lights. His daring had brought him into the presence of something that was, to him, incomprehensible: a large group of boys in their late teens intent on entering a vast cathedral full of pensioners in order to celebrate a supernatural event.

Now our coach was being rocked by the anti-God demonstrators, pushing reciprocally against it on both sides. Taking matters into his own hands, our burly driver left his seat and shoved Nik out through the door so that he floundered down the steps and into the arms of the policeman, who had at last responded to Lydia's call and waded through the crowd with truncheon drawn. We watched as Nik was clubbed a few times around the head and shoulders and dragged away.

It was only afterwards that I wondered if this had been Nik Komarov after all. The straight dark hair, overcoat, bony cheeks, nervous eyes — these had looked the same. But it was surely unlikely that he would appear in two such disconnected circumstances within a few days? Unless, of course, he was following me.

At last the police decided the crowd had made their point. From somewhere mounted police appeared and crush barriers were produced to form a gangway between bus and cathedral. We walked hurriedly, through the parted but still raging sea of atheists, and into a different reality.

The Cathedral was crammed with standing worshippers, and it was rocking. The almost stifling air sparkled as smoked golden candlelight rebounded from the iconostasis, the shimmering wall of gilded icons that isolated the altar and sanctuary from the people. The candlelight shone not only from the iconostasis but also from the dazzle of the mosaic walls and pillars, from the often tearful eyes of the old women, and from the bald heads of the old men. These males were a minority of the congregation, however, because most of those present were elderly women wearing headscarves knotted under their chins. Everyone carried lighted candles, the women singing in a shrill pitch, waves of ululation that surged up around us, then died away, only to surge again. We were brought to a privileged position beside the screen, close to the Patriarchal throne, where the worshippers continually glanced or frankly stared at us. They knew who we were. Some lit candles for us and pressed them into our hands, breathing heavily in delight at our presence. Others merely smiled and nodded, just as they had in Zagorsk. In fact, looking from face to face, I began to suspect that these were *the same people* as those we'd seen at the monastery. The same headscarves and shabby suits, the same ululating piety, the same breath loaded with garlic and vodka.

The rhythms of the service, and the singing, were governed by cues we could only guess at, as most of the rite — completely unfamiliar to us — went on behind the iconostasis screen and out of the sight of the people. But every few minutes the doors — Royal Doors, so called — swung opened and magnificently bearded, round-paunched old men in sumptuous robes emerged to cense or bless us, intoning in rich *basso profundo*. Meanwhile the Patriarch, planting himself briefly on his throne, assumed a majesty of Bourbon proportions. These appearances lasted no more than a minute before the whole of the clergy disappeared again through the Royal Doors, like water sucked through a plughole, to continue their secret ministrations within.

So it went on for more than an hour and, as midnight approached, the shrillness of the singing edged closer and closer to hysteria. Looking around I noticed one whose attention was not focussed on the iconostasis and the Royal Doors. All I could see of him was his head and shoulders, leaning back against of the pillars, his eyes half closed, but all the time observing our group. In his way he was as strikingly out of place as we were: a middle-aged and sprucely dressed man in a crowd of deeply lined faces, discarded and marginalised by the machinery of state.

Who was he? I looked again and thought he looked a little like the actor Dirk Bogarde, and then realised who I was really looking at. Surely, that was Henry Webster— Henry Webster, *again*. Or not again, as this was not quite the same figure as the one I had glimpsed in that doorway at the Palace of Friendship, the one who had looked like John Gregson. This was a slightly taller man, and rather better groomed. He rose well above the diminutive worshippers that lapped around him, with silver streaked hair smoothly combed, exactly like Henry's. So that other Gregsonian Henry, however reminiscent, had not been the real Henry after all, but a case of mistaken identity. This second more Bogardean Henry was the real one, *the* Henry, and he was watching us through hooded eyes.

I still had (though with increasing nervousness) the package entrusted to me at Victoria Station but, since the incident with Nik Komarov, I hadn't risked leaving it in the hotel room. From a souvenir stall in Zagorsk I had bought a leather shoulder bag embossed with a hammer and sickle, and this I carried looped over my shoulder. Alongside my camera and a map of Moscow, Phyllis's brown paper-wrapped gift for Henry lay in this bag, waiting for Henry to stop me and claim it.

But such a thing was out of the question in this passionately pious crush. I couldn't possibly get through to make the presentation, for now the jam of people was growing thicker as the liturgy drove towards its midnight climax, the dramatic transition to Easter Day. We had been briefed to pay close attention to this moment. The Royal Doors would swing open. The Patriarch would stride out with his retinue, stand for a moment and then with raised arms proclaim the resurrection: *Christos voskrese!* To which we, and all the people, would cry out in a great shout of acclamation *Vayiste voskrese!* He is risen indeed. After the excitement around our arrival, followed by the tiring and repetitive hour or more standing in wait, the moment when it came was unexpectedly uplifting. *Vayiste voskrese!* We were all heady and elated. Faith, usually so elusive to me, so insubstantial, felt in this moment palpable.

And, when I remembered to look in his direction once again, Henry had gone.

Captured

By Easter Monday the "little something" I was carrying was still unclaimed, and we were leaving on *Krasnaya Strela*, the Red Arrow train which connected Moscow with Leningrad. Assembling us in the train's dining car, Valentina gave us a lurid summary of conditions in our destination city during its 872-day starvation siege by the Nazis between 1941 and 1944. Dogs and cats were spitted. Rats and mice were casseroled. Sparrows were roasted. But incredibly, she told us with pride, not one inhabitant of the city's world famous zoo was eaten.

At the Leningrad station an electronic display gave the air temperature as minus 14 degrees. A welcoming committee of students of our own age was awaiting us in shivering groups, carrying bunches of tulips. Brokowsky and I were picked out by two girls who by presenting their flowers took possession of us. Parker-Fitch, Morrison and the others were similarly taken (as you might say) into custody. Our own two captors, named Yelena and Nina, announced that we were coming to Yelena's home for dinner that night but first we were to spend the day visiting the Winter Palace of Nikolai Romanov, and many of the other sights that the city of Leningrad had to offer.

Standing in the great, enclosed courtyard of the palace I thought of the Tsar with his trimmed dark beard, in military cap, uniform and riding boots, pacing around the courtyard with the Tsarina, talking of family, and then of state. He knew he wasn't up to the job but knew, too, that he mustn't show it. For Russians, the holiest one had never been the Patriarch. It was Nikolai Romanov, the Emperor but also the Pope of Russia and, as such, constrained never to show a moment's doubt or weakness. A pity, then, that indecisiveness was his worst fault.

Then I thought about the four little girls playing chase and rolling hoops in their sailor hats and flouncy day-dresses, who would one day be machine-gunned in a cellar with surprise on their faces and jewels sewn into their underwear. I thought too of the Tsarevitch, the haemophiliac boy with his gushing nosebleeds, ever-seeping knee-scrapes and swollen bruises, finally bleeding out on a floor thick with dust and broken bricks. This weird and fated family's ghosts had long ago departed the vast birthday cake of the Winter Palace, built after all for show, not living. It was on show to this day, but with a different label attached.

After a week of Moscow museum visits, with their displays of rocket engines and tractor motors, it was a relief to come into the Hermitage's room of Picassos and Matisses. We had previously passed through room after room of hyperbolic Soviet realism, all muscled arms, heroic hammers and resolute hay-rakes. With all their entanglements of tribal mask faces and anyhow limbs, this Parisian modernism, brought to Russia by plutocratic collectors on the eve of revolution, stuffed a defiant thumb into the inhuman Soviet eye.

'That's the life I want,' I said.

Brokowsky and I were standing in front of Picasso's 'Composition with Skull', a jumble of eliding studio accoutrements on red and pink planes around a goggle-wearing death's head.

'What life?'

'Paris. Fun. Freedom. The smell of paints. The artistic life.'

'But as far as I know you can't paint,' he pointed out.

'That is my tragedy.'

Veterok, Ugolyok and Pickles

'My father says, do your fathers let you drink alcohol?'

Yelena's eyes were on me for every second of my time in her home. Her face was non-committal but I thought the way she relayed her parents' questions had an anxious undertone, as if it was vitally important to her that I perform well.

'Yes, they do,' I said. 'At least mine does.'

Brokowsky, Nina's captive, said something in halting Russian, which I assumed approximated what I had said in English because it began with 'Da'. Delighted at my friend knowing some — any — Russian, Yelena's father began to rattle off a series of questions, which Brokowsky couldn't begin to follow. Nina translated for him.

'He says you are too young to have vodka but Soviet beer is good.'

Brokowsky's confidence in Russian deserted him and, glancing at me, he went on in English.

'Then we would like some of that, please.'

'My father says there's no need to say please,' said Yelena. 'It is our pleasure

The apartment consisted of a sequence of rooms giving onto each other with no mediating corridors. The style of furnishing approximated to the vernacular of the 1950s: sub-Swedish, or heavily diluted Bauhaus, none new and none comfortable in any way that I understood. Mr Gilmore had told us in, a briefing that afternoon, that all the homes we visited would be those of solid party members. Once inside, he said, we should be at all times diplomatic.

We sat at the dinner table to address bowls of borsht accompanied by dense chunks of bread, brought to us by Yelena's mother who, we learned, was a telephonist at Moscow's central exchange. She stayed almost silent throughout the evening, but listened with care to everything that was said. Her husband, a schoolteacher, possessed a more forceful, more bullish personality.

In the Hermitage Yelena and Nina had appeared unimpressed by the West European modernist paintings, but would not be drawn into telling us their own favourite artists. Yelena's father had no such inhibitions and, as the subject came up of our visit to the Hermitage, he instructed us that Picasso, Braque, Matisse and the rest were 'formalists' unable to touch the human soul. Aleksandr Dejneka and Boris Ioganson were the men for him, and the woman sculptor Vera Muhkina. These were all great revolutionary soul-touching artists.

'Mukhina,' I said. 'She made the big sculpture of a man and a woman on top of the Soviet pavilion at the Paris Exhibition.'

Yelena's father — his name was Mikhail — had been chewing a piece of bread. Now he stopped mid-chew.

'Is Vera Mukhina famous in England?' he asked, via his daughter.

'Not really,' I said. 'And, I'm sorry to say neither is your other great sculptor of monuments, Yevgeny Vucetich.'

Hearing this name spoken by western lips made Mikhail's eyes gleam in delight. He stood up and delivered a speech that lasted up to a minute. Yelena summarised.

'My father says it is a very large honour that you Christopher, and you Andrew, come in our home, for you have great knowledge of the languages and also of the arts. Now he will play some music in honour for our guests.'

Mikhail drained his shot of vodka and walked into the adjoining room. He came back with a long-playing record, shielding its cover from us, opened the lid of a boxy record player on a side table and slid the disc from its sleeve. He placed it on the turntable, dropped the pick-up into the groove and stood back, watching the record revolve and crackle. After a moment a sequence of four falling notes from a brass section blared out, and Mikhail hit the heavy orchestral chord that followed with a downward punch of his arm. The sequence repeated once, and then again, followed by a new rising sequence of thumping piano chords against a honeyed waltz tune from the violins. All of this was vigorously conducted by Mikhail.

Soon the piano settled down to some serious fast-fingered solo work, and Mikhail dropped his arms and returned to the table. He raised a spoonful of borscht while examining us with one of his eyebrows twitching, like a quizmaster. But I had hit lucky for a second time.

'It's Tchaikovsky, isn't it?' I said. 'The First Piano Concerto.'

When his daughter translated Mikhail dropped his spoon, spattering borscht on the tablecloth, and gave a cry of delight. Next thing he was thumping me on the back and pouring beer into my glass. All awkwardness between us dissolved and after that the rest of the evening was easy.

Walking us back to the Moskvitch Hotel our two young hostesses wanted to talk about dogs.

'Do you like our dogs Veterok and Ugolyok?' said Nina.

'Your dogs? I didn't see any dogs at the flat.'

The girls laughed.

'They are not our *family* dogs, of course,' said Nina. 'They are Soviet space dogs. They just came back from the space flight orbiting three weeks in duration. They are very famous, our space dogs. Everybody knows them.'

'We haven't got any space dogs in England, famous or otherwise,' said Brokowsky.

'But however,' said Yelena, 'you have one famous dog. Peeckle, yes?'

I misheard.

'What? A beagle?'

'She means Pickles, idiot,' said Brokowsky. 'The mutt that found the World Cup.'

The previous week the stolen Jules Rimet trophy had been unearthed from under a bush by a border collie being walked in a London park. He had become a national celebrity as a result, though it was a surprise to hear his fame had penetrated the Iron Curtain.

'How on earth have you heard about that?' I said.

'On television,' said Nina. 'We know all the news about World Cup. Soviet team will win this year, of course.'

'Well one thing's for sure,' said Brokowsky. 'It won't be England.'

Back in our rooms in the vast Gagarin Hotel we found a brown cardboard package waiting for us. Brokovsky tore it open and took out six large bottles of yellowish liquid, and a message card which he read.

'My God,' he said, after reading the card. 'My relations have come good. My family, they've smuggled this over from Poland. They live just by the border. They say *nazdrowie* — cheers.'

'It's alcohol?'

He unscrewed the top of a bottle and took a swig, grimacing as he swallowed, then smacking his lips.

'You bet it is. Polish vodka, that's why it's yellow. My parents must have told them I was staying here. Come on, let's get some of the others in here and have a party.'

Not Having Been Written by a Communist

Before our time in the Soviet Union was up there were more stamina-sapping exhibitions of technical prowess, a two-hour film about the Siege of Leningrad, a tour of the city's World War Two fortifications, and finally a flight in a propeller-driven aircraft to Riga, all endured by those of us who had access to Brokovsky's relations' vodka with excruciating hangovers. According to Rudge, the aircraft was a converted World War Two bomber: the fuselage rattled as if half its rivets had dropped out, and the engines sounded like a chorus of roaring two-stroke lawn mowers. By the time we bumped down in Riga the thought of our spiralling plunge to earth in flames had shaken us all.

At Riga a ship was waiting to bring us down the Baltic, across the North Sea and back to Tilbury Docks. It was a small cruise ship onto which other school groups had already embarked, including the party from Camden High School.

About a quarter of an hour before we were due to cast off Parker-Fitch and I were settling into our two-berth cabin. We unpacked our cases as the engine started to rumble and the ship to hum and vibrate. Then the cabin door swung open.

'Hello, Christopher.'

A middle-aged man stood there with, standing behind him, a thug with crew cut hair and a top-heavy physique. The first man wore a tailored suit and tie, had plentiful, carefully-groomed black hair, rather modified by silver grey, and seemed perfectly relaxed. He somewhat resembled the Gregsonian Henry I had seen in the Palace of Friendship, as well as being rather like the Henry that had been in Yelokhovsky Cathedral, the Bogardean Henry with the hooded eyes. And yet, in the present location, at the present time, he was clearly not either of those doubtful Henrys but quite certainly the real Henry Webster.

'Hello Henry,' I said.

'Would you ask your friend to skedaddle, just for a minute or two?'

'Who's this?' said Parker-Fitch.

'Never mind,' said Henry. 'Though you might be interested to know the guy with me's a footsoldier of the KGB, with the tattoos to prove it.'

At this Parker-Fitch looked alarmed. He may have alleged there was 'no Cold War', but he wasn't betting on it. He turned to me.

'You all right, Christopher?'

'Yes,' I said. 'It's fine. I know him. Don't worry.'

Looking incredulous, Parker-Fitch left the cabin after which Henry slipped in and closed the door, leaving his minder outside.

'I suppose you want the package from Phyllis,' I said. 'Why didn't you contact me in Moscow? She told me that's where you live.'

'There were complications so I had to intercept you here. Hell of a job to organise.'

Picking up the Zagorsk bag I brought out the package and handed it over. He tucked it into his armpit.

'Thank you, Christopher. I always saw you as a chap one might rely on. This is — well, it means a lot.'

'Don't you have anything for Phyllis I can take back? A message even?'

He tensed his lips, breathing in through the nose.

'Just, um, tell her I miss her, will you? Same to Harriet. Miss them all terribly. Just say that.'

He swung round and grasped the door handle.

'So what's in it, Henry?' I said.

He half turned back to me.

'What?'

I pointed to package.

'That. I'd like to know.'

He touched it with the ends of two fingers, hesitating.

'Oh, you know, it's a just a book.'

'What book? I've carted it all this way for you.'

It wasn't that Henry was embarrassed, but more that he was wondering whether to trust me with something that could be construed as embarrassing.

'It's *Ulysses* actually. Best book ever written. Can't get it here in exchange for love, money or even the secret measurements of C. P. Snow.'

I laughed, but still had the feeling that, covered by the joke about C. P. Snow, he was keeping something back. There was a pause, then he said something that on the face of it seemed wildly off the subject.

'Did you know that the woman who turned Byron into Russian did so while she was doing a ten-year stretch banged up by Stalin? While she was in the jug — labour camp actually — she translated *Don Juan* entirely from memory, all sixteen thousand lines of it. And after Uncle Joe died it got published here and was a raging success.'

'That's amazing.'

'The people in this country are.'

He tapped Phyllis's package.

'Somewhere or other in this fabulous and mystical nation there is sure to be a Russian fan of James Joyce who knows *this* book by heart. Fortunately, you have saved me the trouble of tracking her, or him, down. So thank you, Christopher. I am very much in your debt, though sadly not in a position to see you get paid.'

'It's good you've got it,' I said. 'I haven't read it yet.'

'You must. It's a very wise book that seems to acquire more wisdom as it gets older. And, by the way, it is all the better for not having been written by a communist. Good-bye, Christopher. Thanks again.'

He pulled open the door and instantly was gone, his escort hurrying along behind him.

It was only then that I remembered I had promised Phyllis I would take a photograph. I seized my Brownie 127, that I'd had since the age of twelve, and ran out after him. I reached the boat deck rail just in time to see Henry and his shadow descending the gangplank and striding together along the quay just below me. They were intercepted by a third man who'd emerged from a doorway leading into the quayside building, a slim, blond haired youngish man with a cigarette in his mouth who shook Henry's hand gravely. I knew him at once. I had last seen him leaning against his father's limousine while on chauffering duty outside Henry Webster's house in Sussex. He was Serge Windt, son of Wim and Magda.

I got a shot of this group as they paused below me, and another of them heading towards the door through which Serge had come. As I took the camera off my eye, I saw from the cover of a different quayside doorway another figure stealing out. He started after Henry's group and, looking down from my high perspective, I thought there was something familiar about him too: his gait, his greasy hair and olive green overcoat. When he looked back over his shoulder and showed me his face I felt sure that, yes, it was Nik Komarov turning up again. Raising the camera I got off a shot of him, with Henry, Serge Windt and the KGB man still in view beyond. After that the three men turned into a shed along the quay and Nik quickened his step behind them. A few seconds later he reached the same spot. I took another photo as Nik peered into the shed, his head lost in the shadow. Satisfied that he could follow safely, he went in after them.

I turned away from the rail. The gangplank was being pulled inboard. Sailors were releasing heavy ropes from the bollards over which they were looped. The ship let off a long, hoarse warning hoot. The rattly throb of the engine increased and after a few more moments we were moving.

When, back in England, I eventually developed the film, the pictures of Henry with Serge Windt on the quayside was sharp and unmistakable. I sent it on to Phyllis. She might even have had some idea of Serge's role in all this. Of the second and third shots, of the figure who emerged, and followed them, every aspect was in focus except the face. That was a blur I supposed because he had been moving his head to look back just as I pressed the button.

Perhaps it had not been Nik Komarov at all. Did it matter? We had a two-day voyage ahead of us, in the company of the Camden High for Girls, and there was still some of Brokovsky's vodka left. Anything might happen.

The Interview

1966

Wounded Knee

Interviews of scholarship candidates for the University of Cambridge were held across two days in mid-November, starting at ten o'clock on a Thursday morning and finishing on Friday afternoon. On the Wednesday I travelled from school in Yorkshire to London, where I had arranged to stay overnight with the Nagys.

In Kensington I found that the baby they had so long been "trying for" was now well on the way — almost through the door, in fact. I was startled by the planetary roundness of Romy's pregnancy. I had never knowingly been so close to a woman so close to giving birth. Although Romy's outline was transformed, it was not distorted. In pregnancy she was no less beautiful, no less herself. Her skin still bloomed. Her eyes still shot out their sparks. Her movements went on being graceful with nothing impulsive, nothing sudden about them. And there was a glorious assertive quality in her ballooning belly.

These days thoughts of Romy, not just about her as a singer, or as a mother–to–be, but others of a more secret kind sometimes kept me awake at night.

'Would you prefer it to be a boy, or a girl?' I asked her.

I regretted the question at once as being a dull, obvious line. But she took it as if she had never been asked before, and returned another equally well used reply. But melody corrects clichés.

'Oh, you know, whatever God sends will be fine by us. We'll know in a couple of weeks time.'

'But I'll tell you something funny,' she said. 'The other day Pieter's mother came round and asked for a reel of cotton. She made me take off my wedding ring, and hung it on a thread which she dangled over my tummy. She said that in Hungary, if a ring circles clockwise, it's a sure sign the baby's a boy and if it's anti-clockwise it's a girl.'

'Which way did it circle?'

'Clockwise.'

'A boy, then.'

'But the problem is we weren't in Hungary. In London, the odds are by no means so certain, apparently.'

'Probably about fifty-fifty.'

The marvellous melisma of her laugh.

'Probably.'

'Have you chosen any names?'

She sighed.

'Peter wants Augustine or Agnes. I want Bartholomew or Beatrice. Maybe we'll settle on Charlie or Charlotte.'

'Or Donald or Deirdre?'

'Edward or Edith.'

'Fred or Fatima.'

'Guglielmo or Galatea'.

We got as far as M before the game ran out of energy.

I had Romy to myself for a full hour before Pieter came home and we sat down to dinner. He wanted to know why I had made Cambridge my first choice of university.

'It's where my uncle James went,' I said. 'That's my mother's brother. I'm applying to St Saviour, his old college.'

'You know Cambridge is where I met Romy? I had an organ scholarsip at St John's. At Newnham she was known as The Voice on Legs and no one could say which was the more sexy, the voice or the legs.'

'Pieter!' said Romy. 'Such rubbish!'

'What's St Saviour like?' I asked.

'It's a fine old college, slightly off centre geographically. I don't recall anyone from there reading music, not in my time. I remember it as very hearty and full of hefty rowers and beefy rugger-buggers.'

'There's no danger that I'll be rowing, or playing rugger.'

'Good for you. What will you to read, if they take you?'

'English.'

Pieter held up his index finger.

'Well, you beware, young Christopher. According to my information Cambridge these days is infested with Marxists of all stripes, and especially the English Faculty. They're Godless, clueless and shameless. Don't let them get you in their clutches. They are vampires.'

'Darling, don't alarm poor Christopher,' said Romy. 'Not on the day before his interview.'

'The Catholic centre's a place called Fisher House,' said Peter. 'An old building next to the Corn Exchange, which was once a pub, apparently. The council keeps condemning it and then un-condemning it following noisy protests, and so it carries on. It had a very good set-up in our time, when Monsignor Juniper held sway, didn't it darling?'

He sighed.

'But of course now he's out. Got the elbow after Vatican Council fanatics lobbied against him.'

'If you can be here on Saturday you'll meet Monsignor Juniper,' said Romy. 'He's coming to lunch. He is such a wonderful man. And not at all bitter about the way he was treated.'

After the interview I was due to return to the Nagys because Romy had been given a pair of tickets for one of the Royal Ballet's gala Saturday evening performances. Nureyev and Fonteyn were performing and, as once before when we'd seen Olivier's Othello, I was drafted in as Pieter's proxy. Pieter detested ballet.

'So how was he treated?' I asked.

'The bishop ordered him to start saying Mass in English,' said Pieter. 'Not only that, Fisher House was amalgamated with the catholic women's centre, over Juniper's head, who never wanted to let women in. As full members, I mean. So after that he felt he had no choice but to walk.'

'To be absolutely fair, he does come over as a touch out of touch,' said Romy. 'The way he dresses looks positively nineteenth century. That hat he wears is quite literally *vieux chapeau.*'

'I'm delighted he's behind the times,' said Pieter. 'Underneath that dotty patrician manner Juniper's completely sound on the fundamentals, like the importance of retaining the old rite — the Latin Mass and so on. I wish there were more like him. You didn't hear that bloody priest on *Ten to Eight* last week? Talk about heresy! Which day was it on, darling?'

'Now don't start browbeating poor Christopher with theology from the radio, Pieter. He's here to enjoy himself.'

'Enjoy himself? No! He should be steeling himself for his ordeal tomorrow.'

'Oh I shouldn't think it'll be an ordeal,' she said. 'You'll sail through, won't you Christopher?'

But Pieter persisted.

'Have you thought about what they'll ask you?'

'Our head of English says question one is always what are you reading at the moment?'

'To which you will reply?'

'I thought maybe Dickens would be a safe bet.'

'And are you? Reading Dickens?'

'No. I mean I've read quite a few. And we had a Greek master who thought Dickens was the greatest writer who ever lived. When he got bored with teaching Greek he used to read us long extracts, which I can remember surprisingly well.'

'Are you quite sure about that? What if you confuse Mr Merdle and Mr Murdstone? Or Little Dorrit and Little Nell? Or Eatanswill and Muggleton?

There's such a hell of lot of names in Dickens. It's the names that'll catch you out.'

'What's wrong with what you're really reading anyway?' said Romy. 'Don't tell me it's *The Peanuts Annual*, or something equally trivial.'

'Actually it's a novel by William Golding.'

'Oh yes,' said Pieter. 'He wrote that terrible thing *The Spire*. The fellow knows spit-all about medieval spirituality.'

'Well this one goes a bit further back than that — *The Inheritors*. I'm really enjoying it.'

'I've read it,' said Romy. 'It's all about the destruction of the Neanderthals by Homo Sapiens. The Neanderthals are lovely, gentle souls, while the New Men are devious, nasty and violent. It's like a kind of original sin story. Or perhaps I mean Cain and Abel.'

'The Neanderthals were dreamers,' said Pieter. 'Idealists who thought everything would turn out for the best. Panglossian, if you like. What they hadn't factored in was the arrival of Hom Sap to spoil the party. Hom Sap's original sin is cynicism, against which the Neanderthals had no defence. In a nutshell they died of optimism.'

'William Golding seems to think it was more because Homo Sapiens had technology,' I said, 'Things like bows and arrows, which the Neanderthals couldn't compete with. It's a bit like what the white man did to the Indians in America. Have you heard of the Battle of Wounded Knee?'

'I certainly have,' said Romy, 'and if you like I can even sing you a song that ends up at Wounded Knee. Shall I? The words are by Stephen Vincent Benét and it's incredibly beautiful. Come on, Pieter. Let's go through to the piano. Coming, Christopher?'

The idea of Romy singing just for me was a little intoxicating, like an unearned reward.

'Oh yes please. I'd love to hear you sing.'

Holding her swollen belly softly with both hands she began in light and sunny style, suiting the song's cowboy optimism as it hymned the geography of the Midwest.

> *I have fallen in love with American names,*
> *The sharp names that never get fat,*
> *The snakeskin-titles of mining-claims,*
> *The plumed war-bonnet of Medicine Hat …*

At the end, moving into the final stanza, Romy's phrasing slowed, as she turned a folksy melody into sombre threnody.

> *You may bury my body in Sussex grass,*
> *You may bury my tongue at Champmédy.*
> *I shall not be there, I'll rise and pass,*
> *Till you bury my heart at Wounded Knee.*

To convey the real effect of music is not possible in words. A woman's voice, perfectly pitched and under perfect control, is so far out of the reach of words that, when Romy finished, nothing I might say in her praise could possibly fit. Instead, as Pieter closed the keyboard lid and Romy went off to the kitchen to make coffee I asked him a practical question.

'Who wrote the music?'

'Guilty as charged, m'lord,' said Pieter.

'Really? You? I didn't know you were a composer.'

'*Were* is right. I don't any more. Too many knockbacks. Too many rejections.'

'Well I thought that song was terribly good. I mean, *really.*'

That sounded so lame, which makes my point. In face of music, language is more or less redundant.

'Terribly good, or goodly terrible,' Pieter said. 'It doesn't much matter.'

'I could tell Romy loved singing it, though. You mustn't stop writing songs for her. You really mustn't.'

'I know, and I haven't,' he said.

Culture

'Do you mean to say you've never read Brian Wilkins's *Society and Its Culture*?' said the candidate sitting next to me on the next evening at dinner 'in Hall'. He had already told me that his name was Gavin and that, like me, he was hoping to read English here at St Saviour College.

We had assembled earlier, in the late morning, for a talk about the college by the Senior Tutor Dr Lamplugh. He had made great play of St Saviour's ancient heritage.

'The first foundation on this site was a nunnery founded in 1312 and dedicated to St Salomé.'

He had looked around the group of us with a thin smile.

'I know what you're thinking. Did he say St *Salomé*? She of the seven *veils*? Who required John the Baptist's *head* on a platter? Surely not! And you'd be quite right. It's exactly the same name but it's that of a saint rather than a sinner. According to apocryphal sources, much believed in during the Middle Ages, St Salomé was the reputed midwife at the birth of Jesus. So, we at Saviour's hope the college will be the midwife of your future shining careers.'

We all smiled automatically, and some even laughed. It had the ring of an annual joke: the candidates' first taste of donnish humour.

For the next half hour Lamplugh gave us a run down of the college's catalogue of founders, donors and early alumni, a gallery more or less of rogues, adventurers, profiteers and slave traders, with one or two poets and philosophers thrown in. Later in the afternoon we were taken in a group around the college. The core buildings were ancient and all the others were old, except for a single modern accommodation block in front of which Lamplugh gathered us together.

'The Windt Building, which we have here, wouldn't exist without the munificence of The Wim and Magda Windt Foundation, which operates as a modern donor in exactly the same tradition as I was describing earlier. They also give grants and scholarships to facilitate exchanges between Saviour men at every level and counterparts in the USSR — a welcome extension of International Fellowship. Talking of which, right beside it is the Fellows' Garden, though I'm afraid it is strictly reserved for senior members of the college. Moving on, we have in front of us the squash courts.'

Later there was sherry with the Master, a lugubrious biochemist with a New Zealand accent. By the time we went into Hall for dinner I had talked to two other candidates in particular. One said he aimed to read Moral Sciences and was the stepson of an American free verse poet.

'If you're going to read English Literature, you'll have heard of him,' he said. 'Black Mountain School.'

I hadn't heard of him, or the Black Mountain School.

The other man, having applied to read engineering, had travelled all the way on a series of buses from the Scottish Highlands. His name was Hamish and he was the only one of us who wasn't in his heart intimidated by the college.

'I made four changes to get here,' he said, 'and it was nae worth it. I can't believe just how dingy this place is and the sheer dreich of it all.'

Huddled together for dinner in the middle of a long refectory table, we had found ourselves surrounded by confident, chattering undergraduates in their black gowns, below walls hung with portraits of the college worthies whose deeds and misdeeds we had earlier been regaled with.

'You really should, you know,' Gavin went on, after a pause during which he forked, chewed and swallowed.

'What?'

209

'Have read *Society and its Culture*. But it's too late now, so bad luck you.'

He was inches taller than me and built for a rugby scrum, with a growling voice and a shadow of black stubble along his jaw-line. He had earlier explained, with some emphasis, that he was at a Midlands grammar school and his father was a postman, which he claimed would do him plenty of good with Wilkins, who was himself the son of a postie.

'But a title like that,' I said. 'I mean, it doesn't sound as if the book's really about English literature. More like sociology.'

Gavin almost choked on his food.

'Of course it's not *sociology*, not on any day of the week. Sociology! I ask you!'

He said the word as if it were an obscenity.

'What is it then?'

'The clue's in the title, man. Culture. And it's Marxist, of course. I've read it twice. It's incredibly famous, so the teachers at your school can't be up to much if that's not on your reading list.'

'My teachers don't go in for Marxism very much. What's the book about?'

'It's an examination of the components and structures of feeling in writers and society.'

'Blimey,' I said. 'I've read *The Allegory of Love* but that sounds a bit like *The Airfix Model of Love*.'

Gavin gave a humourless, indeed scornful snort, then fixed me with an unmistakeably triumphant leer.

'You do realise Brian Wilkins'll be our Director of Studies, if we get in? *Big* if, in your case, as long as you go around joking like that.'

The others were debating what to do after dinner. One of them, who was knowledgeable about the university (his brother having been at Trinity Hall), said,

'I know. Let's have a go at the King Street Run. King Street's just around the corner.'

'What's the King Street Run?' said somebody.

'It's against the clock. You have to have a pint in each of the seven pubs along the street, without peeing or puking, and then a final one in the pub where you started. It all has to be done in less than one hour.'

Schoolboys that we still were, we proved far from ready to conquer this Everest of all pub-crawls. Our King Street Run ended lamely, though by mutual agreement, at only the fourth pub in the sequence, the Champion of the Thames. Nevertheless with four gulped pints inside me I noticed I was now unable to walk quite straight. I also noticed that, taking no chances, friend Gavin was largely sober. He had confined himself to three half pints. Meanwhile the blond man and I, weaving our way back to college, both threw up over the pavement

The interview next morning was in an oak-panelled room, with my interrogators ranged behind a chunky oaken table. I was facing a tribunal: Professor Wilkins on the left (pipe), the Senior Tutor Dr Lamplugh on the right (Player's Number 6) and, sitting in between them, the gigantic bulk of Duncan Collinshaw's Aunt Cyril inhaling on a cheroot. I had never for a moment reckoned with the possibility of meeting her at my interview. I looked for signs that she remembered me, but could see none.

Then again, my ability this morning to perceive nuances of expression was crippled. I had a scything headache and the heaviness of what felt like a haematoma the size of a fist lying my stomach. My eyesight was occluded and hazy, as that of someone who has only a moment ago groped his way out of bed.

The panel's opening salvo took the expected form.

'So, Mr Conroy,' said Lamplugh, giving a bright lift to his voice so as to sound friendly, 'tell us what book is on your bedside table.'

However hard I strove to remember them, neither the name of William Golding nor the title of his book presented themselves. Determined at all costs not to mention Dickens, I allowed a dim process of unwanted association to break through. I blurted out,

'*Peanuts.*'

'I'm sorry?' said Lamplugh.

It was too late to go back.

'*Peanuts,*' I repeated. 'By Charles M. Schulz.'

With a horrified jolt I knew I had stumbled into disaster, but at least the shock cleared my King Street hangover. It also largely re-sharpened my eyesight. I glanced from face to face to gauge the reaction of the panel. Lamplugh looked puzzled. Aunt Cyril's face wore a faintly amused expression. Wilkins, however, did something unexpected. He flashed a wide smile, as if signalling to a friend. My choice of book apparently delighted him.

'Ah yes, splendid! A cartoon book. And Schulz's work is very much a case for study — of American names, if nothing else. Linus, Lucy Van Pelt, Franklin, Schroeder, Woodstock. That *diversity*, you know.'

He looked at me with new interest.

'So what do you make of Charlie Brown?' he said. 'An existential hero, or merely a marker of failed social integration?'

Was he taking the piss? I didn't know then that the author of *Society and its Culture* almost never attempted a joke. I also didn't know of his recently published articles in the *New Left Review*, 'Dialectics and Contemporary Comic Books' and 'The Seven Labours of Superman'. It was pure good luck, then, that I chose to follow Gavin's advice and take Professor Wilkins seriously.

'Oh,' I said, 'I'd say perhaps he's more like someone in Beckett. Always failing, always bouncing back for more.'

Aunt Cyril gave a wheezing laugh.

'Bouncing back. I like that,' she said. 'But to get on to your papers, I was struck by your exam essay on Eliot, Mr Conroy. You seem to have a pretty good grasp of theme and character in both *Prufrock* and *The Waste Land*. But there was one thing I noticed in particular. At a certain point you mention the question of why *The Canterbury Tales* and *The Waste Land* both begin by invoking the month of April. Then you let it go by. Would you like to enlarge on that here, for us?'

I had thrown this into my essay because Sammy Pritchard, the most amusing of our English teachers, had remarked on the opening lines of the two poems as being a curious confluence, and perhaps not coincidental. But Sammy had himself not gone on to make anything of it, so now I was left adrift with no readymade follow up. I improvised.

'I think Eliot did it on purpose. Maybe he wanted to highlight his depressive outlook against the optimism of *The Canterbury Tales.* Chaucer's full of humour and vitality while *The Waste Land* is, well, a bit downbeat and depressed.'

'Go on.'

'It's almost the complete opposite sort of poem isn't it? But at the same time, both poems have an amazing range of characters in them: all those different voices and ideas from mythology and from the real world, from different classes of people too.'

I was speaking too fast. I took a breath.

'I think Eliot wrote the line about April because he wanted to show that he was living in the same kind of world as Chaucer. [Another pause]. That the two poems are alike in their difference, if you see what I mean. [A longer pause]. They're, um, both part of the tradition he wrote about in one of his essays.'

I looked at them in turn, from face to face. What the hell had I just said? They stared at me in silence. I couldn't tell if they were unimpressed or stumped. I just knew I had made a complete arse of myself, until, that is, Wilkins shook out the match with which he had been firing up his pipe and said,

'Yes, you're onto something there. Historical conditions being completely different, I grant you, but *mutatis mutandi* perhaps there is a commonality in the social positions of Chaucer and Eliot that we should not ignore.'

He observed me like a quizmaster expecting an answer.

'Do you mean because they both had real jobs, and were not just poets?' I said 'Eliot worked in a bank and Chaucer in the customs.'

'Ye-es,' said Wilkins, as if I had not quite taken the line he was hoping for.

But before he could go on, Aunt Cyril butted back in.

'And they both read widely in Italian. That can't be said for most English poets, can it? Milton, of course.'

'And what about Byron?' I said. 'He used an Italian verse form in *Don Juan*.'

Pritchard's voice came back to me from the classroom, praising the virtuosity of Byron's use of *ottava rima*, 'a breeze in Italian, incredibly difficult in English'. But I could tell by the slight deepening of a crease to the side of Wilkins's chin that the career of Byron was not a path he much wanted to follow.

'Oh, Byron,' he said, striking another match. 'He's an aristocratic entertainer, wouldn't you agree? *Lord* Byron. Some would say he's not much more than a titled smart-arse coming up with a lot of jokes, but very little of substance.'

Once Pritchard had read to us Byron's maiden speech to the House of Lords. The poet had spoken up for the Luddites and frame-breakers, thrown out of work by the new machinery. 'In the foolishness of their hearts,' said Byron, 'they imagine that the well-being of the industrious poor is of greater importance than the enrichment of a few individuals'. It was not as champion of the poor but for his 'lordly irony' that Pritchard liked Byron. Not me.

'Byron was dead against Capitalist exploitation of the poor,' I told the tribunal. 'He said so in his speech in Parliament.'

'But we might think of that as opportunistic, mightn't we?' said Wilkins puffing his pipe. 'Something like Auden in Spain. "Today the struggle"

214

and all that. It doesn't follow that Lord Byron was actually progressive. It's a question of sincerity, isn't it?'

'Well I think Byron *was* sincerely progressive. Doesn't he have quite a following in the USSR?'

I had suddenly remembered the port of Riga and Henry Webster, standing with his back to my cabin door, talking about how *Don Juan* had been translated into Russian entirely from memory.

'*Don Juan* was a best-seller in Russia, when it finally came out after Stalin's death,' I went on, recklessly. 'I expect they think he meant what he said. They do take their literature rather seriously there, so I believe.'

Aunt Cyril wheezed with laughter.

'Brian, he's dead right, you know. Your great pals the Soviets simply adore *Don Juan*.'

Twenty minutes later, coming out of the interview room, I found Gavin sitting on a stone bench in Memorial Court, smoking a Woodbine and waiting his turn to go in.

'How did you get on?' he said.

I didn't know how to answer this fully, so I simply told him that I had argued with Wilkins over Byron. Gavin looked astounded.

'You did *what*?'

I gave him a few more details and he shook his head as if shaking rainwater off his hair.

'You mean to say you contradicted him? What the hell got into you? Your goose is properly cooked, mate.'

Walking away after this exchange, I realised I wanted more than anything to be accepted by Brian Wilkins and St Saviour. Hardly less than that, I wanted friend Gavin to be sent packing.

French Lessons

Andy Brokovsky had left school the previous July and was living in the comfort of his parents' home in

Chelsea while cramming to retake his A Levels at Westminster Tutors. I rang him on his home number that afternoon from St Saviour, and we arranged to meet up in London.

'Get yourself to Leicester Square,' he said. 'I'll meet you outside the Odeon at seven.'

I hadn't seen him for four months. He had grown his hair by an inch or two and wore Chelsea boots, narrow twill trousers, a short camel coat with a velvet-faced collar, a pink tab-collared shirt and yellow square ended knitted tie. He was smoking a Benson and Hedges.

'I don't want to see a film, do you?' he said.

The film at the Odeon was called *Winter A-Go-Go*, apparently a farce about Americans on a skiing holiday in Europe.

'Not this one,' I said.

We went to the Tom Cribb pub for some beers and I told Brokovsky about the Cambridge interview.

'Useful to have Collinshaw's aunt on your side,' he said. 'If she is.'

'I rather thought she might be. She's an associate fellow and does a lot of the Middle English teaching. She liked what I had to say about *The Waste Land*, anyway.'

'Christ, I'd hate to be stuck for three years doing nothing but Billy Shakespeare and Silly Shelley, not to mention "Toilets" Eliot.'

'It's all I want to do. And don't be rude about Eliot. He's one of my heroes.'

'If I ever do get my sodding A levels I'm applying to do Economics. As I intend to be seriously rich I reckon I'll need to properly understand money.'

'How are you going to get seriously rich? You could manage a successful rock band, I suppose.'

He wafted the air with his hand.

'Oh, that's far too speculative. There are plenty of sure ways of getting rich quick in the City. Commodity trading or commercial property, as my father keeps telling me. Or I might just take the direct route and marry an heiress.'

He went for a piss and I got another round at the bar. The pictures hanging on the walls were early nineteenth century boxing prints and, on Brokovsky's return, I told him I'd been reminded by these of the show-down between Carani and Nelson at the Castle with boxing gloves.

'You know about Carani?' he said when I'd finished.

'I know he's still at Shed and he's doing the Oxford exam. He still boxes, too. And he's got a pet kestrel that he feeds with raw meat.'

'Does he keep it actually at Shed? I mean, on the premises?'

'He boards it out at a local farm.'

'Did you know Carani's heading into the army as soon as he leaves? He told me they'll pay him to go to Oxford and then give him a fast track commission in the Guards. He obviously likes fighting as much as ever.'

'Remember when he played Henry V? That's why he was so convincing. He didn't need to act. So, have you seen him, or what?'

'Yes, last summer at Mass at the Oratory. We went for a drink afterwards.'

'You still go to Mass?'

'With the old mother I do. When we've had these shall we get some dinner? I know a great place in Chinatown. It's so cheap they're practically paying you to eat there. The food's marvellous, provided you like Dim Sum dumplings.'

Later, with too many bottles of Tsing Tao inside us, we were making our way along Wardour Street with Brokovsky keeping an eye on every passing doorway. He was noting the bell pushes until he came to one in particular that atttracted him. A card, slotted into a brass frame beside it, read in a careful printed hand *'Brigitte French Lessons 1st Floor'*.

'I bet she's not really called Brigitte,' I said.

'Let's go up. You can ask her.'

Before I could say anything to stop him Brokovsky had pressed the bell and pushed open the door. Immediately inside a steep, uncarpeted stair confronted us, which Brokovsky began to climb. I couldn't very well stay behind on the street so I followed.

On the first landing was just one door with Brigitte's card and its educational promise sellotaped onto it. Brokovsky was just raising his hand to knock when it was snatched open from the inside.

To me the woman looked perhaps forty. She wore her copper-dyed hair in a beehive and, clutched around her plump body, a Japanese gown. Her face and eyes were heavily made up.

'Well now, *boys!*' she said offering us an artificial smile. 'What brings you to my door so late?'

She had a strong Liverpool accent, and the husky voice of a heavy smoker.

'French lessons,' said Brokovsky, with mock seriousness and a knowing glance at me. 'We've got money.'

'*Money*, now. That is something I suppose. Do you know any French or are you novices, like?'

She looked directly at me and I felt my cheeks blushing.

'Actually I've got French A Level,' I said.

Brokovsky sniggered.

'And I failed mine, so I need to cram it. Are you Brigitte?'

Instead of answering directly she gave a sigh and I noticed how her cheeks sagged over a crease from somewhere by her chin up towards the cheekbone. It was a sad, resigned sigh, insofar as I could interpret it. She was probably older than forty and I could not be sure she was younger than fifty.

'Well, come in then.'

She stood aside and we sidled past her. The room was less like what I imagined a whore's boudoir might be, and more like the waiting room of a bucket shop for cheap charter flights. The light was glaring: a hundred watt bulb in a tasselled shade hanging from the ceiling. The dusty imitation of a Persian rug covered the floor. There was a pair of bentwood chairs and a low table holding a spider plant and magazines: Playboy, Esquire, Stud. Another door led into what I imagined to be the business side of the apartment.

'Wait here.'

She left by the interior door, through which we could then hear muffled conversation. One of the voices was male. After a few uncertain moments trying to pick out what was being said, we each took one of the upright chairs.

'What in God's name are we doing here?' I said. 'Have you ever done this before?'

Brokovsky shrugged, picked up a magazine and started leafing through it.

'First time for everything.'

'No, Andy. Let's get the hell out of here.'

As I started to rise from my chair a man in a shiny blue suit, with thinning oiled hair, came in through the same door by which the old tart had left us. The many rings festooning his thick and stubby fingers gleamed like gold knuckledusters.

'Hello, boys,' he said. 'Raquel in there says you got money.'

'Who's Raquel?' said Brokovsky, replacing the magazine on the pile. 'Wasn't that Brigitte?'

Ringo fixed Brokovsky with a blank stare.

'Tell me this, sonny. What colour's her hair?'

'Well, it's reddish.'

'Then her name's never Brigitte, is it?'

He snapped his fingers in the air between us.

'So, if we're going to do business, I need to see this money you say you got. It's a score I'm looking for.'

Brokovsky looked blank as must I have.

'That's a twenty quid note. Each. Or two tens, four fivers, it doesn't matter how it comes.'

His smile was reptilian. I sat tight. I knew that all I had after the expenses of the evening was a five pound note and some small change. I looked at Brokovsky. He took out his wallet, then hesitated, upon which Ringo leaned across, picked the wallet from his fingers and efficiently removed two ten-pound notes. He returned the wallet and looked towards me.

'And you?'

'I haven't got twenty pounds.'

'What you got?'

'Five.'

'All right, give.'

'But you said—.'

The snap of his fingers somehow carried more menace this time.

'*Give!*'

So I gave. Instantly our twenty-five pounds was folded and trousered into Ringo's back pocket. He then took two rapid steps to the landing door and yanked it open.

'Now fuck off out of here and don't waste any more of my time.'

It was past midnight when I got back to Kensington. Pieter opened the door in his pyjamas.

'I'm terribly sorry,' I said, 'but I—.'

Before I could say more I threw up on Pieter's bare feet. Over his shoulder he called back to Romy in a tired, resigned sort of voice.

'Darling, you'd better come. Christopher's come back pissed.'

Sedevacantism

'I don't want you to worry about last night,' said Romy in the morning. 'There's no need for your parents to know you had one over the eight. You got back safe, that's the main thing.'

I had woken up at ten the morning and found Romy preparing lunch for two guests, Monsignor Alfred Juniper and a priest from the African mission called Father Carwardine.

'The missionary might interest you, as apparently you're related by marriage,' said Pieter, who had made no reference to having washed my vomit off his toes at half past midnight. 'It seems William Carwardine's ex-wife, Rose Foley from Accrington, is your father's cousin. She now lives in America.'

'Yes, that's possible. My grandmother was a Foley.'

'William and Rose Carwardine got into very hot water in the war. They were interned for a while. Fanatical Mosleyites.'

'You mean they were actually fascists?'

'I'm afraid so. All forgotten now, of course, and Father Carwardine's become a reformed character by taking Holy Orders.'

'But hang on. If he's a priest how can he have an ex-wife?'

'Nevertheless, he has. She went off with a GI in the war and Carwardine wangled some arrangement with Rome. Beats me how, though I believe it's not unheard of. You'll have to ask him. He's a clever devil, that's for sure.'

Juniper arrived first, a tall slim figure wearing an extraordinary costume of black silk stockings, knee-breeches, double-fronted waistcoat and Victorian frock coat. On arrival he handed his wide-brimmed clerical hat to Romy with a flourish.

'Monsignor Juniper is the unofficial chaplain at Bellamy's Club,' Pieter told me during our introductions. 'It's where he's been living since his retirement from Cambridge. He ministers to the Catholic members.'

He raised his voice to speak to the Monsignor who was evidently a little deaf.

'Christopher is hoping to get into Cambridge, Alfred. Saviour College. He's just had the interview, yesterday.'

Juniper beamed at Christopher.

'Oh really? Well, Saviour's is quite a good choice.'

Juniper had a light, rapid and very precise way of speaking. He seemed to be in his sixties and bore a slight — and misleading — resemblance to the Pope.

'Save's is not so grand as Trinity, less snobby than Magdalene and less political than King's, although political enough. They all are, these days. You'll enjoy it if you can put up with the New Left, who really are everywhere now. Awfully solemn people, I find.'

Father Carwardine arrived. He was ten years younger than Juniper and gaunt, with cheekbones and Adam's apple both prominent. His eyes had a way of constantly flicking from face to face. He struck me as being the kind of man who could never quite be at rest.

Lunch was what I would have called pasta pie, but more properly lasagne. It was the first time I had eaten the dish in its proper Italian form.

'These priests love to pig out on pasta and Sangiovese,' Pieter had said. 'It reminds them of their time as carefree students in Rome.'

The meal itself was dominated by an argument between the two clerics, who hadn't previously met. Although it was superficially polite the underlying disagreement was palpable, even though it began by the two men finding common ground with Pieter on the subject of the New Mass.

'This vernacular Mass is just a *bit* of an unfortunate turning, in my belief,' said Juniper. 'I'm lucky. I am allowed to use the old rite — a special dispensation.'

'I insist on using it,' said Carwardine. 'Though I don't tell the bishop, who's a Vatican Two yes-man. I just carry on as before.'

'I applaud the spirit of resistance, Father,' said Pieter.

'I'm a natural resister and I don't like the irrational stampede for change. It's a herd mentality, while I make up my own mind.'

He rapped the table with his finger.

'*And* in Africa I can get away with it because I'm out in the bush and the bishop, who's a black incidentally, is a hundred plus miles away. Anyway my parishioners only speak Zulu or Xhosa so English, Latin, it's much the same to them.'

Listening carefully to this the Monsignor tipped his head fractionally back as he sipped his wine, then dabbed his lips with his napkin. I saw that there wouldn't be any difference between how he drank wine at the lunch table than he did at the altar.

'I can't help thinking,' he said mildly as he refolded his napkin, 'that you will appear to be setting yourself up in opposition to the Holy Father. Quite without meaning to, I'm sure. But you did say you think change is unreasonable. Perhaps I should remind you that he called the Vatican Council to effect change. That's reason enough, surely, even if we don't quite like it.'

'Reason's beside the point. I don't go by reason but by faith. *The* Faith, which is the truth. The unchanging truth.'

After an awkward moment of silence, Pieter cleared his throat.

'Father Carwardine has introduced me to a publisher's house called the Britons' Catholic Library,' he said. 'I am interested in them. They sincerely believe the Church has fallen into error over this.'

'Error? You cannot mean that, Pieter!' exclaimed Monsignor Juniper. 'I know you've had your doubts about some of the decisions of the Council. So have I. But don't tell me you go so far as to think they are errors.'

He sounded for the first time a little shocked by what he was hearing.

'If you ask me, I don't think error is a strong enough word,' said Carwardine. 'The Pope is talking the language of socialism, which is against everything we believe. It's a most serious wrong.'

'But surely,' I put in, 'I mean, in Catholic terms the Pope can do no wrong, can he? He's infallible.'

The Monsignor smiled, pleased that he'd found a way to lighten this dangerous conversation.

'That's a common misconception, Christopher. The doctrine is that the Holy Father is only infallible on Faith and Morals. He can err like anyone when he bets on the Grand National.'

'And has he now bet on the Vernacular Mass,' I said, 'as opposed to the Latin?'

Juniper laughed.

'He has, Christopher, and the race is still on. I myself would back the old rite winning out in the end, but we shall see the outcome in due course. '

This was too much for Father Carwardine.

'No, no, no!' he cried. 'I am shocked indeed to hear you, Monsignor, mouthing such things. To speak of the Mass as you have done is blasphemy. Blasphemy.'

He repeated the word with angry emphasis. Juniper's mouth fell open in dismay.

'Father,' he said mildly, 'I really think we are—.'

'No, Monsignor! I haven't finished. I quote the third true Pope, St Clement: "We should be obedient unto God, and hold those in abomination who in their arrogance and violence set themselves up to lead us into heresy and sin."'

'He was a great saint of course, but those words don't mean—.'

'Clement was beaten and thrown into the sea, tied to an anchor. Do you know why they did that? To make a mockery of baptism, although to no avail because "in the water he did bear witness". No, Monsignor by mocking the sacraments you throw your lot in with the persecutors and heretics, not to mention the Protestants. Have you heard the word Sedevacantism? It means the belief that the seat is vacant. The seat of St Peter itself. Sedevacantists hold that this Pope is not a true Pope because he is, in fact, a heretic. *Ergo*, at this time there is no Pope. And this is a growing belief in the Church, which we hope eventually will prevail and that a new and true Pope will be given us, who understands and holds to the importance of the sacraments and, above all, of the true Mass.'

I was agog to hear what the Monsignor would have to say in answer to this extraordinary rant. In the event he said nothing. He sat quite still, looking down at his plate on which remained a rind of cheese and a smear of butter. Several seconds of silence followed until, with a flourish, Juniper produced a fob watch from his waistcoat pocket and flipped open the lid.

'Oh my goodness, is that really the time?' he said. 'I must be going.'

He rose and, with a brief nod of goodbye to the centre of the table, headed for the door. Romy and Pieter hurried after him into the hall.

With Juniper out of the room Carwardine's passion at once subsided. He smiled into the space in front of him, as if in secret triumph at having put the Monsignor to flight. He turned to me.

'Pieter mentioned you are going to St Saviour College.'

'Just hoping to, at this stage.'

'As a matter of fact I know someone there — Johnny Lamplugh.'

'The Senior Tutor? He was on my interview panel.'

'Well look, I'm going to Cambridge in a few days. I could put in a word if you like.'

Much as I wanted to get into St Saviour, I didn't want it to be on the recommendation of any outside person, let alone an ex-fascist Catholic priest. I said,

'Oh no, please don't. Don't say anything.'

'As you wish. After that I'm going on to Yorkshire, the old school. It'll be nostalgic. I haven't seen the Shed since I was a boy. But I've kept up with Father Albinus. He's an old chum. Housemaster now, I believe.'

He was hinting at a long association with the school; even at having been a pupil there. But a real ex-pupil would know to call it simply Shed, without the article.

'Well look, young Christopher, now that we've met you mustn't be a stranger. I'm not going back to Africa for several months. Why don't we meet up for a meal one night, if you're in London in the meantime? I know a particularly good little Polish place just beside South Ken station.'

He produced a biro and his wallet from which he took out a card. On this he scribbled a string of numbers and handed it to me.

'It's my old ordination card. I still have so many left. I've written the phone number of the place I've been staying at in London. If I'm not there they'll always know where to find me.'

On the printed side of the card was the usual information about the ordination of William Alphonsus Carwardine and a prayer for the success of his ministry. In the lower margin he had written a London number. I turned the card over: it showed Dali's bird's eye view of the crucifixion, just as it had appeared on another ordination card, one which I still had among the flimsy pages of my missal — that of Father Sylvester Prewitt.

In the Taxi

'What's that he's playing?'

It was half past six and we were leaving for the ballet, I in my Sunday suit and Romy dressed in a silk maternity dress in pale yellow and a stole of fox fur around her shoulders. As we went out Peter was striking emphatic piano chords in the sitting room.

'It's *Totentanz*,' said Romy, as she closed the flat door behind us. 'The Dance of Death, by Hugo Distler.'

'I've never heard of him.'

'Rather a tragic figure. Pieter's obsessed with him at the moment, and this piece in particular. It's an etherial choral work that he's been rearranging for solo voice and piano. He wants me to sing it in a recital. It rather gives me the creeps, actually, but I suppose I'll have to do it.'

'I think Pieter's a very good composer. I mean judging by the song you sang on Thursday night.'

'Yes, that is a lovely piece. He always had a great feeling for melody, which he says is the last thing anyone wants in music these days. But he's convinced he's lost even that now.'

'Lost it?'

'Yes, it's how he feels about his music. He says it's rather like losing your faith. You know it's there somewhere but for an unknown reason it's slipped from your grasp. And you're terrified you'll never get it back.'

In the taxi Romy said,

'To be honest, Christopher, I've been genuinely worried about Pieter. I don't like the influence of that priest Carwardine, who Pieter insisted on inviting to lunch with Alfred Gilbert. Well, you were there. It was a just awful. Luckily Alfred's a forgiving soul, and he doesn't look for a fight, which cannot be said for Father Carwardine. He's been trying to involve Pieter with the people behind this Briton's Catholic Library, who really are fanatics, and absolutely horrid.'

'In what way horrid?'

'I mean, this idea that the Holy Father's teaching on the Mass is heresy. They've more than half convinced Pieter and it's tearing him apart. I found him sobbing the other day. He can't talk to me about it. He just cuts himself off and goes deeper and deeper into the glooms.'

'I'm sure it'll be all right,' I said. 'But shouldn't he see a doctor? It might help. He might be prescribed something.'

She took my hand and squeezed it.

'Dearest Christopher! We've done that. He's been prescribed pills of every colour in the rainbow.'

Age Difference

The first half was a ballet on *Paradise Lost*, with modern music by a French composer who I hadn't heard of. Nureyev and Fonteyn both wore nothing but ballet shoes and pale pink body-stockings, with Nureyev as Adam more or less acting the character Michelangelo imagined for him in the Sistine Chapel. At the start he even adopted the same languid pose, lying on the floor, one leg crooked as he extends his finger to receive the spark of life: a resting athlete, an awakening lover. Yet in spite of Nureyev's animal power it was Eve I was looking at. Quite unlike the lumpy country girl who springs from Adam's side on Michelangelo's ceiling, and just as different from the prim ballet doll that she so often played, Fonteyn was sinuous and snake-like, sensuous and dangerous, as she worked on Nureyev, circling him, caressing him, cajoling him and finally entwining herself around him.

I thought, he's 23, she's 42. But the age difference means nothing. They dance together like lovers who belong together.

'Of course, Nureyev's incredibly virile,' said Romy as we went out for the interval. 'But no one usually associates Fonteyn with sex. That was so erotic, don't you think?

'It was rather.'

'Look, I need the Ladies. I'll catch you here OK?'

I wandered about waiting for her, passing group after group of balletomanes huddled around ice buckets of champagne while discussing Rudi and Margot just as you might gossip about people who lived in your own Home Counties village. After ten minutes a middle-aged woman came up to him.

'Are you Christopher Conroy?'

I said I was.

'Romy sent me to find you. I've just been in the Ladies with her and, well, the thing is her waters have broken.'

'I'm sorry? What did you say?'

'Her waters, Christopher. It means she'll soon go into labour. We're going to get her to hospital. She says, will you phone her husband and tell him to join her there at once?'

'Of course. Which hospital is it?'

'It'll be Barts. And she said to give you these.'

She handed across a five-pound note and some keys.

'The money's for a taxi back to Kensington. By the time you get there her husband will have gone off to the hospital, so you'll need the keys to let yourself in.'

I had a gratifying sense of being part of an emergency, of being relied on by Romy to take prompt and decisive action on her behalf. I asked a programme seller who pointed me towards an office, where they let me use the phone. I dialled the Nagys' number and let it ring unanswered for almost a minute before I hung up. Perhaps Pieter had gone out for cigarettes, or to the off-licence. To hell with the phone, I'd go straight back to Kensington and tell him to his face that he was about to be a father. I went out into the street and hailed a cab.

In the taxi I had a vision of Romy lying there, legs apart and crying out, as she pushed and pushed the baby, bloodied with her blood, out into the harsh light of the birthing room.

Death by Water

After letting myself in, I had a sense of the flat being deserted. I walked into the kitchen and put my hand on the kettle. It was cold. In the sitting room the television also was cold, although the air was heavy with cigarette smoke. On top of the piano lay a sheaf of manuscript paper and a page torn from a pocket notebook, all held together by a paper clip. Pieter had written a message. *Finished. It's for you. Sing it for me. I love you.* I lifted the note and saw the music's title. *Totentanz.*

So where was he? If, when I'd phoned, he had gone to the corner shop he'd surely be back by now. I went through the various rooms of the flat, leaving the Nagys' bedroom until last. Here the only light appeared to be from a lamp at the bedside. The Nagys' bed itself was undisturbed although some neatly folded clothes lay on it. Then I noticed the strip of light under their bathroom door. I called out.

'Pieter! Are you in there?'

I went to the bathroom door and knocked.

'Pieter! It's me, Christopher. Romy's gone to Barts hospital. Her waters broke. You're needed. She's going to have the baby.'

I put my ear to the door and heard the hollow drip of water into water. Tentatively I tried the door handle. The lock was not engaged. The door squeaked as it gave way to my gentle push.

'Pieter,' I said again.

As it swung open, the door's squeak turned to a creak on a rising note. I looked at the bath and saw that it was full of water, and full of Pieter. With a gasp I stepped back into the bedroom, then forward to look again. Pieter was not moving. Pieter was submerged. Pieter's mouth was gaping, and his popping eyes stared up like a gargoyle from beneath the surface. Only his feet floated, the toes out in the air. Next to the bath, on a stool, was an empty tumbler, an empty bottle of Scotch and an empty brown pill bottle.

Totentanz

Pieter was a fortnight dead, and Peter his son a fortnight old, when I attended the funeral. I had not seen Romy in the meantime. I would have done if I'd given evidence to the inquest in person, which is what I wanted to do. But the school insisted on arranging with the Coroner, in consideration of my being still seventeen, for my evidence to be submitted in a written affidavit. After a short hearing, and in spite of the whisky and pills found beside the body, the verdict had been accidental drowning.

The funeral took place on the day after my last day at school. On that day I had said goodbye for a final time to the monks who had ruled my life for the past ten years. I felt no regret. As I saw it, or thought about it, I could now at last begin to live on my own terms.

Taking the train once again from Yorkshire to King's Cross I went directly to the Oratory church, where the Requiem Mass, celebrated by Alfred Juniper, had already got as far as the Offertory. It was being staged in all solemnity, with a full choir of men and boys, clouds of incense and a cohort of black-vested deacons alongside the Monsignor. Even before I had spotted the place where my parents were sitting, I saw Father William Carwardine amongst the congregation. He gave me a faintly coy grin and I raised a hand but avoided anything more than momentary eye contact.

Afterwards at the post-funeral gathering I circled around Romy, waiting from a distance for a chance to have a word. She moved between the people talking quietly to one after another while cradling the baby Peter in her arms. When I placed myself directly in her eyeline she looked away immediately but I'd seen that she'd been crying. Twice more I caught her eye and twice more she avoided my gaze, in a way that could only be described as deliberate. Discouraged I wandered off, then noticed Andy Brokovsky pouring himself a glass of wine at the drinks table. I went up to him.

'I didn't know that you knew the Nagys,' I said.

'Christopher! I didn't know *you* did. It's my mother who knows them, not me. I just came along for the free alcohol. Do you want to go out for a smoke?'

It was raining. We went around the corner and lit up under the awning of a flower shop.

'So how did you know the dear departed?' Brokovsky asked.

'The Nagys are friends of my parents. I've stopped over with them quite often when I've been in London. I was staying there that weekend, you know, the one when we had our adventure in Wardour Street.'

'Oh God, that. I was so wiped out. Something about French lessons, wasn't it?'

He gave his snuffling, sniggering laugh. I said,

'Yes and when I got back to the Nagys' flat I threw up over Pieter's feet. He was quite nice about it. And twenty four hours later he was dead.'

'The rumour is he killed himself. Is it true?'

I thought about telling how I'd found Pieter in the bath, but then realised, for some reason, I didn't want to trust Brokovsky with the knowledge. I only said,

'The inquest verdict was accidental death.'

Brokovsky wrinkled his nose.

'They always say that, if they possibly can. You don't have to believe it. Of course if he had officially topped himself he couldn't have had a Requiem Mass, or be buried in hallowed ground.'

'How can you *officially* top yourself?'

'Ha-ha. You're a funny man.'

He dropped his cigarette and ground it out with his shoe.

'Come on, we'd better get back or my mother will be suspicious.'

We Who Were Dying

As the train beat its way northwards I looked out through the compartment window streaked with rain. My mother sat beside me reading and my father impatiently smoked. Hardly taking notice of the landscape we were sweeping through, I was thinking of Romy Purvis as I'd seen her a few hours earlier, holding the baby among the funeral guests and weeping. She had swerved from any contact with me. Why? Could she not face the one who had been the

232

first to see her husband dead? But, even suppose she had allowed me to speak to her, I knew I would have been unable to find any words that mattered or meant anything. In the privacy of my own head I loved her with a unique and inextinguishable love and would do anything for her. But Romy's grief had reared up between us, forming an insuperable barrier. What she was feeling now had become greater than anything I could understand, or imagine, or match.

At some point north of Crewe the thought of Pieter returned, submerged naked in the bath with frog-like eyes, mouth gaping and the only part of his body above the surface his toes. Peter's intense idea of religion, Pieter tortured by faith and enraged by doubt, made him seem finally like one of those dismembered martyrs, St Hippolytus for one, who was so-called because he had been tied between two wild horses and torn apart. Pieter in his mind and his spirit had also been torn apart.

And then, in the finality of that long rail journey, a few words from *The Waste Land* came back to me, pounding in the rhythm of the carriage wheels:

> *He who was living is now dead*
> *We who were dying are now living*

When at last we arrived home there lay, waiting on the hall mat, a congratulatory telegram from St Saviour College.